Tobal has secrets, but doesn't every demon? Of course, his secret is a big one since he's the prince of Hell's secret brother, but he doesn't mean any harm. He never thought he'd have a chance at getting to know Berith, or that he'd ever see his foster brother again, yet here he is, living in a palace and spending time with both of them.

He just wishes people would stop trying to use him to kill Berith.

Lon knows Tobal is hiding something, but he isn't sure what. He's convinced it has to do with the many attacks on the prince and his family, and as head of security, it hits him hard. He has to do something, even though Berith doesn't believe Tobal is involved.

And even though Lon finds Tobal sexy and adorable, he doesn't want to believe he could do something like this.

When Tobal meets a shady guy in an even shadier tavern, Lon knows he was right, but when he corners Tobal, he finds out what his secret is. Tobal is involved in the attacks, but not in the way Lon thought.

No, Berith's enemies are bigger and stronger, and it's Lon's job to take them on and defeat them.

This book is a work of fiction. Names, characters, places, and incidents either are products of the author's imagination or are used fictitiously. Any resemblance to actual events or locales or persons, living or dead, is entirely coincidental.

A Demon's Fortune
Copyright © 2023 Catherine Lievens
ISBN: 978-1-4874-3780-0
Cover art by Angela Waters

Published by eXtasy Books Inc

Look for us online at:
www.eXtasybooks.com

A Demon's Fortune
Demons' Destinies 4

By

Catherine Lievens

CHAPTER ONE

Sometimes, it was hard to believe that this was Tobal's life. He looked down at the table, unsure where to start. He'd never had this much food at his disposal before, and he still wasn't used to it. His instinct was to grab as much as he could and hoard it in his room, but it wouldn't do to behave that way, and it wasn't necessary. If he was hungry, he just had to ask one of the many servants hanging around the palace.

They made Tobal uncomfortable, almost as much as the abundance of food and everything else. He wasn't used to having someone do things for him. All his life, he'd had to fight for what he needed, including food. Here, he didn't have to do anything. He only had to ask, and someone did whatever he needed for him. When he tried to do things on his own, servants usually appeared flustered because he was doing their job. He'd made sure to ask if they were happy here, if they needed anything, but it looked like Berith was a good prince and ruler. Everyone seemed satisfied, which wasn't something Tobal was used to, either.

"You look like you don't know where to start," a gentle voice said.

Tobal looked up to peer at Sabin, his brother's partner. "That's because I don't."

Sabin's expression was both sad and sweet. "Zeno behaves the same way."

"I'm fine," Zeno said gruffly.

He'd never admit otherwise, but Sabin and Tobal knew him. That was one of the reasons Sabin had decided to live away from the palace. Zeno could never have lived there, but Sabin couldn't be away because of his job. They'd found a compromise by having a home built in the palace's extensive gardens, and that was where Zeno spent most of his time.

Tobal didn't blame him. He liked it here, and it was a massive difference from where they'd grown up. He was fine living in the palace, though. It allowed him more time to explore the place and to give Zeno and Sabin space.

"You can eat whatever you want," Sabin said. "And if what you want isn't on the table, it'll be brought to you."

"We're fine," Zeno insisted.

And they were. Even though they had no idea how to behave, they were both settling down into palace life. Tobal was starting to feel restless, but it was better than being out there, wondering where his next meal would come from and having to fight to stay alive. Besides, moving into the palace had allowed him to be closer to his brother, which wasn't something he'd ever expected to happen. He hadn't thought he'd see Zeno again after Zeno left their little town, and now that he had, he wasn't letting go easily.

He didn't regret anything that had happened in the past. His childhood and his entire life, really, had been harsh, but the same went for most demons. Very few of them grew up in luxury like the prince had and like his daughter still was. Tobal couldn't imagine growing up in different circumstances than the ones he'd had to face, but he couldn't help but wonder what his life would have been like if he'd been born at the palace rather than in the middle of the desert.

He pushed those thoughts away and took a sip of juice from his glass. Wondering wouldn't bring anything good. If he'd grown up here, he'd never have met Zeno, and that wasn't something he was willing to wrap his mind around. They might not be related by blood, but that didn't mean Zeno was any less his brother, and Tobal cared about him.

Besides, he couldn't change the past. No one could.

"What will you do today?" Sabin asked Zeno.

Zeno shrugged one shoulder. "Not sure. Someone reached out to hire me, so I'm meeting them, but I don't have anything else planned."

Sabin nodded. He didn't tell Zeno he didn't have to work, probably because he knew that wouldn't go down well. "Just remember, nothing that would put you in danger," he warned with a smile.

"I wouldn't dare," Zeno promised.

Tobal had never seen his brother like this, but then he didn't think his brother had ever been in love. Sabin had done the unthinkable and found a way to Zeno's heart, and Tobal couldn't have been happier. He didn't know much about Zeno's adult life, but they'd grown up together. He'd seen what Zeno had gone through, and he deserved Sabin — and so much more. He deserved everything he'd ever wanted, and Tobal hoped Zeno would get it.

"What about you?" Zeno asked, turning his attention to Tobal. "Do you have any plans today?"

Tobal shrugged. "Not really. I'm going to have to find something to do soon, but for now, I don't have plans."

"I know it's useless to tell both of you that Berith doesn't need you to do anything, but I just wanted to make sure you were aware of that," Sabin said. "You're family to him. He can support you through everything you might want to try, but there's no rush for you to find what you want to do with your new life."

Zeno had stars in his eyes when he reached for Sabin's hand over the table. "Thank you," he murmured.

"It's not me you have to thank for this. Besides, Berith did it for all of us."

"Still. We realize how lucky we are."

"We do," Tobal confirmed.

And he felt like an asshole for everything he was hiding.

He couldn't tell anyone, least of all Zeno, who would attempt to fix things for him. No one could fix any of this. The only thing Tobal could do to make things better would be to talk to Berith, but he had no idea how that would end, and he wasn't that brave.

Actually, he was terrified at the thought of talking to Berith.

Tobal turned his attention back to the fruit on his plate and picked at it while Sabin and Zeno softly talked to each other. He was happy for his brother and for himself, but Zeno had been gone for a long time. He didn't know most of what Tobal had gone through recently.

He didn't know about Tobal's father and his brother.

Tobal should tell him. If anything, he should tell Berith, because he was involved, even though he didn't know anything about it. It was easier to keep his secrets to himself, though. Telling anyone might put the life he had now in jeopardy, and he wasn't willing to do that. It had nothing to do with living at the palace, having an abundance of food and whatever else he wanted, and everything to do with Zeno and how he stood to lose him. He wasn't ready for that to happen, which meant the secret would stay his.

Even though it was starting to weigh heavily on his shoulders.

But watching Zeno with Sabin, Tobal knew this was the only thing he *could* do. If he wanted a place in his brother's life, he'd have to learn to deal with the fact that he might have to keep his secret for a while, if not forever. If it meant having Zeno and maybe even Berith by his side, he was willing to do exactly that and so much more.

Lon rubbed the sleep out of his eyes, or at least, he tried to.

He was exhausted, but he didn't want Berith to notice. The prince already had enough troubles to deal with on his own, and he didn't need Lon to add more to the pile, especially problems there was nothing he could do about.

It was infuriating. Lon should be used to it by now, but he still couldn't wrap his mind around the fact that demons managed to find a way into the palace and tried to kill Berith on a regular basis. Every time he thought he'd found the way they'd come in and made it so that no one else would be able to do it again, they found a new way to do so, usually more complicated. Most of the assassins bribed servants or were servants themselves. Some climbed the walls separating the palace from the town and the desert. Others were snuck in, sometimes by people who had no idea what they were doing, other times by people whose aim was to kill the prince.

And Lon was supposed to protect Berith from all of them.

That wasn't his only job. He was head of palace security, which meant that he kept both Berith and his family safe, along with keeping an eye on all the guards, making sure they did their job, arranging shifts, keeping up with the trainees, and many other things he couldn't remember right now.

That was how tired he was.

He sighed and took a sip of strong coffee, hoping it would help. He had a long list of things he needed to do today, and the sooner he started on it, the sooner it would be over.

He almost snorted out loud. When was his list of things to do ever over?

But looking around the table, he reminded himself that he wouldn't have this any other way. He was protecting his family, the people he cared the most about, and that was all he'd ever wanted to do.

He frowned when he realized Sabin wasn't at the table. "Has anyone seen Sabin?" Berith's personal assistant and their best friend wasn't usually one to get himself in trouble, but recently, he had, so Lon worried when he didn't see him.

Sabin had been sent on a mission, and he'd come home with a lover known in Hell for being a formidable assassin, amongst other things. Lon hadn't been sure what to think of Zeno, and he still wasn't. Having someone like him hanging around the palace and the people he loved made him nervous, but Sabin had chosen Zeno, and Lon would never ask him to choose differently. For some reason, Zeno made Sabin happy, and that was all both Berith and Lon wanted.

But did Sabin really have to find happiness with The Mercenary?

"He's eating at home with Zeno and Tobal," Mel, the prince's consort, said. He was out of place at the table, surrounded by demons, but the way Berith looked at him was enough to tell anyone who saw him exactly why Mel was here.

That left only Lon.

He was the only one of their little friendship trio who hadn't fallen in love, and that was perfectly fine with him. He didn't need love, and in his case, it would be a complication He had to focus on his work and being the head of security Berith needed, and that took precedence over anything and anyone. He doubted that any partner he might find would understand that, so it was better this way. It didn't matter that sometimes it was lonely. Lon could deal with loneliness. He couldn't deal with something happening to Berith.

He needed a distraction, so he latched on the most obvious one. "Tobal went there?"

Berith chuckled from the other side of the table. "I know you don't trust him, but I truly believe there's no reason not to. He's Zeno's brother. He wouldn't do anything to hurt anyone here."

"You can't know that. I understand why you trust Zeno, although I'm not sure I do just yet, but Tobal is unknown. He could be planning on attacking you."

Berith shrugged. "And if he does, I'll defend myself. He's not here to hurt me, though. You need to stop being so suspicious of everyone."

Lon snorted. "How am I supposed to do that when I'm your head of security? Being suspicious is part of my job."

"I suppose it is. Sometimes, though, I wonder if you're using the job to hide."

Berith had always been able to read Lon too easily. Lon glared at him, but for once, Berith didn't grin back. He seemed sincerely worried, which wouldn't do. He was one of the princes of Hell, which meant he had better things to focus on than Lon's non-existent love life.

"I'm perfectly fine," Lon insisted. "I don't need you to worry about me. Worry about our territory, or even better, about Mel."

The human's cheeks flushed. "You don't have to worry," he quickly said. "I'm fine."

Berith patted his hand. "I know you are. Lon is deflecting, but he should know better than to think it will work."

Lon groaned. "Can't you just leave me alone? I have a job to do."

"And you're incredibly good at it. It doesn't mean you need to stay away from people. I know you haven't had anyone in your bed in a while now."

Lon risked a glance toward the end of the table, but Cyarea, Berith's daughter, was reading a book while she ate breakfast. She wasn't the least bit focused on what the adults were saying, which was a relief. Demons didn't usually have much of a childhood, but Berith was doing everything he could to ensure his daughter was happy and didn't have to grow up too fast.

Berith leaned over the table. "Seriously. When was the last time you released a bit of *stress*?" he asked, wiggling his eyebrows at the last word.

He was ridiculous, but Lon loved him with all his heart. He understood where Berith was coming from, too. He'd been worried about Berith before in very much the same way. Berith had been alone, but he wasn't anymore. Mel was a perfect fit for him, even though no one would have imagined that by seeing him. He'd made himself at home at the palace, and Lon was happy to see that. He trusted Mel with Berith's heart, just like he trusted Zeno with Sabin's.

But he didn't trust Tobal one bit.

On the surface, he should. Tobal was Zeno's brother, and he'd come to the palace both because he wanted to be with his brother. and besides, who would have said no to being offered a spot here? Tobal didn't have to worry about anything anymore. He had a roof over his head, food in his stomach, and people who did everything for him. He had an easy life now. He would have been a fool not to want to travel here with Sabin and Zeno, and most stupid demons didn't survive to adult hood. Tobal had, which meant he wasn't an idiot.

But that didn't mean he wasn't planning something.

Lon was suspicious because of the circumstances that surrounded Tobal's reappearance in Zeno's life. From what he and Zeno had explained, the two of them had grown up together in a foster home. Zeno had left as soon as he could, abandoning Tobal. He'd expected Tobal to be long gone by the time he went back to their small town as Sabin's bodyguard, but Tobal had still been there. After the two brothers reunited, they'd both decided it would be best for Tobal to move to the palace with Zeno.

It was a heartwarming story, and everyone got tears in their eyes when they were told about it.

Not Lon.

He couldn't trust Tobal, and he wished Berith understood why. Maybe he trusted him, but he was the prince, not the head of security. It wasn't his job to worry about Tobal or anyone else.

It was Lon's, and he'd find out what Tobal was hiding. He had to.

Berith sighed. "I can see I won't change your mind about Tobal, but that's okay. You'll eventually come to trust him, and maybe then you'll be more relaxed. In the meantime, you should probably find companionship. It'll help you release stress."

Lon resisted the urge to bump his forehead against the table. "I never stick my nose into your private life, and I'd appreciate it if you didn't, either."

"I won't insist, but both Sabin and I are worried about you. You're overworked, never take a day off, and spend your free time with us. We love you, and we're always happy to see you, but you need more than friends and family."

Maybe he was right, but even if Lon did need more, he didn't have time for it. Perhaps when he found out what Tobal was up to and managed to stop him, he could allow himself to relax.

But until then, he'd keep an eye on Tobal and on any demon who tried hurting Berith or anyone from their family. It was his job, and he wouldn't fail them.

"I'll see you later tonight," Sabin said, leaning over Zeno to kiss him goodbye.

Tobal looked away. Seeing Zeno and Sabin together made him want what they had, but he wasn't sure it would ever be in the works for him. It certainly wasn't now, at least until he managed to solve the many problems he'd brought with him to the palace. It wouldn't be good to pull someone else into them, and he'd never do that to anyone, least of all someone he cared about.

That was one of the reasons he hadn't told Zeno about this mess.

Both of them watched Sabin walk away. Tobal couldn't deny Sabin was beautiful, but he knew that wasn't what had pulled Zeno in. He'd fallen in love with Sabin's gentleness and fierceness, and Tobal couldn't blame him for that, even though it wasn't what he wanted for himself. He was more into strong, silent types. He loved feeling protected and like he didn't have a worry in the world.

He supposed he *shouldn't* have a worry in the world, not anymore, but he was hiding too many things to be able to let go of the past.

"So, what are you hiding?" Zeno asked as he leaned back in his chair.

Tobal eyed him. He was tempted to tell his brother he wasn't hiding anything, but Zeno wasn't an idiot. He'd always been able to see through Tobal, which clearly hadn't changed, even though years had passed.

"What are *you* hiding?" Tobal asked instead of answering.

Zeno laughed. "Good point."

"Thank you."

"You're not going to tell me?"

"No."

"You're making me worry."

Tobal sighed. "That's not my intention, so I'm sorry you feel that way. This is something I have to deal with on my own for now. I promise I'll tell you if I need anything, but you need to leave me be right now."

Zeno stared at him for a moment before nodding. "Just remember that you're not alone. Whatever mess you're in, I'll always have your back. I didn't in the past, so I understand why you're wary of telling me anything, but things are different now." He hesitated. "I'm sorry for leaving."

Tobal had known this conversation was coming. He was

surprised it hadn't happened sooner, but they'd both been distracted by the building of the new house Zeno and Sabin shared and settling in. Tobal had also tried to avoid having serious conversations because he was terrified. No matter what Zeno had done in the past, Tobal had done worse, and he'd never been angry at his brother for leaving.

How could he have been? Anyone who could do so left. Zeno had seen an opportunity and had taken it, and while Tobal wished he could have gone with him, he'd been happy that his brother was free. He'd also been afraid something might happen to Zeno without him watching his back, but Zeno had done well.

Tobal leaned closer and patted Zeno's shoulder. They'd never been overly affectionate, because it would have drawn too much attention to their relationship, so Tobal didn't linger, but he needed that gentle touch. "I don't blame you for leaving. I would have in your place, too."

"You'd have waited for me."

"Maybe, maybe not. There's no way for us to find out what we would have done if the circumstances had been different, and I'm fine with that. I don't blame you, and you shouldn't, either. The past is over. Let's focus on the future, yeah?"

Zeno didn't look convinced, but he nodded. "I was surprised not to see the house when I got there."

"That's because I burned it down." And Tobal was damn proud of that.

He'd made sure no one who didn't deserve it was inside when he'd done it. He'd been pissed, but not at the other kids. He'd found out that the people who'd taken him and Zeno in had known his mother and had kept some of her things but had never given them to him. They probably would have sold them if they could have, but the items had only been diaries and a few other knickknacks, so Tobal suspected his foster parents had just dumped all of it in the attic and forgotten about it.

That was where he'd found them. It was where he'd read his mother's diary and found out who his father was.

Where he'd found out he was Berith's half-brother.

He still wasn't entirely convinced that what he'd read was the truth, but he couldn't deny it sounded good. Apparently, his mother had been a servant here at the palace when she was young. She'd met Berith's father, and they'd had a fling. She'd always known there couldn't be anything more between them, so she hadn't been surprised when, after she'd told him she was pregnant, he'd paid her to leave. He'd already been married and had a son, Berith, and he wasn't willing to welcome Tobal. Tobal's mother had left, just like she'd been ordered to.

He and she had been happy when he was a child, but she'd been killed, and he'd been left alone. It wouldn't have changed anything for him to know who his father was, and it hadn't until he'd met Sabin and Zeno had explained who the demon was. Tobal had known he couldn't ignore the coincidence. Sabin and Zeno had been his way into the palace, and while he still felt guilty about not telling them the entire truth, he wasn't ready. Besides, he wasn't exactly using them. He'd have been here even if he'd had nothing to do with Berith. He was at the palace for Zeno, mostly, but he wouldn't avoid Berith.

He was fine with never telling anyone about his apparent family links if it meant he could be close to Zeno.

"I didn't know you had it in you," Zeno teased.

"I didn't, either, but they pushed me too far. I did what I had to do, and I don't regret it."

Zeno stared for a moment before nodding. "I wouldn't regret it, either, if I were you. I'm proud of what you did, Tobal. I'm proud that you managed to survive."

"Same."

Tobal had done what he'd had to do, and he'd continue doing so. He hadn't thought he'd ever see his brother again, but with Zeno in his life, it was easy to forget who Berith was.

And that someone was trying to use Tobal to get to the prince.

Lon was already exhausted by the time he reached his office after breakfast. He carried the biggest cup of coffee he'd been able to find, routinely sipping on it as he walked. He'd always loved his job and had been proud of it, but recently, he'd started dreading spending any length of time behind his desk.

Things had been easier when he'd just been a guard. He'd always known he wouldn't stay a guard for long, and sure enough, as soon as Berith had climbed onto the throne, he'd assigned security to Lon. In the beginning, Lon had apprenticed with the old head of security, but after a few years, the man had retired, which was a small miracle for a demon. They usually died violent deaths, but the old man had a small house on a pond and spent his days fishing.

That sounded boring as Hell.

Right now, though, Lon would do pretty much anything if it took him away from his office, including fishing. Unfortunately for him, he didn't have a choice, so he pushed open the door and slipped in.

His ass had barely touched the chair when someone knocked on the door. Lon groaned and stared at it, hoping that whoever was there would leave if he didn't answer, but he should have known better. There was another knock, then the door slowly opened, and his second in command, Mikal, leaned in.

He grinned when he saw that Lon was there, opened the door wider, and slipped in. "Are you hiding?" he asked.

Lon glared at him. "You'd be hiding, too, if you were in my

place."

Mikal closed the door behind himself and grimaced. "I probably would, but I'm *not* in your place."

"Yet."

Mikal's eyes went wide. "You're not planning on retiring, are you? Because I'm not ready for this."

Lon was tempted to tell Mikal he'd retire next month or something just as ridiculous, but he kind of wanted to at the moment. He couldn't afford to have that kind of dream, so he shook his head instead. "Where would I go? This is my life."

Mikal chewed on his bottom lip. "Maybe that's the problem. Maybe you just need some time away from the job, but not so much that it would be retirement."

"Like a vacation? When would I have time for that?"

Mikal shrugged. "Eventually, you're going to have to trust me."

"I do trust you. But as long as I know someone is after Berith, I can't relax or leave this territory."

"You do realize there'll always be someone after Berith, right? He's the prince. Some people hate him just because of that, while others want to take his place. You won't be able to do anything about that."

"I'm very much aware of that, and I don't need you to remind me of it. Now, I see you have more reports."

Mikal sighed but came to sit in front of Lon. Together, they went over the reports Mikal had brought, which were mostly boring stuff about how the trainees were doing and various incidents that had happened over the past few days. Lon supposed he'd rather be bored than be fighting for his or Berith's life. Still, he had a hard time focusing, and of course, Mikal noticed.

He leaned back in his chair and crossed his arms over his chest as he stared. "What's up with you?"

"Nothing. Is there anything else you need from me?"

"To know why you're distracted. I mean, I'll be the first to admit this isn't exactly fun, but it's the job."

Lon tapped his fingertips onto the desk as he thought. "Have you looked into Tobal?" he eventually asked.

Mikal didn't seem surprised by the question. "So that's what you've been obsessing over."

"I'm not obsessing over it. I'm worried because Berith doesn't seem to realize he shouldn't trust Tobal."

"I'm not saying we should trust him, but what proof do we have that we shouldn't?"

"I never said we shouldn't trust him."

"But you don't."

"He appeared from out of nowhere."

"So did Zeno."

"Yes, but Zeno has a reason to be here. He and Sabin are together, so it makes sense for him to follow Sabin back to the palace."

"And he's Tobal's brother, so it makes sense for Tobal to follow him."

"Maybe, but Zeno hadn't seen him in years. What are the odds that he'd suddenly appear to rekindle their relationship just as Zeno is moving into the palace?"

"Okay, I won't say you're wrong, because I'm not sure you are, and it is a massive coincidence. You can't spend your life not trusting anyone, though."

"I have people I trust. You're one of them."

Mikal sighed. "Well, I've been looking into him, but so far, I haven't found anything, or rather, nothing other than I'd have found about any other demon. He grew up with his mother until she was killed when someone broke into their house to steal stuff. The same people who took in Zeno took in Tobal, too. Tobal stayed back even when Zeno left, but eventually, the house caught fire, and he had to find a new place. He's been in that small town since then, so I don't think it's odd that he found Zeno again, since Zeno was the one who went there. I'd have found it weird if he *hadn't* reached out to Zeno once he saw him."

Everything Mikal was saying made sense, but something still told Lon that Tobal was hiding something. "Dig deeper," he ordered.

Mikal nodded. It didn't matter that he disagreed with Lon. Lon knew he'd do what he asked, and not just because he was his second in command. They were friends as well as coworkers.

"I'll see what I can do," Mikal promised. "Now, we need to review the new recruits list."

Lon groaned. "Do we have to?"

"Yes. Unless you'd rather continue talking about your crush on Tobal?"

Lon glared. "I do *not* have a crush on Tobal. You'll never say anything about that ever again unless you want me to mention your crush on Reyni."

Mikal's cheeks flushed, and he looked down at the papers he was holding. "I don't have a crush on the healer."

They both knew it was a lie, but it was enough for Mikal to finally refocus on their work, which was what Lon was aiming for.

He was done thinking about Tobal and talking about him. He had work to do, and he needed to do it to keep Berith safe.

Even though it was the most boring work in the world.

CHAPTER TWO

Tobal was bored.

Zeno had ended up accepting the job about which he'd met that person a few days ago, so he was out of the palace. Sabin had been okay with it because it wasn't dangerous, and Zeno wouldn't stay away long, but it left Tobal with no one to talk to.

He supposed he could go to Sabin, but he didn't want to bother the prince's personal assistant. Sabin was important and had a lot of work to do, and Tobal was unwilling to interrupt him. He didn't have any other friends, though, so he was on his way to the library.

Tobal had never been a reader. He'd never had the opportunity to become one, but his mother had taught him to read, and he hadn't lost the ability. He was hoping he'd be able to find some of her old favorites, but even if he couldn't, at least it would give him something to do. He still had no idea what his future would look like, but he couldn't continue hanging around the palace without doing anything. Eventually, he'd die of boredom, and that wasn't something he wanted.

He hoped the library would distract him, but his thoughts kept returning to Berith. Now that he was getting to know the prince, Tobal wondered what the next step should be. It probably wouldn't be the best idea to just go up to him and blurt out that they were brothers, even though Tobal was tempted. He couldn't exactly tell Berith that his father had cheated on his mother, since he wanted to keep his head attached to his body.

Eventually, though, he'd have to say something. It wasn't right to hide this from Berith, and the only reason Tobal kept hiding it was that he couldn't know if Berith was safe. There was at least one plot against him, as far as Tobal knew, and he wanted nothing to do with it, even though they'd tried pulling him into it. That was one of the reasons he'd left with Zeno and Sabin, although he still wondered how these people had found out he was Berith's brother. He hadn't known more than a few years, himself.

He turned a corner, eager to get to the library so he could find a book to distract himself, but his step faltered as he saw the scene in front of him.

The hallway was empty except for him, or rather, it would have been empty if there hadn't been a dead person on the floor. There was no doubt that the man wearing the servant's uniform had been killed violently. The pool of blood splattered around his head was a pretty good indication of that. The symbol that had been drawn on the wall with his blood also was.

Tobal was frozen. Like every demon, he was familiar with death. It wasn't the first time he'd seen a dead body, and it probably wouldn't be the last, no matter how much he disliked it.

But what was he supposed to do? Scream for someone to come? It was clear the demon was dead, but even then, Tobal inched closer. He crouched, careful of the blood, and pressed two fingertips against the demon's throat. He couldn't feel anything, so he started getting to his feet, which was when he lost his balance. He swore, but unfortunately, he had to touch the body to stay on his feet, getting dirty with blood.

That was when someone else turned the corner.

The female demon saw him and started screaming instantly. He raised his hands, intent on showing her he wasn't planning on hurting her, but since they were bloody, it only caused her to scream louder. Tobal wasn't sure what to do to make her stop. She sounded terrified, and it only took a few minutes for guards to appear running.

Tobal was in trouble.

Of course he was. His entire life, he'd been in trouble, sometimes because of his own behavior, other times because he'd fallen into it. He hadn't done anything wrong this time, but he recognized the symbol on the wall, and it made his stomach churn.

Things didn't get better when Lon arrived.

Tobal had no idea what to think of the demon. He was head of security, and when Tobal had arrived, they'd had a meeting in which Lon had asked him about his past and intentions. It had all been very dramatic, but Tobal had enjoyed it almost as much as he'd enjoyed staring at Lon's ass as the demon paced the length of his office.

There would be no staring now, though. Lon looked from the body to Tobal, who tried cleaning his hand on the floaty pants he was wearing. Thankfully, they were black, but he suspected Lon knew what he was trying to hide anyway.

"What happened?" Lon asked, ignoring the female demon who was now sobbing. One of the guards had gone to her, and she was crying in his arms.

"I have no idea," Tobal said.

Lon's eyes narrowed. "You're going to have to do better than that. Why did you kill the servant?"

Tobal almost rolled his eyes. Of course Lon thought he was the killer. "I didn't."

"Your hands are dirty with his blood."

"It doesn't mean I had anything to do with his death. I was headed to the library, and when I turned the corner, I saw him. I touched his throat to see if he was still breathing, lost my balance, and unfortunately touched the body. That's when the other servant came in and started screaming."

Lon stared at Tobal for a moment. Tobal wondered if he believed him. He wasn't sure he'd believe himself if their roles were reversed. Lon didn't have a reason to, but he also didn't have a reason *not* to.

Lon looked at the body again, then turned his attention to the demon standing next to him. "Take Tobal to my office," he ordered.

The demon nodded. "Should I come back here once he's there?"

"Stay with him until I join you."

"Got it," the second demon agreed before cupping Tobal's elbow and guiding him back from where he'd come from.

He wasn't harsh or anything, which Tobal hoped meant at least he believed him.

"My name is Tobal," he said as they walked down the hallway. He kept trying to hide his hands so no one would see the blood. He didn't have pockets, which was a damn shame.

"I'm Mikal," the demon said.

"You work for Lon?"

"I'm his right-hand man."

So Mikal was important. "That's impressive."

"Thank you. Do you want to tell me what happened again?"

Tobal shook his head. "I'm going to have to repeat it to Lon, right?"

"He'll want to hear it again, yes."

"Then I'd rather wait. But I didn't have anything to do with this. I just tried to help."

But the memory of the symbol on the wall made Tobal want to throw up. He'd recognized that symbol, and its presence meant that the people after him were at the palace, probably watching him. They knew where he was and where he slept, and if they hadn't needed him, they'd probably have killed him instead of the servant. The only reason they hadn't was that they had a use for him. Tobal had no intention of allowing them to use him.

Even if he had to die.

His main goal was to keep Zeno, Sabin, and anyone they cared about safe. He might not be a guard like Lon and Mikal, but that didn't mean he couldn't defend himself. It also didn't mean he wouldn't hesitate to kill himself if things came to that. He'd gladly do it if it was to protect the people he loved.

But he really hoped he wouldn't have to. He liked life at the palace way too much, and now that he'd gotten Zeno back, he had every intention of spending as much time as possible with him.

This was their second chance, and Tobal wasn't wasting it.

Lon waited until Mikal and Tobal were out of sight to turn to the other guards. "Take care of the body," he ordered. "I also need you to go to the servants' quarters and learn more about the man who died and whoever might have witnessed anything. I need all the information available."

The guards nodded and got to work, but Lon stayed where he was. He needed to start working on this case, go to his office and talk to Tobal, but he needed a moment. He stared at the body, his mind working hard.

What had happened? Who had killed the poor demon? It wouldn't be a surprise or a shock anywhere else, but here at the palace, it was. This place was supposed to be safe, and not just for Berith. The servants weren't supposed to be afraid to do their job or to live here. Now, one of them was dead, and Lon had no idea what had happened to him.

But he'd find out. It was his job, and he was damn good at it. He'd also make sure the servant's family was contacted and that they got anything they needed. Berith was generous, and he'd take the fact that this had happened in his palace personally.

Lon stayed around for a while longer, watching as the guards and servants worked. He talked to the woman who'd walked in on Tobal and a few other servants, but no one could say much to him about the demon who'd died. Lon had his name now, and he knew that most of the demons Iskander had worked with considered him quiet but nice, but no one had any idea what had happened. Iskander had been here to work, and he'd died doing his job.

Once the body had been covered and cleanup was on its way, Lon turned around and headed to his office. Tobal had been there, which meant that even if he wasn't involved, he'd seen something. Lon wasn't convinced he had nothing to do with this, though. It wasn't the first time someone was killed at the palace, but Tobal had been present this time. There was no way this was a coincidence, but Lon told himself not to focus on Tobal. He was a friend of the prince, and it wouldn't do to accuse him of killing someone when there was no proof.

Which meant Lon would have to find that proof.

But no matter how much he wanted Tobal to be responsible, it didn't make sense. He believed Tobal was here to get to Berith, so why kill a servant? It would only get Tobal in trouble, and it had. Now, Tobal would know that Lon was keeping an eye on him, even if Lon didn't find anything to link him to Iskander's death, which meant he'd be extra careful about whatever else he was planning. Maybe Iskander had walked in on Tobal doing something he shouldn't have.

Lon had to keep in mind that whatever reason Tobal had to be here, it probably didn't have anything to do with poor Iskander, which meant he couldn't focus on the murder if he wanted to solve the mystery that was Tobal.

When he reached his office, he didn't hesitate to open the door. Mikal stood next to it inside the office, and he nodded at Lon when he walked in. Tobal was sitting in front of Lon's desk, and he jumped to his feet, clearly flustered.

"You can't believe I had anything to do with this," he said.

"What I believe doesn't matter. The only thing that does is whether or not you're involved, and we'll find out soon enough."

Tobal swallowed heavily and sat back on the chair. "Fine. What do you want to know?"

"What happened."

"I already told you what happened. I was on my way to the library. Sabin assured me I could go there and use it, and I was bored, so I thought it was a perfect moment to do just that. I turned the corner and stumbled on the servant on the floor. I could tell he was dead, but I wanted to be sure, so I crouched next to him to check if he was breathing. I lost my footing, almost fell, and caught myself on the body. It was stupid, but it was better than falling face-first in the blood. That's when the other servant walked in and started screaming. I understand why she thought I'd killed the guy, but I truly had nothing to do with it."

Lon stared. It was a plausible explanation, and he didn't have any proof that Tobal had been involved in any other way. Still, he wasn't done. "What about the symbol on the wall?"

Because he'd noticed it. How could he not have? Whoever had killed Iskander had used his blood to draw the symbol on the wall, which meant it was important. It meant something to someone, and it made the death feel like a message. Was it a message for Tobal, though? Or was someone else involved?

Tobal looked away. "I saw it," he confirmed.

"Did you recognize it?"

Tobal shook his head. "I have no idea what that symbol is about, and I don't care. I had nothing to do with the servant's death, and I won't allow you to accuse me when you have no proof."

"Who said I was accusing you of anything?"

Tobal huffed and rubbed his face. "Look, I realize I'm acting guilty, and I understand why you interrogated me and even why you suspect me. I'm the new guy, and it makes sense that you want to accuse me rather than someone who's lived here longer. I'm not sure how to convince you that I'm innocent, but I'm going to have to. I'll do whatever I need, answer whatever question you have."

Lon was dismayed to discover that he believed Tobal. The demon looked flustered and genuinely frightened, and while he might just be a good actor, Lon didn't think so. The fact that he was interrogating him like this made him feel guilty, something he didn't like, but he needed to do his job, which in this case, meant questioning the man who'd been found on the scene with the body.

But he needed to be careful. Berith considered Tobal part of his family now, which meant he wouldn't be happy if he found out about this. He'd agree that Lon needed to do his job, but he'd tell him to be careful and not to treat Tobal like he was guilty, which was what Lon had done.

Lon leaned back in his chair, still staring. Tobal shifted in his chair, clearly uncomfortable, but Lon didn't care. What he cared about was finding Iskander's killer.

"You understand how it looks," he said slowly.

Most people who lived at the palace would have been outraged that Lon suspected them of having killed Iskander. They'd have threatened Lon and gone straight to Berith, but that wasn't what Tobal did. He didn't use his position as Zeno's brother to threaten Lon, and he answered questions easily.

"I do," Tobal said. "And I also know you need to do your job. I don't blame you for having to interrogate me, but I'd really like you to believe me when I tell you that I had nothing to do with this. I didn't have a reason to kill the servant. I'm not even sure who he was."

"You've never seen him around?"

"I might have. I'm honestly not sure. There's been so much happening since I arrived that I couldn't tell you for sure, which makes me feel guilty, because no one should die like that and not be recognized."

Lon was surprised by Tobal's words, but maybe he shouldn't be. For all that he didn't trust Tobal, he didn't seem like a bad person. He didn't behave like one, either. "We know who Iskander was. We'll make sure his family is told what happened and compensated for his death. What will help them the most is to know what happened to him, though."

Tobal nodded. "I can understand that, but I swear to you that I have no idea. I don't know anything."

"Maybe not about his death, but what about the symbol?"

Tobal looked away again, and Lon knew he was right. Tobal might not have had anything to do with the death, but he'd recognized that symbol. He knew who had put it there and what it meant, and he was terrified.

Which meant Lon was on the right track.

Tobal couldn't let Lon know he'd recognized the symbol. If he did, he'd be convinced Tobal had something to do with the servant's death, and Tobal would end up in one of the palace's cells.

Maybe it wouldn't be such a bad thing. At the very least, it would keep him away both from Berith and the people who wanted to use him against his brother. But Tobal didn't want to be locked away. He wanted to spend more time with Zeno and get to know Berith, which wouldn't happen if he was stuck in a cell.

That meant he had to convince Lon that he truly had

25

nothing to do with the death. He wasn't sure there was anything he could do or say to make that happen. He barely knew Lon, but he could tell the demon didn't trust him. He hadn't welcomed Tobal as openly as the others when he'd first arrived, which hadn't surprised Tobal. Tobal didn't blame him. As head of security, Lon was extra careful when adding new people to the palace.

And he might become a problem.

The murder was a warning to Tobal. The people who'd contacted him in the past were telling him they knew he was at the palace and that he could either work for them or die. Tobal wanted to do neither of those things, but he wasn't sure how to get himself out of the situation.

He hadn't done anything to get himself into it. These people had somehow found out he was related to Berith and had decided he'd be a nice pawn in their game. They wanted to kill Berith and put Tobal on the throne in his place, using him as a puppet to get what they wanted, which clearly was more power. Tobal had no intention of letting that happen, but he wasn't sure how to stop it without anyone getting hurt.

He supposed he could leave. He'd do that if he didn't have any other choice, but for now, he'd stay put at the palace and try to avoid being alone in the hallways. Hopefully, the assholes who belonged to this secret society would let him be and find another way to get to Berith.

But Tobal didn't want them to do that, either.

He didn't want anything to happen to Berith. The man had been nothing but nice, even though he was a prince of Hell. He'd welcomed Tobal without hesitation and had made him part of his household. Berith didn't know they were brothers, yet he'd allowed Tobal to become his family. That meant something to Tobal, but what meant even more was that Berith had welcomed Zeno. He'd given Zeno a safe place to live his life, and he'd allowed him to be with Sabin, which was all

Zeno had wanted. Tobal had never seen him so happy, and he didn't want that to change.

He licked his lips. He desperately wanted to tell Lon everything. He needed someone who knew what they were doing to be in charge, but what would Lon do? Tobal suspected he might think that Tobal actually agreed with this secret society bullshit. He'd think Tobal wanted to take Berith's place on the throne and that was why he was here. Nothing could be further from the truth, but Tobal doubted anything he'd say would convince Lon otherwise. He'd tell Berith everything, and Tobal would lose both of his brothers.

He couldn't allow that to happen.

He pressed his lips together. For now, he'd be quiet. Hopefully, the secret society would stay away from him for a while longer. He'd have time to come up with a plan, so when they struck again, he'd know what to do.

Or at least, he hoped so.

"All right," Lon declared, making Tobal jump. "If you have nothing else to tell me, you can go, but I might have to talk to you again."

Tobal got to his feet so fast he almost toppled over the chair. "Well, it's not like I'm going anywhere. You know where to find me if you need to talk to me."

Lon stared for a moment before nodding. "I do. Be careful out there."

Tobal chuckled, aware that he sounded almost hysterical. "Trust me. I don't want to stumble on another body. This isn't how I imagined my day would start."

"I doubt Iskander thought he'd die today."

And now Tobal felt guilty again. He'd had nothing to do with Iskander's murder, but nevertheless, he was involved. The secret society had been here before he arrived, and they wouldn't stop until they got what they wanted, which was Berith's throne, but Tobal couldn't help but wonder if maybe he could have done something to save Iskander. The servant hadn't deserved to die, but then, most demons didn't. They were caught in a game of power and blood, and it looked like Tobal was, too.

And he had no idea how he'd get himself out of it. He wasn't even sure he *could* get himself out of it.

Lon was already back to work, having dismissed Tobal. Tobal didn't hesitate and rushed toward the door, next to which Mikal was still standing. He gave Tobal a small smile and opened the door, but before Tobal left, he lightly touched his arm. "Do you want me to walk you back to your rooms?"

Tobal wanted to say yes, but he shook his head. "I'll be fine."

"Are you sure?"

Tobal wasn't, but he couldn't take Mikal away from his work. "I am, but thank you for the offer."

Mikal nodded and let go, and Tobal strode out. The sooner he got back to his rooms, the sooner he could break down. He wanted to cry and scream at the same time, but he didn't allow himself to do so in the hallways. There weren't many people around, but when he did cross paths with a few servants, they stared. They no doubt already knew what had happened, and he wondered if some of them thought he'd killed Iskander. Was that what his reputation would be like from now on? Would the people in the palace think he was a murderer? He hoped the answer to that was no, but he could tell that wouldn't happen. Unless someone was arrested for Iskander's murder, Tobal would always look guilty.

He turned the corner, relieved to be in the prince's private wing. He'd been surprised when Berith had given him a set of rooms here, even more so when Berith had explained he wanted his entire family to be close by. Sabin might have moved out because he and Zeno lived in the garden, but Tobal was perfectly fine here, as close to his second brother as possible.

The wing was silent as he made his way through it. He was almost running, and he did run as soon as he saw the door to his rooms. He threw it open, rushed in, and slammed it shut.

That was when he was attacked.

The demon had been waiting for him in the room and reacted as soon as Tobal was there. He threw himself at Tobal, and Tobal grabbed the first thing he could find to defend himself.

Luckily, Tobal had been raised on the streets. He'd had a weapon on him since he'd become an orphan, and even at the palace, he was never without his trusted knife. It was in his hand before he could even think about it, and when the demon tried grabbing him, Tobal sank it into the demon's arm.

The demon cried out, but he wasn't done. He had a knife, too, and he raised it, ready to kill Tobal. Tobal danced out of the way, and the knife hit the wall. The demon was dripping blood everywhere, but he was a professional. He swung at Tobal, and Tobal was lucky when he managed to avoid the knife aimed at his gut. The small victory wouldn't last long, though. Tobal might know how to fight, but that didn't mean he was a fighter. He could defend himself for a while, but not forever. He had to do something, but what?

When the demon reached for him again, Tobal raised a foot and kicked the demon in the stomach. The demon staggered back, and Tobal moved as quickly as he could. He stepped forward, aiming for the demon's throat because it would be the quickest way to dispatch him. The demon moved, but not swiftly enough. The knife sank into the demon's neck. It made a horrible sucking sound when Tobal tried pulling it out to stab him again, so he left it there. He staggered back, watching as the demon touched his neck, then dropped to the floor.

Tobal had done that. He'd killed this demon.

He took a moment to get his breath back, but he couldn't

linger. He couldn't risk having someone walk in on him and a dead demon, so as soon as he was physically able to, he dragged the body out of his room, found the nearest alcove, and stuffed him there. Someone would find him eventually, but hopefully, they'd focus on the fact that the demon had been in the prince's wing rather than on the fact that Tobal's rooms were close by. Hopefully, everyone would think he'd been there to kill Berith. He'd probably also been the one who killed the servant, and some of the guilt Tobal felt eased at that thought.

Still, he didn't breathe easier until he was back in his room, alone and safe.

But *was* he safe?

Lon's next stop was the healer, and he wasn't surprised when Mikal offered to go with him. His second in command had a crush on Reyni, and he visited him any chance he had. The problem was that Mikal couldn't see him often enough because to do that, he'd have to be wounded, or that was what Mikal seemed to believe. Lon had told him several times that he just needed to talk to Reyni, but Mikal always behaved like he didn't know what Lon was talking about. Lon had decided to let it go, but he was amused at how flustered Mikal was.

"He's not going to eat you," he pointed out as they reached Reyni's domain.

The healer didn't treat just Berith and his family, but also anyone who lived and worked at the palace. He had a small army of assistants, and the infirmary was bigger than some hospitals Lon had seen in smaller towns. Everything was sparkling clean, and the air smelled of disinfectant. There was a separate area for dead bodies since it wasn't the first time they had to deal with one, and that was where Lon headed, Mikal at his heels. One of Reyni's assistants came out of the room as Lon and Mikal reached it, but she didn't try to stop them.

Lon quickly knocked on the door, then peeked in.

He wasn't surprised to find Reyni leaning over Iskander's body. He'd already cleaned it up, so there was no blood to be seen. He'd covered Iskander's groin, which meant he'd probably already examined him.

"I thought you'd be coming by sooner," Reyni said without looking back.

Lon stepped in. "I wanted to, but I had someone to interrogate. What can you tell me?"

Reyni stepped aside and pointed at the body. Lon didn't need him to do that to see the wound at the base of Iskander's skull.

"Whoever did this was a professional. I don't think Iskander even realized someone was behind him. There was only one hit, straight to the spine, and it severed it. Iskander didn't feel anything."

Lon supposed that would be a relief for the family, but it didn't tell him much. "Anything else?"

"Not as far as I can see. I want to catch this bastard as much as you do, but that's all I have."

Lon thought of Tobal. He'd started this investigation with the conviction that Tobal had been the one to kill Iskander, and he might still be right, but what if he wasn't? That meant someone was in the palace, possibly planning to kill someone else. Considering everything, it was probable that the person was here for Berith.

Lon swore and turned to leave, but a guard burst in before he could go anywhere. He looked at the body on the table, his face turning slightly green. Lon snapped his fingers in front of the guard's face, trying to get his attention.

"What is it?" he snapped.

He wasn't usually one to lose his patience with the people

who worked for him, but right now, he was exhausted and needed to find whoever had killed Iskander as soon as possible. He had to warn Berith that someone was in the palace, planning to kill him. Berith wouldn't be surprised and insist on going on with his everyday life, but he'd make sure Lon put more guards with Mel and the rest of their family.

As if Lon needed Berith to tell him to do so.

"Another body," the guard stuttered.

Lon swore. "Take me there."

The dread that had already been present deep in his gut worsened when the guard led Lon and Mikal to the prince's wing. Lon lived there, along with Berith and his family, and he wasn't surprised to find out that was where the killer had gone.

"Who is it this time?" he asked the guard.

The demon shook his head. "Not a servant. As far as I know, no one recognized him, and he wasn't dressed as a guard, either."

Lon frowned. "Yet he was in the prince's wing." And the family and the guards, along with selected servants and heal ers, were the only ones allowed there.

"We found a knife on him. It was bloody, so it might be the knife that killed Iskander," the guard offered.

Lon and Mikal exchanged a glance. That would be the best outcome, but it created another problem.

If this second body belonged to the killer who'd murdered Iskander, who had killed *him*?

The questions swirled in Lon's mind as they reached the body. As Lon looked around, he noticed they were close to Tobal's rooms. He wasn't the only one who lived in this area of the wing, so it didn't mean he'd been the one to kill this guy, but it also might have been him.

Lon rubbed his face. "We'll need to talk to Tobal again," he said.

Mikal was frowning. "You think he did this?"

"I don't know, but he was going back to his rooms, and they're right there. Even if he didn't have anything to do with this, he might have heard something."

"You think he killed both this guy and Iskander?"

Lon had initially believed Tobal could have killed Iskander, but no longer. Unless Tobal had a personal relationship with Iskander, he wouldn't have had a reason to kill him. On the other hand, this guy was dressed like someone who'd snuck in. He was in all black, with a hood over his head and a face covering that had been pulled down to his chin. He couldn't be here for good reasons, so it would make sense that he'd been Iskander's murderer.

But maybe Tobal had killed this guy.

"I don't know," Lon said with a sigh. "Right now, I don't know anything." And he wasn't sure that would change. He had dozens of questions and no answers. How was he supposed to find out what happened when he didn't even know where to start looking?

CHAPTER THREE

Tobal had been distracted, which was a problem, because Zeno had noticed. Tobal wasn't surprised. His brother had been observant before, and clearly, that hadn't changed when he'd become a mercenary. He'd needed to see everything to survive, and it meant that now, he knew Tobal was hiding something.

Zeno hadn't asked yet, but Tobal was sure he would eventually. He was probably waiting to give Tobal time, but even though they hadn't seen each other in years, Tobal knew him. He wouldn't wait forever. He wanted to know what was going on and whether there was something he could do to help, and if Tobal didn't volunteer the information, he'd push and prod until he found it himself.

Which was a really big fucking problem.

"You haven't eaten much," Zeno said, staring at Tobal's plate.

They were having lunch together in the house Zeno and Sabin shared in the garden. Tobal had taken to spending most of his time there, at least while Zeno was home. He wasn't fully comfortable with Sabin yet, and besides, when Sabin was home, he and Zeno would rather spend time together than have Tobal as a third wheel. During the day, though, he was always welcome, which was one of the reasons he was here.

Another reason was that he was glad to be able to spend time with his brother. The main one was that he wanted to be away from the palace in case someone else was sent to kill him.

He wasn't sure why that demon had tried killing him. The society had reached out to Tobal several times, and he'd told them to fuck off on every occasion, but now, he was here at the palace. Why wouldn't they try talking to him again? Or maybe the demon hadn't been supposed to kill him. Maybe he was only meant to threaten Tobal or even hurt him, but not kill him. It would have shown Tobal how serious the society was, and he might have broken down and agreed to go along with their plan.

But now the demon was dead, and Tobal was free.

He wasn't sure how long that would last.

"Tobal?" Zeno asked.

Tobal plastered a smile on his lips and speared a piece of meat with his fork. "Sorry. I guess I'm just not used to having so much food available all the time yet. I ate a lot more than I should have at breakfast."

Zeno stared at Tobal with an expression that told Tobal he wasn't buying it.

Dammit.

He sighed. "Fine. There's more," he admitted.

Zeno cocked his head. "I'm glad you're finally ready to tell me."

"I don't want to."

Zeno looked hurt, which was the last thing Tobal wanted. "You don't have to tell me if you'd rather not," Zeno said.

"It's not that I don't want to be honest with you. I just don't want you to get in trouble."

That was the wrong thing to say. Zeno's eyes narrowed, and he leaned closer. "Which means that *you're* in trouble. What's happening? What did you do?"

Tobal tried to make a joke. "So ready to think I did something."

"Does it have to do with the two dead bodies from the other day?"

Zeno had always been like this. Once he focused on something, no one could distract him except maybe Sabin, but he wasn't here right now.

"Look, you have a marvelous life with Sabin. There's no need for you to stick your nose into this," Tobal tried.

"How can you say that? You're my brother. If you're in danger, I want to know. I'll protect you."

"I don't doubt that." Tobal thought about what he could tell Zeno. "I *am* in trouble," he eventually admitted. "Someone is after me. They want me to do something I'm not willing to do, and they won't take no for an answer. For now, I'm fine, though."

"The bodies the other day?"

"I didn't touch the servant. I did kill the other one, though. He was in my rooms, and he attacked me."

Zeno nodded. "So you're in trouble."

"I already admitted as much."

"But you won't tell me what's happening."

"Only because I don't want you to be involved. You have too much to lose."

"You're right. I do have too much to lose, and that includes my brother. I promise I won't judge you if that's what you're afraid of."

Tobal had been a little afraid of that. "For now, I'm fine," he said. He needed Zeno to stay out of this. "But I'll tell you if anyone tries anything else."

Zeno hesitated. "I can understand if you don't trust me, but you should talk to Lon, at the very least. He needs to know what's happening."

"I already thought about doing that, but he suspected me of killing the servant. Do you really think he'll believe me?"

"His only goal is to protect Berith and the family. You're part of the family, which means he'll protect you, too."

"*You* might believe I'm part of the family, but I don't think

Lon does. I also don't think he likes me very much."

"He doesn't need to like you to protect you. Please. I don't want you to have to face this alone."

Tobal considered his options. He'd been thinking about telling someone, mostly because he had no idea what he was doing. The next time he was attacked, he might not be as lucky as he had been this time, and the thought of dying before he could tell his brothers how much he loved them terrified him. What options did he have, though?

He could tell Zeno and pull his brother into this mess. Zeno wouldn't hesitate to help him, but could Tobal do that? Zeno had finally found what he wanted in life. He was settling down with Sabin, and Tobal couldn't find it in himself to put him in danger. He didn't want to lose Zeno, and he didn't want Sabin to be hurt.

But if not Zeno, who? There was no one else Tobal trusted. The most logical option would be Lon, but Tobal couldn't be sure the head of security wouldn't lock his ass up both for being involved and for not telling Berith they were brothers. Besides, who was to say that Lon would listen to Tobal and believe him? As soon as Tobal mentioned he knew part of what was going on, Lon would probably take it as an admission of guilt. Then, Tobal would lose everyone, and he couldn't deal with that.

That left him alone, unfortunately.

"I'll be careful, and I promise I'll talk to someone if things take a wrong turn," he said.

Zeno stared at him. "That's not what I said. You need to tell someone. You can't afford to wait."

"I'll be fine," Tobal promised.

"You can't know that. Someone's already tried to kill you, and it's because of whatever you're hiding. What is it?" Zeno leaned forward. "You're not planning on killing Berith, are you?"

Tobal wasn't surprised that was where Zeno's mind had gone. He was slightly hurt that his brother could think he'd do something like that, but he shouldn't be, considering the situation. "I promise I'm not planning on hurting Berith or anyone else. You know me. I wouldn't do that."

"Then why keep this secret?"

"Because I have no choice."

"We always have a choice."

Tobal wanted to believe Zeno, but he wasn't sure he could. Eventually, he'd have to make a decision. He wasn't looking forward to it, but it would be necessary.

And once he made his decision, he'd lose everything. He'd get kicked out of the palace, and Zeno might never want to see him again.

So, the longer he managed to keep all of this to himself, the better. He couldn't stand to lose his brother so soon after finding him again.

Lon knew Tobal was involved. The problem was that Tobal would never admit to it, which meant Lon would have to find proof he was right in the middle of this, whatever *this* was.

But no matter how many ways he looked at the situation and poked at it, he couldn't find anything.

He believed that the demon who'd been found in the prince's wing was responsible for Iskander's death. No one had recognized the second body, but being dressed the way he'd been and in Berith's wing, there was only one reason for that demon to have been there. That meant that whoever had killed him had probably saved Berith's life, which was a good thing, but it still didn't tell Lon what the fuck was happening.

He rubbed his face with his hands and stared at his desk. What now?

So Iskander's murder had been solved. The murderer had

been taken care of, hopefully giving Iskander's family some relief. That still left Lon with another murder. Who had killed the assassin?

He believed it was Tobal, but it was complicated. For one, why would Tobal have killed that demon? He'd told Lon he didn't know anything about Iskander's death, and Lon believed him. He'd been too pale and shocked to have been involved.

Maybe he'd walked in on the assassin. If that was the case, though, why hadn't Tobal told anyone? Lon had found out that the demon hadn't died where he'd been found, which meant he'd been moved. Why would Tobal have moved him? If he'd been the one who killed that demon, he'd done a good thing. Yet he was hiding it.

None of this made sense.

Lon got to his feet. He didn't know what was happening, and he didn't like it. He was sure Tobal was involved, though, which meant he had to talk to Berith.

He headed to Berith's office, passing through Sabin's first. Sabin waved him in, which meant Berith wasn't in any meeting and that hopefully, he'd have time to listen to Lon.

Lon knocked on the office door, then opened it when Berith called for him.

Berith grinned when he saw him. "Are you here to complain?"

Lon found himself smiling. "Always. Do you have time for me?"

"Always," Berith echoed. "Why don't you sit down?"

Sitting down wouldn't help make the news better, but Lon obeyed. Once he was on his ass, he went straight to the point. "I think Tobal is involved with that demon found in your wing," he declared.

Berith stared for a moment before nodding. "I expected you to say that. Can you tell me why you suspect him?"

"To begin with, I think it's too big a coincidence that Zeno found him again as he decided to move into the palace." Even though there was something to Mikal's thought that since Tobal had never left their hometown, it made sense that he'd found Zeno again when Zeno had visited.

"Wasn't he still living in their hometown? Technically, isn't it Zeno who found him again?"

Lon glared. "That's not my only problem."

"Tell me the other ones."

"We don't know him. I asked Mikal to look into him, and everything appears normal, but he's hiding something. I'm sure he recognized the symbol drawn on the wall next to Iskander's body, but he hasn't told me about it. It's almost as if he's frightened, which doesn't bode well."

Berith tapped his fingertips onto his desk. "Haven't you thought that maybe he's afraid of *you*?"

"Why would he be afraid of me?"

"Because you've been gunning for him since he arrived. You don't trust him, and you've made that obvious to anyone who was willing to listen to you. You don't even treat Zeno that way, which I don't understand, considering he's probably more dangerous than his brother."

Lon groaned and leaned back in the chair. "There's something about Tobal that I don't trust."

"I understand that. I'm not dismissing how you feel about this or your suspicions, but maybe you're not seeing things the way they are. You're exhausted. You've been running yourself ragged, trying to keep everyone safe. Why don't you let Mikal take over for a bit? That's what you're training him for, and it'll allow you to get a good night's sleep."

Lon wanted to say yes because he was exhausted, but this was too important. "I can continue working."

Berith sighed. "I know you can. It doesn't mean you *should*. Look, what if Tobal has nothing to do with this? You're focused on him, but what if you're wrong and someone else is planning something? You'll never forgive yourself if you don't see it in time."

That much was true. Lon didn't understand why he was so focused on Tobal, but it needed to stop. Tobal wasn't going anywhere. He was here for Zeno, or at least, that was what he'd said. So far, it appeared it might be true. He'd been spending most of his days with his brother, catching up and just being together. He hadn't given signs that he was planning on going anywhere, which meant he probably wasn't. Whatever he was planning, he needed to be here to make it happen.

"I'll get some sleep," Lon finally agreed.

"Good. I'm sure things will be clearer once you've rested."

"I'm not too sure about that. I still believe Tobal is involved."

Berith chuckled. "I know, just like I know I'm not going to change your mind. If he truly is involved, I trust you to find out what's happening."

"But you don't believe he has anything to do with it." It was frustrating, but just like Lon felt a certain way toward Tobal, Berith had his own opinions and feelings.

"I do believe he's hiding something. Who isn't, though? I have secrets, too. I hope Tobal's aren't dangerous or a threat to anyone, but I trust you. If he has nefarious intentions, you'll find out and make sure he doesn't hurt anyone."

That was a lot of trust for Berith to have in Lon, and Lon hoped he wouldn't let his friend down.

Because if he did, it meant someone would be hurt, and that wasn't something he could live with.

CHAPTER FOUR

The investigation was going nowhere. Lon stared at the documents in front of him, ignoring the tablet Sabin had set him and Berith up with. He should use it, but he was more comfortable with paper, even though Sabin teased him that he was an old man every time he saw him use that.

Lon didn't care about being an old man. What he did care about was keeping Berith and his family safe, and he felt like he was failing at it.

That was probably because he *was* failing.

He still had no idea what had happened beyond the fact that the unknown demon who'd been found dead in the prince's wing had killed Iskander. Iskander's murder had been solved, but who had killed the murderer? Everyone had been telling Lon to let go of his suspicions of Tobal, and he was tempted to, if only to keep the peace, but he couldn't shake the feeling that Tobal was hiding something. If that something had to do with hurting Berith, Lon couldn't let it go.

The problem was that investigating Tobal hadn't brought anything to the table. He was still living his life as if nothing had happened, and it was hard to believe he'd been involved. No matter how many times Lon talked to him, he couldn't get Tobal to admit to anything. He'd been watching him, but Tobal was careful not to do anything stupid in front of people who'd know to tell Lon about it.

That left Lon only one option.

He glanced at the wall. He didn't like the thought of spying on someone, especially since he couldn't be a hundred percent sure that person had nefarious intentions, but if it was the only way to protect Berith, he'd do it. He'd have to do it himself, because only a few people knew about the secret passages in the walls, but that wouldn't be a problem. As long as he told Mikal he was investigating and that he might disappear from his office without warning, Mikal would know what to expect.

Lon got to his feet. He'd told Mikal he'd be unavailable for the next hour, which would hopefully give him enough time to learn more about what Tobal was up to. He made sure his office door was locked, then went to the door and opened the secret passage.

It had been well constructed, and it was nearly impossible to see it if one didn't know it was there. One pull on the lamp by the bookshelves, and the wall opened.

Lon slipped in without hesitation. He didn't like what he was doing, but it was necessary, which meant he felt no shame. If Tobal was innocent, he'd understand. If he had something to do with what was happening, Lon didn't care how he felt.

He had to be careful not to make too much noise. He didn't want anyone to realize someone was in the walls, least of all Tobal. It would be bad if Berith found out about this, too. He'd tease Lon to no end, and while Lon didn't care about that, he did care about the fact that Berith didn't seem to see how dangerous the situation could be. They'd talked about Tobal possibly having plans to kill Berith, but Berith had dismissed it and promised Lon that if that was the case, he was more than capable of defending himself.

Lon had never doubted that. That didn't mean he was comfortable with having Tobal so close to Berith and his family, but since Berith wouldn't listen to his concerns, he was taking things into his own hands.

Lon's office was at the edge of the private wing in which he and the others lived, so it didn't take him long to head back and find Tobal's rooms. He almost got turned around once, because it was hard to understand where he was without a map, but peering out one of the many openings in the passage walls told him he was headed the right way.

Hopefully, Tobal would be in his rooms, doing something he shouldn't be doing. Lon hoped he wouldn't have to use the secret passages for too long, but he'd do it until he found proof that Tobal was involved in something unsavory.

When he reached Tobal's rooms, he took a deep breath, then slowly opened the tiny hole in the wall. Several gave onto Tobal's rooms, but for now, Lon would stick to the main living area. He didn't want to spy on Tobal in his bedroom, mostly because he was pretty sure he wouldn't like whatever he'd see if he did.

Or at least, that was what he was trying to convince himself of.

Lon should have realized things wouldn't be that easy. He'd decided to stick to the living area so he wouldn't see Tobal in a vulnerable position, but he hadn't counted on the fact that Tobal might enjoy being naked in every room, not only in the bathing room and bedroom.

There he stood, gloriously naked, sipping on a cup of coffee as he stared out the window. Lon told himself he should look away, but he couldn't seem to be able to. His gaze was pulled to Tobal's body, and what a body it was.

Tobal wasn't as tall as Lon, but he wasn't short, either. The red marks on his skin guided Lon's gaze over his body, from his toes to his tail, up to the stumpy horns poking from his messy dark hair. There had to be some djin in him, since his feet and hands were a dark red, while the color appeared in swirls over the rest of his pale skin. That wasn't all Tobal was, considering the third eye on his forehead. It was yellow, like the other two, and while mesmerizing, it wasn't what kept Lon's attention.

No, that would be Tobal's round ass.

Lon scowled. He wasn't here to stare at Tobal's naked body, dammit. He was here to find out what Tobal was up to.

He almost groaned at what his words made him think of.

He looked away, because it wasn't right for him to spy on Tobal in this state of nakedness. He wasn't sure Tobal would mind, but since he wasn't about to ask, it was the only thing he could do.

It was useless for him to stay. Clearly, Tobal wasn't up to anything that would warrant Lon's presence here, and Lon wasn't going to stick around and spy on him just because he enjoyed what was in front of him.

He slowly closed the hole in the wall, sucked in a breath, and went back the way he'd come. He hadn't discovered anything for now, but this was his first day of spying on Tobal. He was convinced that eventually, Tobal would take the wrong step, and when he did, Lon would be there to arrest him for putting the prince in danger. It would destroy Zeno, and Lon was sorry about that, but he couldn't afford to have someone who was dangerous so close to Berith.

He had no way of knowing if Tobal was planning something in particular, but he wouldn't be. Maybe Tobal was even involved with one of the many groups who wanted to get Berith off the throne. Lon had lost count of how many there were, but he had no doubt that several had people in the palace. It was infuriating, but there wasn't anything he could do about it. He worked with Mikal and Berith's spymaster to ensure no one got hurt, but sometimes, it was better to keep their enemies close rather than expose them. At least they knew who they needed to keep an eye on.

Once Lon returned to his office, he unlocked his door so it would be open if anyone needed to talk to him. Then he slid behind his desk and stared at his documents again.

He had a plan. He'd continue spying on Tobal until he found something. Tobal didn't seem like a professional assassin, although he might just be good at hiding it. It was in the family, after all. But even if he wasn't a professional, it didn't mean he couldn't be dangerous. Berith didn't believe so, but Lon didn't trust anyone with his best friend's safety, especially someone they barely knew. Whatever reason Tobal had to be here, he'd eventually expose himself, and when he did, Lon would be there.

Someone knocked on the door, and it opened before Lon could tell whoever it was to come in. He glared until he saw it was Berith, then he allowed himself to relax.

It only lasted for a moment.

"You weren't here when I came around a few minutes ago," Berith said, leaning against the doorframe.

"Well, unlike you, I work hard."

Berith grinned. "Mmm. I noticed the door to the circuit passages was open. What hard work were you doing in the passages?"

Dammit. "I don't know what you're talking about."

"Sure you don't. Are you spying on him?"

Berith didn't have to say a name for both of them to know who he was talking about. "I'm doing what needs to be done." There was no reason for him to deny what he'd been doing. He'd been planning on telling Berith anyway.

"If you say so. Some people might think you're obsessed with him, though."

"Some people might think I'm doing everything I can to keep you safe."

"I have no doubt you are. Usually, I trust your instincts, but I believe they're wrong this time."

"Yet they're yelling at me to keep an eye on Tobal."

Berith arched a brow. "Are you sure that's because you

think he's dangerous?"

"Why else?"

Thankfully, Berith didn't answer. Instead, he stared at Lon until Lon wanted to wiggle in his chair.

Damn his best friend. He'd always been able to read Lon way too easily.

Tobal loved early mornings. Most of the palace was still asleep, and he could enjoy the quietness of the moment. He had no doubt the servants were already at work, but they didn't come to the private wing until later, and if they did, they were incredibly quiet about it. Tobal's morning coffee was always in his living area when he got up, and he still had no idea who brought it.

He enjoyed watching the sky as he drank his first coffee and thought about his plans for the day. To his own surprise, he had something planned. He was meeting Zeno and Sabin, and they were coming to the palace this time. Apparently, Sabin enjoyed having breakfast with his family a couple times a week, and since Zeno would do pretty much anything for him, he came along.

Tobal had seen Zeno with the others a few times, and it had been clear he was uncomfortable. Tobal didn't blame him. Eating breakfast with a prince of Hell was nerve-racking, even though Berith was one of the good ones. It had to be even worse for Zeno because he was dating one of Berith's best friends. Berith was no doubt keeping an eye on him, just in case Zeno decided to hurt Sabin.

That wasn't something Zeno would do. He loved Sabin, and it was obvious to anyone who saw them together.

Tobal shook himself. He was happy for his brother, but wondering if he could have the same would only lead to heartache. He couldn't afford to put anyone in danger. Just his presence was enough to do so, and he didn't like it, but he didn't have a choice. That was why he'd been trying to stay away from Zeno, but his brother would have none of it, even after Tobal had admitted someone was after him. Zeno had always been stubborn, even when they were children. It was good to see that hadn't changed as he grew up, even though it was putting Tobal in a hard spot.

So instead of staying in his rooms like he wanted, Tobal got ready for the day. Once he finished his cup of coffee, he washed up, got dressed, and headed out. He'd been taking most of his meals in the dining room, so he knew where he was going. He nodded at a few servants he walked past, his stomach churning as he thought of Iskander. He hadn't known the man, but he still felt guilty about his death. He'd done everything he could to help him, though, and even killed his murderer.

It didn't feel like enough.

Tobal was relieved to see his brother and Sabin were already there when he reached the dining room. They weren't alone, and he hesitated when he saw Mel, Berith's human consort, sitting there. Mel looked up and smiled, then gestured at him to take a seat. There was no saying no to him, even if Tobal had wanted to. He didn't, though. He was curious about the human and how he'd ended up here, of all places, dating a prince of Hell.

"Good morning," Sabin said with a smile.

"Good morning." Tobal looked around the table. "Are we expecting anyone else?"

"Berith and Lon had breakfast earlier," Mel explained. He'd been reading something but turned his attention to Tobal now. "As for Cyarea, she has a stomach bug, so she and her mother are staying in their rooms today."

"I hope she's feeling all right," Tobal said as he reached for a plate to fill.

"Not really, but she'll be fine."

Tobal nodded and got to work getting his breakfast together. He still wasn't used to being able to choose from so many different dishes, but he'd learned not to eat too much, so he was careful not to overcrowd his plate. Once he was back at the table, he started eating, listening to the conversation between Sabin and Zeno. They were talking about Zeno's most recent job, leaning against each other as they did so.

Tobal wasn't jealous. Really, he wasn't.

He was happy that Zeno and Sabin had each other, but sometimes he wondered what it would be like to have someone. Maybe he'd be able to tell them what was happening with the society. Maybe they could help him get out of this situation without him losing anyone.

But he didn't have anyone, and it was better that way.

Tobal thought as he ate. Everyone here had a job. Mel was the prince's consort, but that wasn't all he did. He was also a teacher, and from what Tobal had heard, he was damn good at it. Sabin was Berith's best friend, but he was also his personal assistant. As for Zeno, he was still a mercenary, and while he'd been taking fewer jobs since he'd moved into the palace, he was still working.

But Tobal wasn't doing anything, and he didn't like it.

He was used to working. He'd done it his entire life, as soon as he'd been taken in by his foster parents. They hadn't behaved like parents but rather like abusers, and Tobal and the other kids who lived there had been forced into compliance. They hadn't had a choice. If they wanted to eat, they needed to work.

But right now, Tobal was relying entirely on Berith's generosity. It didn't sit well with him, especially knowing that Berith was his brother and that he was in danger. Tobal wanted to do more, but he doubted anything would help him feel any less guilty about not telling Berith the entire truth.

"You're thinking so loud I can hear it," Zeno suddenly teased.

Tobal blinked at him. "I don't think that's possible."

Zeno shrugged. "I don't know. What's going on, though? Is it about what we had that conversation about the other day?"

Tobal narrowed his eyes to warn him, but Zeno ignored him. Thankfully, it was fairly easy to redirect the conversation. "I was thinking that everyone here has a job except for me. It doesn't feel right."

"Well, that should be easily dealt with," Mel offered. "What do you feel like doing?"

"That's the problem. I have no idea. Before, I had to work to survive, so I did pretty much anything I could find."

Mel nodded. "But here, you have a choice and don't want to make the wrong one."

"Exactly. There's so much I could do that it almost scares me."

"You and Zeno have a unique point of view. Unlike most people in the palace, you know how life is out there. Berith and I have been trying to improve things, but it's hard. Maybe you could help us with that?"

Tobal leaned closer. "At the very least, I'm interested in hearing more about that idea."

Mel smiled. "It's not much for now, because we have no idea what we're doing, which is why it sounds like a good idea to get you involved. You know what the children out there need. You were one of them. Maybe we could set up a meeting? You can start working with Sabin and getting lists together. It won't be easy, and it won't be quick, but Berith wants to change things in his territory, and I want him to succeed."

"Why? We're demons. We're in Hell. Our lives are supposed to be hard."

Mel cocked his head. "Are they?"

Tobal wasn't sure what to say to that. His life had never been easy, and Mel clearly didn't know what he was talking about.

But that was why Mel wanted to involve Tobal. From what Tobal had seen, Mel was a good person. A bit odd, but it probably was because he was the only human Tobal had ever met. No matter what he was, he wanted to make things better for children, and that was something Tobal could get behind. He *had* been one of those kids. If he could make even one child's life better, he wanted to be involved.

He grinned at the prince's consort. "I'm in."

Watching over Berith during his many meetings was one of the aspects of the job that Lon disliked the most. It was boring, both because of what was being said at the table and because his only job at the moment was to stand behind Berith and keep an eye on the ministers sitting around, arguing about one thing or another. It was endless bickering, and Lon could have done without it.

But his place was next to Berith, and he was already doing a bad job keeping his prince safe. The least he could do was to listen to the ministers droning on and on about what they believed Berith should do. Usually, Berith told them to fuck off at one point or another, which was always entertaining.

"I don't see why we should set up these places," one of the ministers said.

Her eyes were black pools that didn't give away anything. Lon had no idea what she was thinking, and he didn't care. Just like every other demon around the table, she was dangerous.

That was why Lon was here.

Berith looked seconds from strangling her. "Because these

are *children*. They live in my territory, and I don't want them to suffer."

"It'll take gold."

Berith almost growled. "We have plenty of that," he said, gesturing at the opulent room they were meeting in, then at her. "Look at you, Nowla. The tunic you have on and the jewelry could probably fund a dozen of these safe houses. We have the means to do this."

"But they're not our problem. Their parents should take care of them."

"What if they're dead?"

Nowla delicately shrugged. "Then I suppose those children will die, too. Again, I don't see how this is our problem. We've never done anything like this, and I don't see a need for us to start. Some children will die, but so what? We'll be overrun in a few years if we keep every child alive *alive*."

And there was the main reason she didn't want to help kids. She was afraid lesser demons would eventually take over and take everything from her, including her luxurious house and jewelry.

Lon couldn't deny it was a fear they all had, but that wouldn't stop Berith. Hopefully, keeping children and people happy would mean they were loyal to Berith.

Berith had never wanted to lead his territory with fear and power like most other princes of Hell did. He wanted his people to like him, and he'd been working hard to make that happen. Sometimes, he stumbled, because he didn't know how to do it. No one else did, after all, which meant he was a trailblazer. That was probably why, for the most part, he'd gone the easy way, but that had changed when Mel had come into his life. The human was horrified that even one child had to go hungry or was abused. He wanted to keep all of them safe, which probably had to do with his job as a teacher, but Lon couldn't blame him. He didn't want children to suffer, either.

"I'm not surprised you feel that way, but I don't," Berith snapped. "I *will* open these houses, even if I have to pay for them myself. It won't be the first time I've had do something like that, anyway."

"If you're going to do whatever you want, why are you asking for advice?" Nowla asked, her black eyes narrowing.

"I thought I could make you see that this was important." Berith's tone was icy. "Things are changing. Things *should* change, and if you stay back, you'll miss out on them."

"This is still Hell," Huward, another minister, said. "People are supposed to suffer."

Berith arched a brow. "Because you do?"

Huward had the good taste to look bashful. "I did. I didn't get to where I am because people were handing out things."

"I don't see it as a handout. I see it as helping the most vulnerable of our people. Doesn't anyone at this table agree with me that it's the right thing to do?" Berith looked around, hoping for someone to speak up.

Lon held his breath. He didn't have a lot of faith in these ministers. Most days, he wondered what Berith needed them for. He ended up making his own decisions anyway.

But they did a lot of work that would fall back on Berith's shoulders if he didn't have them. That much Lon knew. Maybe it was time for Berith to choose better ministers, though. Surely not everyone in their territory thought the way Nowla and Huward did.

"I agree with Berith," Sira said. "I've seen the state of some of these children. I've tried helping them, but there's not much I can do on my own. I've welcomed several orphans in my home, and I'm glad that someone came up with a solution to help others."

Berith's glance toward him was appreciative. "I didn't know you'd taken in orphans."

Sira shrugged. "It's part of my private life, and I don't see the need to talk about it. But yes. I don't want children to suffer. No one should want that."

The rest of the ministers grumbled but eventually agreed with Berith and Sira. Lon was surprised. Most of them went on and on when they were convinced they were right, and he'd expected the meeting to go on for hours. Berith would have won in the end. Even if the ministers had refused to fund his safe houses for children, he'd have used his personal wealth, and he had plenty of it.

But it was good that the ministers had approved this. It meant the houses would be official and, hopefully, that there would be even more money to build them.

Lon made a mental note to keep an eye on Nowla and Huward, who'd been so opposed to Berith's suggestion. It was probably nothing, but better safe than sorry, especially when it came to the prince.

The ministers eventually started leaving the room, but Lon stayed behind with Berith. He wouldn't be going anywhere without his prince, and it was good to see that Berith was taking a moment to breathe.

"That could have gone much worse," Lon said as soon as the door was closed behind them.

"For a moment, I thought it would," Berith admitted. "I knew it wouldn't be easy to make them accept the idea that no one deserves to suffer. We might be demons, but we're not monsters, at least most of us. I don't understand how so many of my ministers oppose this plan. Why would they want children to die?"

"They're using being demons to justify themselves."

Berith nodded. "They are. I'm glad that a few of them agreed this was a good idea."

"Don't go giving Sira a promotion now," Lon warned.

Berith laughed. "If I could, I'd give him my throne."

That was probably true. Berith had never been comfortable

being prince, but he'd accepted the job because it was the right thing to do. He was great at it, too, better than most of the princes Lon had heard about. Whether it would be enough to keep him on the throne for years to come was still to see, but as long as Lon was by Berith's side, he'd make sure nothing happened to him.

Or at least, he'd try to. Right now, he felt like he wasn't good at his job and should have put Mikal in control. He wasn't about to do that when his best friend was in danger, but all of this made him think.

What if he couldn't find out what Tobal was up to? What if he was planning on hurting Berith, and Lon wasn't in time to stop him?

And what about the other demons who wanted Berith dead? He didn't just have enemies in other territories. He didn't even just have enemies outside of the palace. Some of them were right here, and without knowing who they were, it was next to impossible to stop them.

CHAPTER FIVE

"Where would you start?" Sabin asked.

He stared at Tobal until Tobal wanted to run away screaming. He'd known this meeting wouldn't be easy, but he hadn't expected it to be so complicated. He'd thought Sabin already had a vague idea of what would be needed to help the kids, but it seemed he'd been waiting for Tobal.

Tobal swallowed. "It depends on what Berith wants to do."

Sabin shook his head. "If you think something is necessary, he'll listen to you. You have much more experience than any of us." He hesitated. "Why don't you tell me about your childhood? You don't have to go into details if they're too painful, but I think it would give me a better idea of how a child can end up having to work to survive."

Tobal leaned back. He was sitting at Sabin's desk, ready to work, but he should have known he'd have to talk about his past. He didn't mind. It *had* been painful, but it had been years, and he couldn't regret anything that happened to him, because it meant he was here today.

"I grew up with my mother," he began. "My father was never in the picture, but she loved me and did everything she could to give me a good childhood. It was, for the most part. It wasn't easy for her to feed me and give me everything I needed, but she loved me, and that was all that mattered."

"She sounds like she was a good person."

"She was. She was alone in the world except for me, but we made it work."

"What happened to her?"

"She was killed. Someone broke into our house to steal things, and while she managed to hide me, there wasn't time for her to hide. She defended herself, but the demon killed her. I stayed with her body for the rest of the night. We were friends with the neighbors, and one of them always kept an eye on me while my mother was at work. She came to check in on us when she didn't see us. She found my mom and ensured she was taken care of."

"What happened to the demon who killed her?"

"Nothing."

Sabin's eyes widened. "How is that possible?"

"No one cared about her enough to investigate. Like I said, we didn't have anyone."

"But surely your town had guards."

"Yeah, but those guards are to protect the mayor and the other few officials we have. They were never to help us, especially when she was already dead."

Sabin looked horrified, and unless Tobal was mistaken, there were tears in his eyes. He hadn't wanted to make Sabin sad, but this was what had happened to him when he was a child, and Sabin had wanted to know.

"Why didn't the neighbor take you in?" Sabin asked.

He was taking notes, and Tobal was curious as to what he was writing. Maybe Sabin would show him when this conversation was over. "She already had three kids of her own. She couldn't afford to take me in, and I never blamed her for that. My mom wouldn't have, either."

"And that's how you ended up in that place?"

It was cute how Sabin couldn't even say the word. "It is. They took in a lot of orphan kids, and that was all anyone was interested in. It meant they didn't have to see children running around the town alone, starving to death. We were fed, but we were also worked down to the bone."

Sabin nodded. "And it's where you met Zeno."

"We shared the same room. Well, we shared it with a dozen other kids, but we also shared a bed, which is how we became friends. He was always there for me, and we made many plans about what we'd do once we left."

Sabin's expression did a complicated thing. He knew about part of Tobal's past because he knew about Zeno's. "But he left without you," Sabin whispered.

"He did, but I'll never blame him for that."

"He's worried you do."

"I understand, but I'll tell him until he believes me. If I'd had the opportunity, I would have left, too."

"Why didn't you?"

Tobal shrugged. "I guess it was easier for me to stay. It was the only thing I knew, and I wasn't as brave as Zeno. Eventually, I burned the house down, but I was an adult when I did that. I should have done more to protect the kids I left behind once I was old enough to go."

"Why did you burn the place down?"

Tobal wasn't about to tell Sabin the truth about it, at least not entirely. "I found out they had some of my mother's things. I went back because I wanted to find out if my father was still alive, but they couldn't tell me anything. They didn't know."

"Did you find your father?"

Tobal shook his head. "I've been told he's dead. There was nothing anyone could have done to help me out of that place. I made it out anyway, but many other children weren't that lucky. Many of them are worked to death, and that's one of the things I want to prevent."

Sabin nodded. "We want the same thing. So, what do we do about it?"

Tobal leaned over the desk to check Sabin's notes. "Well, you have good ideas. I suppose that the first thing we could do is build a safe house for children in as many towns as we can. You'll need people there who can help the kids and know where to find them. Especially in the beginning, it will be word of mouth. Once the kids know the place is safe, they'll start coming on their own. Someone will have to be there to take care of them and finish raising them in many ways. You can't stick just anyone there."

"We won't. We're not doing this alone. We need a plan that we can show Berith, but once he agrees with what we come up with, we can hire more people. There are only two of us, so it's impossible to go through every town and find the kids who need help, but we won't have to. We just need to start."

Tobal was terrified he'd do something wrong and ruin the entire project, but now that he knew that doing this was possible, it was dear to his heart. He wanted to help the kids out there who still had a chance at having a good life. He wanted to give them what he hadn't had, and while he wouldn't have had the opportunity to do so if he hadn't found Zeno and moved to the palace, now, he did.

And he'd take full advantage of that.

Lon pressed his forehead against the wall. He hadn't meant to spy on Tobal and hear his conversation with Sabin, but he hadn't been able to leave once he heard what they were talking about.

He'd only meant to check in on Sabin and make sure he was all right with Tobal in his office. What Tobal had said about his childhood was like a punch to the stomach, making Lon want to throw up.

He'd been lucky. Both his parents had been good people, and he'd grown up with Berith. He'd always had everything he needed, from both Berith and his parents. He'd never had to worry about what would happen to him if his father died or if they didn't have enough money to feed themselves.

He'd known that building these safe houses for the kids was a good idea, but he was even more convinced of it now. They were going to do this, and Tobal would help.

But none of what Tobal had said just now meant he wasn't trying to kill Berith. It made Lon want to believe it, but what if he was wrong? What if all of this was a lie?

It couldn't be. Mikal had looked into Tobal, and Lon remembered his report. Everything Tobal had just said was the truth. Lon wasn't sure about some of the details, but why would Tobal lie about those and not about the most important events in his life?

No, Tobal *had* gone through all of this, and the fact that he'd survived was a small miracle.

But where did that leave Lon?

He sighed and pushed away from the wall. He was hidden in the wall's secret passage, which made him feel dirty. Sabin wouldn't care that he was listening to the conversation, but what about Tobal? How would he feel if he found out that he hadn't been telling his story just to Sabin, his brother-in-law, but also to Lon? In his place, Lon would be pissed. He wasn't sure Tobal would be, and it wasn't like he'd ever tell him, but still. It made him feel guilty.

It also made him proud, and he didn't fully understand that feeling. What was there to be proud of? He and Tobal weren't together. Lon shouldn't feel this way about him, yet he did. Most demons would have gone on to hurt people, almost like revenge for how much pain they'd been in. Not Tobal, though, who wanted to help kids have opportunities he hadn't had. If Lon hadn't suspected him of planning something nefarious, he might have stopped resisting.

But he couldn't.

He walked away, even though he could still hear Tobal and Sabin. He made his way back to his office, still thinking about what he'd heard.

He wasn't surprised that Tobal's life had been hard since the very beginning. Berith's territory was nicer than most, but they were still in Hell. Life was hard, and most of the princes made it even harder for the demons who lived in their territories. Many of them had migrated to Berith's when they'd realized he was doing what he could to keep his people happy, but they'd brought trouble. Until recently, Berith had left them to their own accord, but it was clear more needed to be done. The children, at the very least, needed to be protected.

And apparently, Tobal, of all people, would make sure they were.

In the end, Lon hadn't found out anything he didn't already know about Tobal. The only thing he'd seen was more proof that Tobal was a good person, which made him wonder if he was seeing all of this wrong. What if Berith was right and Tobal had nothing to do with any of this? What if Lon was obsessing over the wrong person? It could mean he wouldn't see it when the person who actually wanted to kill Berith attacked, and he couldn't allow that to happen.

So, change of plans. He'd continue keeping an eye on Tobal, but he'd expand the investigation. He'd go over all the reports again just to make sure he hadn't missed anything, and as long as he didn't find anything that pointed to Tobal, he'd leave him alone and try to stop obsessing over him. Everyone was giving Tobal a chance except for Lon. He didn't trust him, but maybe it was time to accept that Tobal was part of their family. He hadn't been here long, but he was making himself at home, and that was possibly all he wanted. It wasn't fair for Lon to continue watching him with suspicion until he did something that would warrant it.

Lon didn't like admitting he was wrong, but in this case, he had been.

Or at least, he hoped so. Many people would be hurt if it

came out that Tobal had been plotting against Berith the entire time he'd been here, and Lon would be one of the people left behind to pick up the pieces.

CHAPTER SIX

It was never a good thing to hear someone run toward his office, so when Lon did, he tensed. He waited, knowing he'd find out what was happening soon.

Sure enough, only a few seconds had passed when a quick knock on his door told him trouble was here. The person on the other side didn't wait for him to answer, instead pushing the door open. Lon would have been pissed at anyone else doing this, but it was Mikal.

"What is it?" Lon asked as he got to his feet.

"The prince was attacked."

Mikal sounded out of breath, possibly because he'd come running all the way from wherever Berith had been attacked. He'd known Lon would want to know as soon as possible, and he'd been right.

"Is he wounded?" Lon asked, already moving to follow.

"He says he's not."

"Well, at least he's well enough to talk."

"That he is. I already had someone fetch a healer."

Lon nodded. Mikal probably would have wanted to get Reyni himself, but he'd chosen to come to Lon instead. Lon was grateful. Mikal could have easily sent another guard, but he'd known Lon would freak out and that his presence would be reassuring. The fact that he was here rather than by Berith's side was an indication that Berith was probably okay.

Lon still had to see him with his own two eyes.

They made their way to the prince, Lon following Mikal. His stomach churned, even though this was far from the first time Berith was attacked. It probably wouldn't be the last, but knowing all of this didn't make Lon feel any better. He was supposed to protect the prince, yet he couldn't seem to stop the demons from sneaking into the palace and attacking him. Sooner or later, one of them would manage to do what they were here to do, and Berith would be hurt or worse. What would Lon do then?

He *had* to put an end to this.

They headed toward the prince's wing but didn't stop there. Mikal continued, crossing the hallway and moving toward the doors that opened to the garden. Lon was relieved when he heard Berith's voice and almost started running. Berith sounded fine, and Lon told himself he had to look the part. He was the palace's head of security, and that came with authority but also expectations. If he showed the guards he was freaked out, they'd freak out, too, and that was the last thing he needed. They had to believe he was in control even though he didn't feel like he was.

They reached one of Mel's favorite spots. The prince's consort enjoyed the gardens and spent a lot of time here when he wasn't with the children he taught. Berith had made it comfortable for Mel, adding couches and a few tables and covering the area with a light gazebo. Mel's skin was very much human and not used to the heat and sun of Hell. This way, he didn't burn.

Berith was sitting on one of the couches, Mel by his side. The human was fussing, but Berith didn't seem to mind. If anything, he leaned into it, visibly happy to have the man he loved taking care of him.

Lon relaxed. As far as he could see, there were no traces of blood on Berith. A body was slumped against the wall a bit further away, but a guard was covering it with a blanket, no doubt so Mel wouldn't have to look at it. Lon was impressed by the fact that Berith seemed to have taken care of his attacker without shedding a single drop of blood.

"What happened?" Lon asked when he reached Berith.

He and Mel weren't the only ones there. Sabin was curled into one of the armchairs, and hovering next to him was Tobal. His focus kept bouncing from Sabin to Berith, as if he wasn't quite sure who he should be taking care of. He'd seemed to decide to stick with Sabin, which was the best choice, since Zeno was nowhere to be seen, either on a job or at the house he and Sabin shared deeper in the garden.

Berith looked up. "Isn't it obvious?"

Lon glared at him. "You were attacked and killed the attacker. I already know that. What I don't know are the details. Speak."

Lon couldn't look away from Tobal. Why was he here? Was he involved in the attack? Berith would have behaved differently if Tobal had been openly involved, but maybe he'd acted behind the scenes. How had the attacker come in? Someone had to have helped them, and that someone could be Tobal just like it could be anyone else.

Lon told himself to stop. He'd promised he'd give Tobal a chance, and that was what he'd been planning on doing. He needed to stop obsessing over Zeno's brother unless he was sure Tobal was involved.

And he wasn't sure yet.

"As you can see, I was attacked," Berith said. "There were two of them. I only managed to kill one, while the other ran."

"Because he was focused on me," Mel intervened. "I was there, and I freaked out. I'm really sorry."

Berith patted Mel's hand. "You have no reason to be sorry. You shouldn't have to worry about being attacked in your home."

The words went straight to Lon's heart. Berith was right. Neither he nor Mel should worry about being attacked while they were relaxing in their garden. It was his job to make sure they weren't, but he wasn't doing it.

He turned to look at Mikal. "Where's the second demon?"

"I sent guards out to find them, but no one has reported back so far."

Lon nodded and looked around. His gaze stopped on Tobal again, and while he didn't say anything about suspecting Tobal was involved, his expression clearly was enough for Tobal to understand what he was thinking.

Tobal's eyes widened, then he glared. "I wasn't the second demon," he said.

"I never said you were." But it was interesting that he was defending himself without Lon even having to ask.

"You don't have to. I know you don't trust me and that you think I'm here to hurt Berith."

"Once again, I never said that."

"You don't trust me."

"I don't," Lon agreed, although, to be fair, he didn't trust most people.

"Can we not do this?" Sabin snapped. "Tobal was with me, so stop thinking he was involved, because he wasn't. Shouldn't you be focused on catching the other demon instead of accusing Tobal of something he didn't do?"

Lon wanted to snap back, but Sabin was right. He hadn't truly believed Tobal was involved, at least not openly, and the fact that he'd been with Sabin when the demons had attacked meant he wouldn't have to worry about possibly missing something. As far as everyone was aware, Tobal was innocent of anything.

He nodded curtly. "I don't suspect you," he told Tobal. "But I have to talk to all of you."

Berith sighed. "Of course you do. What's happening, Lon? Why are so many demons attacking recently?"

Lon didn't have an answer to that question, unfortunately. He'd been looking into it, but he hadn't found anything out of the usual.

There had always been people who wanted to kill Berith for one reason or another. Most of the time, Lon managed to stop them before they even snuck into the palace. The fact that demons kept getting to Berith made him think that someone was working against him from the palace. Whoever these demons were, whoever they worked for, they had inside help, and maybe that was what Lon needed to focus on. If he'd taken care of whoever was sneaking them in, they wouldn't have a way into the palace anymore.

His gaze flickered to Tobal again. He told himself that this kind of trouble had started way before Tobal moved into the palace, which meant he wasn't the person letting the demons in.

But it didn't mean he wasn't involved.

Tobal understood why Lon was suspicious. He couldn't even blame him, since in a way, he *was* involved. He was hiding enough that Lon would feel vindicated if he ever found out about it.

But Tobal had nothing to do with this attack. He hadn't known about it, had never met the dead demon slumped against the garden wall, and he'd been with Sabin when the attack had happened. Sabin had freaked out, and Tobal had spent some time trying to reassure him. It had been easier after they'd seen that Berith was all right, but Tobal couldn't help but wonder.

Was this the society?

He was ready to bet that it was. They were still trying to get to Berith, even though they weren't using Tobal to do so at the moment. He was glad, because he didn't want anything to do with any of it, but it wouldn't last. They wanted to use him, and if he continued saying no, they wouldn't hesitate to get rid of him. He knew too much, and they were very much aware of that.

Tobal needed to defend himself, and he needed to defend Berith and the others. He'd never have forgiven himself if Berith or Mel had been hurt. What could he do, though? He wouldn't be able to stop the society. It wasn't like they'd listen to him if he asked them to, because he was nothing more than a pawn in their game. They thought that having him on their side would give them legitimacy, that he'd let them use him as a puppet, but nothing could be further from the truth.

He had no intention of ever being prince, real or fake, which meant he needed Berith to be alive and on the throne. He'd hoped the society would let it go once they realized he didn't want to be involved, but he'd been an idiot. He should have known they wouldn't let go of him so easily.

Where did that leave him?

He wasn't sure. He hated that Lon always suspected him first, even though Lon was right to do so. He wanted to help keep Berith and the others safe, but the only way to do that would be to tell them about the society, and in turn, about him being Berith's brother.

And he wasn't sure he could do that.

He cleared his throat. "I can come with you to your office, if you want to interrogate me," he told Lon.

They might as well get this out of the way. Lon had wanted to interrogate him when Iskander had been killed, and since he still suspected him, he'd probably want to do the same now. Besides, maybe Tobal would be able to get more details about what happened. Lon didn't know much at the moment, but that wouldn't last long. He was the head of security, and the guards would tell him every single detail. Tobal wanted to know them, too, and the best way to get them was to be in Lon's office when the guards reported to him.

Or at least, he hoped so.

But Lon shook his head, surprising Tobal. "There's no need for you to come to my office. Sabin just vouched for you, and anyway, I didn't believe you were involved."

"Why not? You did before."

Lon arched a brow. "You sound sorry that I don't suspect you this time around."

Tobal wasn't, although he wouldn't have said no to spending more time with Lon — as long as he didn't accuse him of trying to kill his brother.

Lon was handsome. He wasn't pretty, like Mel and Sabin, but that wasn't the kind of demon Tobal usually went for anyway. No, Lon was rugged, with broad shoulders and thick, black horns that curled away from his face. His light red skin was pretty and usually hidden under his uniform, but Tobal didn't need to see all of it to imagine it. Lon's white eyes seemed to look right into him, making him want to squirm.

"I'm sorry," Tobal quickly said. "I just don't want you to think I'm skirting my responsibilities or whatever." That sounded like something Lon might say.

"I don't believe you are. I apologize if I treated you badly before, but I was investigating a murder. I don't believe you had anything to do with Iskander's death or the attack."

Tobal nodded. "Good, because I didn't." Mostly. He didn't have anything to do with Iskander's death, but he did know more than he'd told anyone. Lon would be pissed if he ever found out about this, but Tobal was starting to wonder if maybe he should. He'd know what to do better than Tobal.

But the thought of telling him was terrifying.

Tobal swallowed. He wasn't stupid. He'd wanted to try keeping all of this a secret, but he'd known it might not be possible. He wasn't the only one in danger, and the society was much bigger than he was. It wouldn't take much for them to hurt someone, and he'd never forgive himself if they did and he hadn't stopped them. He wasn't sure there was anything he could do, but could he deal with not even trying?

This time, Berith had escaped. He was fine, as was everyone else. What about next time, though? What about people like Iskander, who were in the wrong place at the wrong time? And what about Mel and Sabin?

Tobal's head ached, and he still had no more answers. The situation was degenerating, and he feared that every single one of them would eventually be in danger.

Maybe he could leave. It would the coward's way, but if it helped keep the others safe, he'd do it. The problem was that he didn't think it *would* keep anyone safe. The society had already set its eyes on Berith. They wanted his throne, Tobal or no Tobal. If they couldn't have Tobal, they'd put someone else in his place on Berith's throne and call it a day. Tobal would give them more legitimacy because he was Berith's brother, but it wasn't like anyone knew about it. They could always put someone else on the throne and say they were Berith's brother, sister, or anything else, really. No one would check or care.

The goal was to get rid of Berith, and the society was working hard to make that happen. Tobal wanted to do something, but what?

He didn't know, and he wouldn't find out on his own. This wasn't something he knew how to deal with, which meant he had to involve someone else. The demon who made the most sense was Lon, unfortunately. Zeno would help if Tobal told him, and he probably would eventually, but his brother was just Sabin's lover. He didn't have any kind of authority at the palace, while Lon did. If there was one person who knew how to deal with all of this, it was Lon.

Which meant Tobal had to talk to him.

Tobal's mouth tasted like ash. What would happen when he did? Would Lon go straight to Berith and tell him what Tobal had said? Would he demand Tobal do it himself? Or would he tell Tobal he had to leave?

All of those were possible, and Tobal hated every option. He'd never been planning on keeping his link to Berith a secret forever. He just wanted some time to watch Berith and ensure he was a good person. He wanted to know Berith without the added pressure of him knowing they were brothers.

And he had. Berith *was* a good person. He could have told Tobal to fuck off, since Tobal was nothing more than Zeno's brother and not even related by blood. Instead, he'd welcomed Tobal and had given him a home, not expecting anything in return. If telling him meant Tobal had to leave the palace, then he would.

He hoped things wouldn't come to that.

Lon was exhausted when the situation was resolved, or at least as resolved as it would be. He wanted nothing more than to go back to his rooms, take a bath, and sleep for a week, but instead, he headed to his office, Mikal trailing behind him.

They hadn't found the second demon. Whoever it was had either managed to escape or was hiding, but the guards hadn't been able to find them so far. They were still combing through the palace, but no one had much hope they'd find the second attacker. Lon hoped it was because the demon had escaped, but he couldn't help but wonder if it was because that demon was a servant or someone who worked at the palace. That would be the best way for them to hide, and it would make finding them impossible.

"You should get some rest," he told Mikal as they reached the office.

"Look who's talking. You look like you haven't slept in a week."

"I feel like it, too. I'm going to stay awake for a while longer, just in case the guards find something."

Mikal nodded. "I doubt they will."

Damn him for saying out loud what Lon had been trying not to think about. "I feel the same, but we need a win. I don't know what to do." Lon wouldn't have admitted that to anyone else, but Mikal was safe. He worked side by side with Lon, so he knew how much Lon was fretting over all of this.

Mikal patted Lon's shoulder. "You'll find out who's behind this. I have faith in you."

It touched Lon, but he didn't feel like he deserved so much trust. "I hope so. Get some rest. I'll wake you up if there's anything new, but we both know that's not going to happen."

"Whoever the second demon was, they're in the wind."

And no one had recognized the first demon. Lon was having a picture shown to every demon in the palace, but so far, no one had identified the dead demon. Not knowing what was happening was becoming routine, which he wasn't happy with.

Mikal headed out, leaving the door slightly open. Lon didn't have the energy to close it or do anything else. He flopped into his chair behind his desk and closed his eyes, tilting his head up.

The palace was falling silent around him. People were going to bed, where he should be headed, too. He was tempted to go check in with Berith first, but he didn't want to bother him and Mel.

A soft knock on the door made him look up. With it open, he could see it was Tobal, and he had to school his expression so Tobal didn't understand how surprised he was.

"Yes?" he called out.

Tobal opened the door more fully and peeked in. He seemed relieved to find Lon alone, which made Lon perk up. Why was Tobal here?

He'd never been alone with Lon of his own free will. Lon could understand that. No one wanted to meet with him, because it usually meant there was a problem or they were in trouble. Yet Tobal was shuffling his feet, clearly needing to say something.

Lon had to play his cards right. If he was too harsh, he'd send Tobal running, and he couldn't afford that. He might be about to get the truth about what had been happening, and he couldn't jeopardize that.

"What can I do for you?" he asked, keeping his voice gentle.

Tobal hesitated, then seemingly made a decision. He nodded, stepped into the office, and closed the door. "I need to talk to you," he declared.

Lon resisted the urge to dance in victory. "Of course. I'm always available to listen to whatever you have to say."

Tobal snorted. "You could sound less happy."

"I've been waiting for you to do this since you arrived."

Tobal sighed. "I know. I probably should have talked to you sooner, but honestly, I'm still not sure it's the right thing to do."

"Why don't you sit down and start from the beginning? We'll go from there."

Tobal sat on the edge of the chair as if he expected to have to run. Maybe he did. Depending on what he had to say, Lon had no idea how he'd react. He could freak out, although he hoped he'd be able to keep himself under control.

Tobal sucked in a breath. He stared down at his hands in his lap, and while Lon wanted to push, it was clear Tobal needed a moment. Lon wasn't about to ruin everything. He might not trust Tobal, but Berith did. More than that, Tobal was Zeno's brother, and Zeno was Sabin's partner. Lon would never do anything to hurt one of his best friends, which meant that if there was even a chance that Tobal wasn't involved, he needed to consider it. The fact that Tobal was here, ready to talk to him, pointed to the fact that while he could be involved, it clearly weighed on him. He wanted to help, and that might just be what Lon needed to solve this case.

"I don't know if you're aware of how I grew up," Tobal eventually said.

Lon had no idea why he was starting there but decided to go with the flow. "You were an orphan. You grew up with Zeno."

"I did. My mother died when I was young, and I never met my father. I never knew who he was until recently, either. I found out that the people who took Zeno and I in had kept some of my mother's things in their attic. She had diaries, and I read them. My father's name was there."

Lon slowly nodded, wondering where this was going. "Do you need help locating your father?" It wasn't what he'd expected, but if that was what Tobal needed, he might be able to help.

But Tobal shook his head. "He's dead."

"I'm sorry."

"I'm not. I never knew him, and I'm fine with that. I wasn't an only child, though. My father had another son."

That got Lon's attention. "Can you tell me who that son is?"

Tobal licked his lips and finally looked up. His eyes were wide, and he seemed afraid, which didn't make sense. If Lon hadn't known better, he'd have wondered if Tobal was about to tell him *he* was that brother.

"I won't hurt you," Lon said slowly. "No matter who that person is or what he's done."

"He hasn't done anything. I'm just not sure you'll believe me."

"Try me." Something told Lon he needed that name.

Tobal swallowed loudly. "It's Berith. He's my half-brother. He was already born when my mother got pregnant, and his father gave her money to leave. I guess he didn't want the complication of having a bastard son."

Lon was in shock. He didn't know what to say or even if he could say something.

He wasn't surprised by the revelation. Berith's father was known for not keeping his dick in his pants, and Lon had always been surprised he didn't have more children. Berith was the only official one, since he'd been born from the union between his parents, but that didn't always mean much in Hell.

"Anyway, that's one of the reasons I wanted to come to the palace," Tobal continued. "I never thought I'd be able to meet Berith, and I had to take this opportunity when it presented itself. I'm glad I did. I swear to you that I didn't hurt him. I don't want to become the prince in his place or anything like that. Hell, just the thought of being a prince makes me want to scream and run. I don't want anything from him beyond being allowed to get to know him. I had nothing to do with this attack or with what happened to Iskander."

Lon wasn't sure why, but he believed Tobal. It made sense that Berith had a brother—what was surprising was that he only had one—although what kind of coincidence could it be that the brother was Tobal?

Tobal wouldn't be surprised if Lon didn't believe him, but beyond showing him his mother's diaries, Tobal wasn't sure how to convince him he was telling the truth. More importantly, he needed Lon to believe him when he said he didn't have anything to do with the attack, and he wasn't sure how to do that, either. The only thing he could offer was his word, but he doubted it would be enough for Lon.

He was afraid of looking up. He'd glanced up for a split second, but fear had driven him to look back down at his hands. He had no idea if Lon was angry or suspicious or something else.

Probably. Tobal would be suspicious if their roles were reversed. An unknown guy arrived and told him he was the prince's brother? No one would believe that. Tobal wouldn't believe it.

Yet, as far as he knew, it was the truth.

He supposed his mother could have lied, although he didn't see why she would have done something like that. Beyond the money she'd gotten from Berith's father after she got pregnant, Tobal hadn't found any clues that she'd ever contacted him. Why would she have? He'd made it clear he didn't want anything to do with her and Tobal, and she'd been more than happy to raise Tobal on her own. Adding Berith's father to the mix would have made things worse, and Tobal was glad she hadn't. He also wasn't sorry he'd never met his father. Something told him he wouldn't have been impressed.

Lon was still completely silent. Tobal resisted the urge to run and instead finally peeked up, needing to know what was about to happen. Would Lon have him arrested? Would he yell at him? Tobal didn't know, and he didn't like not knowing.

Lon was just staring. The way he was looking at him made Tobal want to squirm, but instead, he raised his chin high.

"You think I'm lying," he said.

That finally got a reaction. "I don't."

Tobal was surprised. He hadn't quite believed any of this the first time he'd read his mother's diaries. "Why not? I'm sure other demons have tried convincing Berith they were related."

"You're not the first," Lon confirmed.

"Then why do you believe me when you didn't believe them?" Or had he? If Berith's father had one son outside of his union with Berith's mother, what were the odds that he had others? Maybe Tobal wasn't the first who'd come here, claiming Berith was his brother. Maybe Lon took care of those

76

demons, and he was going to take care of him, too.

And not in the way Tobal wanted.

"Can you tell me about your mother?" Lon asked instead of answering.

It made sense that he wanted to know more. "Her name was Kamika. She never talked much about her life at the palace, but I do know she used to work here. If you have records, you might be able to find her name."

Lon nodded and took a note on the pad in front of him. "I'll look into it, if anything so you might find out more about your mother."

That was something Tobal had always wanted. She died before he could ask her the many questions he had. It didn't even have anything to do with his father. He'd only known his mother as a child, and he couldn't help but wonder what their relationship would have been if she'd been allowed to grow old as he became an adult. Maybe she'd have told him about his father once he was old enough. Maybe she'd have wanted him to know where he came from.

Or maybe not.

There was no way for Tobal to know, and he couldn't obsess over it. If he did, he'd break his own heart, and that wasn't something he was planning on doing.

"I only know what I read in her diaries," he explained. "I can give them to you if you want, but I'd like them back. There are several volumes, but she meets Berith's father in the second. The first few cover her arrival at the palace. She worked here several years before having to leave."

"And she left because Berith's father asked her to."

Tobal nodded. "He didn't want her around. I guess he didn't want anyone to know he had another son." Which was a pity.

Berith was a few years older than Tobal, and they could have grown up together. He couldn't imagine what it would have been like, although maybe he'd had a taste of it after he and Zeno had met.

They wouldn't have met if Tobal had been born at the palace.

He couldn't be sorry for what had happened to him. He hated that his mother had died, but he loved Zeno and never wanted to lose him. It was hard to feel so conflicted, which was why Tobal tried not to think about it too much.

"You haven't told Berith," Lon said, leaning forward.

"No. What am I supposed to do, go up to him and blurt out that I'm his brother? He wouldn't believe me."

"I don't know about that. He loved his parents, but he wasn't blind to the kind of person his father was. Both of us are surprised there aren't more of his children around. If anything, I think Berith will be happy to know you're related to him. He loves Sabin and me, but he's always wanted a brother or sister."

Tobal had a hard time believing this was so easy. "I don't understand how you can believe me on this when you've been convinced I was planning on hurting Berith for weeks, if not since I arrived."

"You haven't?"

Tobal glared. "Of course not. I told you I came here to get to know my brother. Not to kill him."

"But there's more. Or is this your only secret?"

It wasn't, and being Berith's brother wasn't why Tobal had decided to talk to Lon. He needed to tell him everything.

He looked down again, unable to hold Lon's gaze as he explained. "Back when I was still in the town where I grew up, someone contacted me. It was after I found out who my father was, and somehow, they knew. They said that Berith was a monster, that he was hurting people, and that they needed me to take his place on the throne. I told them I wouldn't even consider it because I couldn't think of anything worse, and they promised that I wouldn't have to make any decision. Once I was on the throne, they'd take care of everything, and I'd be able to live a luxurious life and never want for anything. It was tempting, but I knew it wasn't true. I've heard how the other princes of Hell treat their people, and even though my childhood was shitty, it's not the same everywhere. I considered it, but then Zeno came back into the picture. He and Sabin told me about Berith, and there's no one I trust more than my brother. I told this secret society to fuck off and followed Zeno here."

Lon's eyes narrowed. "Secret society?"

"That's what they call themselves. They even have a symbol."

"The one on the wall."

"Yeah. I recognized it. They use it on all of their messages and clearly when they want to send messages, too. I'm so sorry Iskander died because of me."

"You weren't the one who killed him."

"No, but I did kill the other demon you found that day." Tobal might as well be honest about everything.

"He killed Iskander, so I'm not too worried about that. Has the society contacted you again? Beyond the symbol, I mean."

"No, but I found that demon in my room waiting for me. I don't know if he was supposed to kill me or just intimidate me, but he attacked, and I defended myself. I know they're watching me. I expect them to contact me again and try to get me to go along with their plan."

Lon nodded. "I wouldn't be surprised if they did. I'm glad you told me everything. You shouldn't have kept it a secret for so long."

"It's not that I wanted to. I knew I'd need to tell you everything once I started, and I wasn't up for that. I'm still not sure it was the best idea." Because he didn't know what Lon would do now that he knew. He was too afraid to ask.

"I understand why you felt that way, but I'm glad you told me."

"What now?" Tobal needed to know.

Lon stared at him for a moment. Tobal didn't look up, but he could feel it and held his breath. Right now, Lon held Tobal's future in his hands. Tobal had no idea what his decision would be, but he hoped he wouldn't regret being honest.

"Now, we talk to Berith."

Tobal jerked back. "We can't. I can't tell him."

"Well, someone needs to. Either you do it, or I will."

Tobal glared, but Lon wasn't cowed.

"I don't want to take this away from you," he said. "Berith should find out from you, not me. I believe it's important for him to know, either way, especially the secret society part. Personally, I want my best friend to know he has a brother, but professionally, he should know about the secret society."

Tobal could understand that, but he didn't like being given an ultimatum. "So if I don't tell him, you will."

"I'll have to. I hope you'll understand."

Tobal wanted to say he didn't, but it would be a lie. He *did* understand why Lon wanted Berith to be aware of this.

He just wasn't sure what would happen to him once the prince knew.

CHAPTER SEVEN

Tobal had thought he'd have more time. He supposed he should feel lucky that Lon hadn't dragged him to Berith's rooms right after he'd confessed he was Berith's brother. Lon had agreed it could wait until morning, but the morning had arrived, which meant Tobal was about to talk to Berith and tell him the truth.

He swallowed and stared at the door in front of him. Berith was behind it in his office, no doubt working. Lon and Tobal had agreed to meet here, and Tobal had arrived first. He was tempted to make a run for it. He would have if he weren't sure Lon would find him. There was nowhere for him to hide.

"Are you sure you can't tell me why you're here?" Sabin asked from his desk.

People had to pass through Sabin's office to get to Berith's. He'd confirmed that, for now, Berith was alone and had time to see Tobal and Lon, but he was confused because he had no idea why they needed to talk to Berith. Tobal couldn't say it out loud, not yet. Eventually, he'd have to. He needed to tell Zeno about being Berith's brother, which meant that Sabin would find out, too. Tobal didn't have a problem with that. He just needed to get through this first.

He shook his head. "It's nothing bad. It's about my past."

"You seem nervous."

And Sabin seemed worried, although Tobal wasn't sure if it was for Berith or him. "I am, a bit. I'm sure everything will be fine."

"I have no doubt that will be the case. Berith is a good

person."

Tobal agreed. The news that he had a brother would be a surprise for Berith, though, and there was no way to know how he'd react. Tobal wasn't looking forward to finding out.

Unfortunately for him, he couldn't run, because Lon had walked in at that moment. He looked from Sabin to Tobal and arched a brow, so Tobal shook his head, hoping Lon would understand he hadn't told Sabin about any of this. Lon nodded while Sabin stared at them, his body almost vibrating with the need to ask questions.

Tobal was surprised he'd gotten to know Sabin so well that he could read him, but maybe he shouldn't be. He'd been spending a lot of time with Sabin and Zeno, and he loved it. He was getting to know his family.

Including Berith.

"Ready?" Lon asked.

Tobal chuckled darkly. "Would you let me go back to my rooms if I said no?"

"Of course. You don't have to be the one to tell Berith about this."

But if Tobal didn't, Lon would.

Tobal glared at Lon and knocked on the door. He might as well get this over with. The sooner he told Berith, the sooner he'd find out how the prince took the news.

"Come in," Berith called out.

Tobal couldn't move. He was trying to be strong and behave as if he didn't really care, but he did—so much. He didn't want Berith to reject him. He wasn't sure they could have a brother relationship, but he wanted them to try.

Lon gently moved Tobal to the side and opened the door. When Tobal didn't walk in, he pressed a hand against Tobal's back and pushed him forward. Tobal followed his lead, unable to think.

This was it.

Berith was behind his desk and looked up when they came in. He smiled and relaxed, leaning back in his chair. "I can't say I ever expected to see the two of you together. What happened?"

There was a hint of wariness in his voice, which Tobal guessed had to do with the fact that Lon suspected him of being involved in the attacks. Maybe Berith thought Lon had dragged Tobal here to make him confess.

Tobal supposed it did kind of have something to do with the attacks. He'd been the one to kill the demon, and he didn't regret it.

This was going to be a disaster.

He tried turning around, but Lon pushed him toward one of the chairs. Tobal sat, thankful for the support because his legs were shaking. He clutched the arms of the chair, torn between being frozen in his spot and wanting to run away.

"Lon?" Berith asked.

"You were right," Lon said. "Tobal had nothing to do with the attacks."

Berith relaxed. "I'm glad to hear that. It doesn't explain why you're here."

"Because while he *is* innocent of what I believed he'd done, he's been hiding something. That's why we're here. He needs to tell you about it."

"Oh?" Berith asked, moving his focus on Tobal.

This was it. It had been hard to tell Lon all of this, but telling Berith felt impossible. Still, Tobal didn't have a choice. "My mother used to work here at the palace," he quickly said. Unlike when he'd been talking to Lon, he didn't hesitate. "She had an affair with your father, and I'm the result. I'm your brother."

Tobal waited for the explosion, but it never came. He dared look up, unsure what he'd find.

Berith was staring at him.

Tobal tried to read his expression, but he couldn't tell what Berith was thinking. He was frowning, so it possibly wasn't good, but Lon didn't seem worried, so Tobal waited.

"You're my brother?" Berith eventually asked.

Tobal nodded. "I know it's hard to believe, but my mother kept diaries. She's dead, so we can't ask her, but I can lend you the diaries if you want to read them." They were private, so Tobal didn't want to, but if it convinced Berith that he was telling the truth, he would.

Thankfully, Berith waved his words away. "I don't need you to. I'm sure Lon's already looked into it. You believe him?" he asked, turning to Lon.

"I do. Everything he said made sense, and I had Mikal look up his mother. She's on the records as working here for years."

Berith got up and walked around the desk. Tobal held his breath, wondering what was about to happen. He hadn't realized Lon had found the time to look into his story, but he should have. Did the man even sleep?

He had no idea what to expect, but he was stunned when Berith grabbed his arm and pulled him to his feet, only to hug him.

Tobal looked at Lon in panic. What was he supposed to do?

Lon wasn't any help. He seemed amused, with a slight smile playing on his lips. The smile made Tobal want to both hit him and kiss him, so instead, he focused on hugging his brother back.

"It's a pleasure to meet you as my brother," Berith said when he leaned back. "I always wanted a sibling."

"Really?"

Berith nodded. "You thought I wouldn't be happy."

"I wasn't even sure you'd believe me."

"I know my father. Even though he wasn't a bad man, he wasn't a saint. I'm not surprised he had other children. I'm glad one of those children is you."

Berith sat on the edge of the desk, and Tobal flopped back into the chair.

He'd done it. He'd told Berith they were brothers, and Berith seemed happy about it.

"I'll understand if you'd rather wait, but I'd like to make a public announcement," Berith said.

Tobal's eyes widened. "What?"

"Whenever you want. I'm not going to keep you a secret, though. I see no reason for that."

Tobal looked at Lon, knowing the demon would understand why this was a bad idea.

Lon sighed. "Unfortunately, before you do that, we have something else to tell you."

Berith didn't look happy. "I'm not going to like whatever it is, am I?"

"You're not," Lon confirmed.

Thankfully, he'd be the one to explain the next bit. Tobal wasn't sure he'd have made sense, even if he'd tried. He needed a few moments to gather his thoughts and to allow himself to believe that even though he'd thought the worst would happen, the best had instead.

Berith was *glad* Tobal was his brother.

Lon wished he didn't have to ruin the reunion between the brothers with more bad news. This had to be said, though, no matter how little he liked it.

He wasn't surprised that Berith was happy to find out Tobal was his brother. Berith had always cherished family, even family who wasn't related to him, like Lon and Sabin. Adding a brother to the mix could only be a good thing in his eyes, and Lon hoped he wouldn't regret it.

"Let's hear it," Berith said.

Tobal and Lon looked at each other. It was clear Tobal didn't want to be the one to tell his brother about the secret society, and that was fine with Lon. He was used to giving Berith bad news.

"Around the time Tobal found out he was your brother, he was contacted by someone who said they belonged to a secret society," Lon said.

He'd asked Tobal for more details, but there really wasn't much there. He couldn't wait to start digging into the society, because no matter how secret they thought they were, someone always talked or did something stupid that led to their discovery.

"A secret society?" Berith asked, his eyebrows rising on his forehead. "Like in those TV series Mel likes to watch?"

"Pretty much," Tobal inserted. "I don't know much about them. They contacted me, and I was curious, so I asked what they wanted."

Berith sighed. "Let me guess. It has something to do with me. They wanted to kill me or, at the very least, incapacitate me."

"Yeah. They told me that you were a bad leader and that since I was your brother, people would accept me if I became prince. It would give them legitimacy or something like that. They promised they'd take care of everything and that I'd be pampered and wouldn't have to think about one thing for the rest of my life. I'm not gonna lie—it was tempting, especially before I got to know you."

Berith stared at Tobal for a moment. "But you said no. If you hadn't, you wouldn't be telling me this."

"I did say no. I have no interest in being the prince, fake or otherwise. Besides, even though my life back then wasn't easy, I wanted to give you the benefit of the doubt. It also happened around the time Zeno and Sabin arrived in town, and when they said they lived at the palace, I knew it was my chance to get to know you and find out whether or not this society was right. I'd already told them to fuck off and not contact me again, and I thought that moving here would help keep them away, but they found me. They killed a servant, drew their symbol on the wall, and sent a demon to intimidate me."

Lon wasn't sure whether the demon had been supposed to intimidate Tobal or kill him, and they'd probably never find out. It would make sense for the society to intimidate Tobal and attempt to force him into accepting their offer again now that he lived at the palace. Or maybe they'd realized Tobal was never going to be on their side, and they'd decided to kill him so he couldn't tell anyone about them. Either way, Lon didn't like anything about this, and he knew Berith well enough to be sure the same went for him.

"Have they tried contacting you again?" Berith asked.

Tobal shook his head. "Not openly. I'm sure they were behind that symbol and the demon in my rooms, but they haven't reached out directly. It's like they're just telling me they're there, waiting. I swear that sometimes, I can feel people watching me, even though I'm alone."

Lon very deliberately didn't look at Berith. He had no doubt his best friend knew that what Tobal had said was linked to Lon, but this wasn't the right moment to say anything about it.

"I'm sure it's just an impression," Berith said, barely repressed amusement in his voice. "As for the society, I'm going to ask Lon to put a bodyguard on you."

"I don't think that's the best idea," Lon said.

Berith arched a brow. "You don't think that protecting my brother is a good idea?"

"Let's be honest. The secret society is probably behind all the demons getting into the palace. We don't know much about them, but what are the odds that they don't have inside help? I thought maybe it could be a servant, but I'm starting to wonder if it's someone higher up, and I don't like it. I'm not planning on using Tobal as bait, but putting a bodyguard on him would tell the society we know what's going on. They might react badly, and that's not what we want."

"They've already reacted badly. They sent a demon to attack Tobal, for fuck's sake."

"We don't know if it was to kill him or for another reason, and we won't find out if we're not careful about our next step. Tobal is safe here. I'll keep an eye on him, but it's for the best if the society doesn't realize he told us about them."

Berith still didn't look happy. "I don't want anything to happen to him."

"I don't, either. I also don't want to use him as bait, but I truly believe this is the best way for us to find out more and get rid of these people."

Tobal cleared his throat. "I'm right here, you know. Shouldn't I have a say in whether or not you use me as bait?"

He should, but there was no way Berith would allow him to have a say. He was fiercely protective of his family. It was a small miracle he allowed Lon to do his job most days, and Tobal was in for a rude awakening if he believed Berith would just step back and let him do what was needed to deal with the society.

"No bait," Berith ordered. "But fine. We can skip the bodyguard for now. As long as I'm sure Tobal is protected, of course."

Lon nodded. "We'll all need to keep our eyes open. We have to find out who's in the society, and it won't be easy."

Berith snorted. "I don't know about that. They already made a big mistake, contacting Tobal. I'm not surprised they tried using him, but I do wonder how they found out he's my brother."

"There's no way to know unless we get our hands on

someone who belongs to the society, and that won't be easy." But Lon was convinced there were members in the palace, and he *would* find them.

It was the only thing he could do to protect his family.

He got to his feet. "I'll get back to work and leave the two of you alone for a chat. I'm sure you can't wait to talk."

The frown on Berith's face vanished, and he nodded. "Thank you."

"You know where to find me if you need me."

Lon could see they couldn't wait to be alone, so he quickly left the room. He waved at Sabin, who was working but waved back and walked into the hallway.

"Lon?" a voice asked behind him.

He turned around to see Tobal had followed him. "Yes?"

Tobal shuffled his feet. "I just wanted to thank you. I don't know if I'd have found the courage to tell Berith who I was if it weren't for you."

"You would have eventually."

"Maybe. Or maybe I'd have waited too long and something would have happened to either me or Berith. I'm glad I told him, and I'm happy he's so welcoming. I didn't expect it."

"Even though he's a prince, Berith is a simple man. His family is the most important thing in his life, and he already considered you a member before. Now that he knows you're blood-related, he'll make sure always to protect you and keep you happy." And Tobal deserved it. Berith did, too. Lon was glad his best friend had found a long-lost brother.

But he couldn't help but wonder what would happen next. It seemed like too big a coincidence that Tobal didn't have anything to do with the secret society, although maybe he'd been telling the truth. Maybe they'd tried involving him, and he'd told them to fuck off, and now, they wanted to kill him, just like he'd said.

Lon wanted all of this to work for Berith's sake, and he was tempted to believe Tobal had nothing to do with any of this beyond what he'd already told them, but just in case, he'd keep an eye on him.

And it had nothing to do with how handsome Tobal was.

CHAPTER EIGHT

It was time to tell Zeno what he'd been hiding, but Tobal wasn't looking forward to it. He didn't think his brother would have a problem with Tobal being Berith's brother, but he'd be hurt that Tobal hadn't felt he could tell him. Tobal hoped Zeno would listen when he told him that wasn't true, that he'd just been scared and confused, but he couldn't be sure. He wanted to have a good relationship with both his brothers, and hopefully, by the end of the day, he'd have that.

Berith had accepted him without blinking, something Tobal still had a hard time believing. He'd been afraid Berith wouldn't believe his father could have a child with a servant, then make her leave, but he hadn't. Tobal had never known his father, and he never would, but maybe that was for the best. He was fine with only getting to know Berith. Berith was a good person, and Tobal was lucky to be his brother, and not only because he was a prince of Hell. Even if Berith were a simple demon living in a small town, he'd be lucky.

Even though he quite enjoyed living at the palace.

"You've been distracted," Zeno suddenly said.

Tobal blinked up at him. He was still clutching his cup of coffee, but he'd barely drunk, and it was getting cold. He took a sip, grimaced, and put it down.

Definitely too cold by now.

"I'm sorry," he murmured.

"You don't have anything to be sorry about. I'm just worried about you. Are you sure you can't tell me who's after you?"

Tobal sucked in a breath. "That's one of the reasons I wanted to have coffee with you. I need to talk to you."

Zeno's back straightened, and he leaned forward, ignoring his cup of coffee. "You're ready to talk?"

"I don't think I'll ever be ready to tell you all of this, but I might as well."

Berith had promised he wouldn't tell anyone Tobal was his brother until Tobal told him he could, but it wasn't fair. Berith should be able to tell Mel, Sabin, and anyone he wanted. He was waiting for Tobal to be ready, and he was. The only thing missing was telling Zeno, and hopefully, after today, that would be over.

"You're making me worry again," Zeno said.

"It wasn't my intention. This is just a lot."

"Whatever it is, we'll face it together."

And that was what gave Tobal the strength to tell Zeno everything. "A while back, I went back to the house." Tobal didn't have to explain what house. Zeno knew. "I'd left some of my things behind and wanted them back. I had to threaten them a little, but they finally told me to check in the attic. When I got there, I realized that was where they kept all the stuff from the kids they adopted, including the things the kids came with. It took me a while, and I had to poke around through a lot of boxes and dust, but I finally found my things. It wasn't the only thing I found, though. I hadn't realized that they truly kept everything, including the things I'd arrived with that first day. My mother's diaries were in a box, along with a few knickknacks."

Zeno sucked in a breath. "Your mother's diaries?"

"I looked for your stuff, too, but the only thing I could find was what you left behind when you ran. There was nothing about your past."

Zeno waved Tobal's words away. "I didn't expect there to be anything. Tell me about your mother's diaries."

Zeno was invested in this. He wanted to know what Tobal had found, and Tobal wanted to tell him. "She mentioned my father. She named him and explained why I never got to meet him. He already had a son when she got pregnant with me."

Tobal licked his lips. How could he have been less scared to tell Berith about this than Zeno? It probably was because he and Zeno had a years-long relationship while he and Berith had just met. It would have hurt to lose Berith, but it would have been more because of the possibility of what they could have been. Losing Zeno would destroy Tobal, though. They'd been brothers since they were children, and he was the most important person in Tobal's life.

"You don't have to tell me if you're not ready," Zeno murmured.

"You need to know. I already told Berith, and he's waiting to tell the rest of his family."

Zeno frowned. "What do you mean?"

Tobal grabbed his cup of coffee just to have something in his hands. "Berith and I have the same father. My mother was a servant here at the palace, and Berith's father got her pregnant with me. He gave her money to leave, and she did. She raised me alone until she died." And now, Zeno knew the rest of the story.

He sat there, staring at Tobal and blinking. Tobal had no doubt he was turning the words in his mind, trying to make sense of them. As soon as he did, he'd have questions, and Tobal prayed he'd be able to answer them.

"You're telling me you and Berith have the same father," Zeno eventually said.

"We do. He's my half-brother."

"You only found out recently?"

"Yeah. I wasn't planning on doing anything with the knowledge, but then you and Sabin appeared, giving me the only possible opportunity I'd have to meet Berith. I wasn't planning on coming to the palace and telling him this before. Honestly, I didn't know what kind of person he was, and I didn't want to risk it."

Zeno flopped back in his chair. "But he's a good person."

"I know that now, but I didn't before. Still, I wasn't sure I should tell him, especially considering I was contacted by people who want to put me on the throne in his place."

Zeno glared. "What else are you hiding?"

Tobal quickly told him about the secret society. He wanted everything to be out of the way and to finally find out what Zeno would do now that he knew all of it.

"What did Lon say about the society?" Zeno eventually asked.

"He wants us to wait and see what happens next. He's not convinced that the demon was sent to kill me, and I think I agree with him. The society has an opportunity they probably don't want to miss. I'm right here at the palace, and now that I've told Berith we're brothers, I'll have even better access to him. Even if they wanted to kill me before because they were afraid I'd tell Berith about them, they'll want to see if they can use me now."

"I don't like this."

"Berith doesn't, either, but I want to do this. If my brother is in danger, I need to know what's happening."

Zeno's eyes narrowed. "That's exactly how I feel." He hesitated. "I'm sorry you felt you couldn't tell me this. I understand my behavior wasn't the best, but I truly want things to change. We're together again. I don't want to lose you."

Tobal leaned forward and quickly patted Zeno's hand. "You won't. Just because I have another brother now doesn't mean I don't consider you my brother. I do. The years you were away don't matter. I can have two brothers, right?"

The small smile on Zeno's lips told Tobal everything would be okay.

And everything *was* okay. Zeno decided to walk Tobal back to his rooms in the palace, even though Tobal knew how uncomfortable it made him. He hoped it was a sign that Zeno was okay with everything. He seemed to be, and there was a new bounce in Tobal's steps as they walked down the hallway and into his rooms.

Unfortunately, that bounce vanished as soon as he walked into his bedroom.

Zeno had stayed back, but he came in running as soon as he realized something had happened. Tobal didn't ask him how he knew. He was too busy staring at the message pinned to the headboard of his bed with a massive knife.

"Fuck," Zeno muttered, reaching for it. He grabbed the knife and pulled, and the message fluttered down to Tobal's bed.

Tobal swallowed. He didn't know what was written on that piece of paper, but he'd recognized the symbol at the bottom of the message.

The secret society.

The knock on the door made Lon groan. He was used to people interrupting him, demanding things or bringing up problems, but sometimes, he wished he didn't have to deal with any of this.

Right now, he was trying to focus on the secret society and finding out who was part of it. He didn't want to use Tobal, but he wasn't sure there was another way to do it. No matter how hard he tried to find more information, there was nothing. The secret society was just that—a secret. What they called themselves might sound ridiculous, but they were clearly good at hiding, at the very least.

"Yes?" he called out.

The door creaked a bit as it opened. Tobal peeked in, but

before Lon could tell him to come in, the door was pushed open, and Zeno strode into the room. He was holding a piece of paper and slammed it onto the desk in front of Lon.

Lon blinked at it, wondering what it was. He reached for the piece of paper, his eyes narrowing when he recognized the symbol at the bottom of it. "What's this?"

"We found it stabbed into Tobal's bed," Zeno said with a growl.

He wasn't happy, but then, neither was Lon. He peered at the message and wasn't one bit surprised at what it contained.

You can either be with us or die with the prince and his family. Choose wisely. We'll contact you soon.

Below that was the same symbol that had been on the wall when Iskander was killed.

Tobal had been right. The society wasn't trying to kill him, at least not for now. They wanted to use him and were warning him that if he didn't go along with that, they'd kill him.

Lon looked up. Tobal seemed shaken, while Zeno was clearly both terrified and pissed. Lon understood how he felt and he had no doubt that if Zeno knew who was part of the society, he'd already be hunting them. He had to feel as useless as Lon, which was never good. Lon wanted to rage and punch something, and he wasn't nearly as deadly as Zeno. It would be a disaster if Zeno lost control.

"Do you want to sit down?" he asked.

"I want to talk to the prince," Zeno said through gritted teeth. "He needs to know, and I want to know how he's planning to keep my brother safe."

Lon looked at Tobal, who was still hovering behind Zeno. "You told him?"

Tobal nodded once. "I did."

"So, Zeno, you know that Berith will do everything he can to keep Tobal safe. Tobal's *his* brother, too."

"I'm aware. He doesn't care about Tobal as much as I do, though. He can't, because they've only recently met, and I wouldn't put it past you to try to use Tobal to stop this society or whatever they are."

"Zeno!" Tobal snapped.

But Zeno wasn't wrong. Lon did want to use Tobal to get to the society. He wished there was another option, because he didn't want Tobal to be hurt, but he couldn't see one. How were they supposed to draw out the society when they didn't even know who was part of it? The only thing they did know was that they were aiming at Berith's throne and that they hoped to use Tobal as a puppet, but it wasn't useful.

"We won't use Tobal without talking to him first," Lon said.

"That's not good enough," Zeno snarled. "You shouldn't use him at all."

Lon raised his hands. He didn't want to fight with Zeno, especially considering this last development. "I don't know if we'll have a choice, but I promise I'll do everything I can to keep him safe." He got to his feet. "But we should talk to Berith. He needs to know about this message."

"It's just a piece of paper," Tobal protested. "We shouldn't bother him for that."

He didn't know Berith all that well yet, but in time, he would, and he'd realize it was foolish to try to keep something like this from him. If they did, Berith would be pissed when he found out, and he would. Nothing stayed a secret for long in the palace, and Berith knew how to use that to his advantage.

Besides, the society was taking another step toward the throne, which meant Berith needed to know what was going on.

"They're threatening you," Zeno said. "We all need to be aware of that and do everything we can to keep you safe."

"I can defend myself," Tobal answered. "I killed the demon who attacked me in my rooms. I'm still here, and he's not."

And it had been damn impressive. Lon wasn't about to say that out loud, though, especially considering the glare on Zeno's face.

"You shouldn't have had to defend yourself that way. The demon shouldn't have been in your rooms."

"I'm not saying that's not true, but Lon is doing everything he can to keep the palace safe. His main focus has to be Berith, not me."

Lon had had enough. He wasn't going to choose between Berith and Tobal, mostly because he didn't know what he'd do if he had to. "No one has to choose anyone," he said. "Now let's go. Berith will want to know this."

Tobal looked like he wanted to protest again, but Zeno grabbed his arm and pulled him toward the door. Lon followed them, his mind whirling with what had just happened. The secret society was taking another step forward. They wouldn't hesitate to kill Tobal if he refused to help them, but they hoped he would. They didn't need him to get to the throne, but having him there, even temporarily, would give them a certain legitimacy they wouldn't have otherwise.

Not that they needed it. Being a prince of Hell wasn't hereditary. Lucifer gave that title to the demons he felt deserved it, so unless whoever took Berith's place on the throne did, they wouldn't be a prince of Hell for long.

But maybe the secret society didn't know that, or maybe they did and thought Lucifer would turn a blind eye. It wouldn't be unheard of for a prince of Hell to be killed, but Lon wasn't going to test any of this. He'd keep both Tobal and Berith safe and in one piece, be it the last thing he did.

They reached Berith's office, but Sabin stopped them before they could knock on the door. "He's in a meeting." Sabin's gaze bounced over all three of them, finally stopping on Zeno. "What's going on?"

Sabin had asked his partner because he knew Zeno would

tell him. Lon didn't have a problem with that. Maybe it would be best for Sabin to be aware of what was happening so he could be safe. Lon didn't know if Berith had already told the others about Tobal being his brother, but if he hadn't, he would soon. Zeno clearly knew, which meant Sabin would, too.

"This is urgent," Lon told Sabin.

"Urgent, as in someone might die if you don't see him?"

Lon hesitated. It wasn't *that* urgent, but his hesitation was enough for Sabin to get into gear. He jumped up from his chair and rushed to the door of Berith's office, quickly knocking before walking in. He didn't tell Lon and the others to wait, but they did and listened to the voices coming from inside the office.

"This meeting isn't over," a woman snapped.

"It is for now," Berith told her, sounding calm but annoyed. "I'm not changing my mind, anyway. The safe houses are a go, whether you agree with them or not."

The woman huffed, and Lon steeled himself. He wasn't surprised to see Nowla stomp out of the office, her black eyes blazing. Her expression made him sit up and notice, but he wasn't surprised that at least one of Berith's ministers hated the prince. Most of those people weren't ministers because they wanted to help the population of Berith's territory. They wanted power and to be rich, and this was the best way for them to obtain that.

She glared at their little group, then walked away, her tunic floating behind her. Lon made a mental note to look into her, just in case. He wouldn't be surprised if she was plotting something, which was the last thing he needed.

"You can go in," Sabin said, stepping out of the office. "But I'm coming, too. Whatever's happening, I want to know."

Zeno and Tobal looked at each other, and Tobal nodded, silently telling his brother he was all right with Zeno telling

Sabin about him and Berith. Zeno wrapped an arm around Sabin's waist and pulled him close, leaning down to whisper something in his ear as they walked into the office. Sabin gasped, but Berith was already on his feet, headed toward them.

"What's going on? Sabin told me it was a matter of life or death."

Lon had carried the piece of paper on which the message was written from his office, and he held it out for Berith to see. "Tobal found it in his bedroom."

Berith took it, his expression darkening. It didn't take him long to read it, and once he had, he looked up. "What now?"

Lon wished he knew the answer to that question.

Tobal swallowed. He had no idea how Berith would take this, and there was only one way to find out, but he was still nervous when it came to his brother. It would be much easier for Berith to kick him out of the palace. That way, he'd keep the rest of his family safe, and he wouldn't have to deal with the society.

Except he would. They weren't giving up, whether Tobal was involved or not. Berith had to know that, and hopefully, it meant he wouldn't leave Tobal hanging.

"What do you think?" Lon asked.

"That you're my head of security. What do you suggest?"

"Things are escalating. I don't like the thought of Tobal being on his own, so I'd like to assign him a bodyguard. I know we decided not to do it before, but things have changed."

Tobal groaned. "I don't need a babysitter."

He didn't want someone following him around. He was used to being on his own and liked things that way. Was he afraid of the society? A bit, mostly because he didn't know where the attack would come from. Would it be enough for him to agree to have someone follow him around the palace? *Nope*. He wasn't doing that.

"Not a babysitter," Berith said. "I'm not risking your life. You read the message. Either you work with them, or you die, and I won't allow that to happen."

"They're not going to kill me tomorrow."

"You can't know that. You don't know anything about them, so stop arguing."

Tobal looked at Zeno for help, but he should have known better. His brother was nodding, which meant he agreed with Berith.

Lon was Tobal's last option. He looked at the head of security and opened his mouth to try to convince him he didn't need a bodyguard, but he never got the words out.

"I want Lon to protect you," Berith added.

Tobal and Lon stared at each other for a moment before Lon turned his attention to Berith. "I can't do that. I have a job, and while I don't want anything to happen to Tobal, it's you I need to keep safe."

"You can, and you will. You'll stick with Tobal. There's no one I trust more with my brother than you."

"I'm touched, but I don't think it's the best idea. I could put Mikal with him."

Berith's eyes narrowed. "*You*. Am I clear?"

Tobal held his breath. Lon and Berith were best friends and had been for years, but right now, it wasn't Berith the demon who was giving orders. It was Berith, Prince of Hell, and Lon had to obey him.

Right?

"I could still act as bait," he suggested. He didn't want Lon and Berith to fight.

Everyone turned to look at him. From their expressions, Tobal was pretty sure the answer would be no.

"You're already in danger. Why do you want to make

things worse?" Berith asked.

"Because we have no other way to stop the society. We don't know who's part of it. We know what they're planning, but we don't know what or how they're going to do it. We need someone inside, just like they have someone inside the palace helping them. I could be that someone."

"I forbid you to do anything that would put you in danger," Berith snapped. "What is it with you two? Tobal, you'll keep yourself safe whether you like it or not. Stay away from the society. Don't answer any of their messages, and if they reach out to you, let Lon know immediately. It won't be a problem because he'll be watching your back as your bodyguard. Lon, you're sticking with Tobal. You used to be my bodyguard, and now, you can do the same for my brother. I don't want anything to happen to him."

Lon's shoulders slumped just a bit. "I'll keep him safe."

Berith seemed satisfied by that answer. He'd gotten what he wanted, but Tobal was bewildered. All his life, the only person who'd cared if he lived or died had been Zeno. When Zeno had left, Tobal had been completely on his own, and no one would have noticed if he'd died. Now, he had an entire family, including a prince of Hell, and he had no idea how to deal with any of it. Going against Berith's wishes wouldn't be a good idea, even if Berith weren't who he was. He was doing this because he cared about Tobal, which was hard to believe.

But Tobal was glad for it. He felt loved for the first time in forever, even though it was a lot to take in. Besides, he wasn't looking forward to dying. Now that he'd found both his brothers, he wanted time with them, which meant he couldn't allow the society to kill him.

And since Berith wouldn't allow him to protect himself, maybe he'd have to take matters into his own hands.

He eyed Lon. It wouldn't be easy to sneak away, but he'd find a way. He always did. He'd grown up on the streets, where he'd needed to think quickly and smartly. It didn't matter that his brothers didn't think he could protect himself. He'd show them otherwise. He'd take on the society, and he'd win.

Just like Zeno and Berith wanted to keep him safe, he wanted to keep *them* safe, and he he'd stop at nothing to make that happen.

"Tobal, you should go back to your rooms. I'll send someone to check them to make sure there isn't another message," Lon declared.

"I'll do it," Zeno grumbled. "No one will get to him as long as I'm with him."

Lon nodded. "I'll need to organize things to free up my time to be with Tobal, but it shouldn't take long. You can stay with him until I'm done."

"I will."

In any other circumstance, Tobal would have been amused. These two didn't have anything in common, but now, they were allies as they tried to protect Tobal.

If he weren't as irritated as he was, Tobal would love it.

But the decisions had been made, even though no one had listened to him. Berith had more work to do, as did Sabin, so Zeno and Tobal left the office. Tobal didn't know what to say. He didn't want to be ungrateful, and he understood why Zeno was freaking out so badly, but he hated feeling like his brother didn't trust him. Berith, he could understand. Zeno, though? How could he not?

"You realize I can do this on my own, right?" he asked once they reached his rooms.

"And you realize you don't have to do it on your own? You're not alone anymore. If things go as they should, you won't ever be alone again. Try to put yourself in our place. How would you feel if I were in danger yet refused to let you help?"

Tobal glared. "Not fair."

Zeno shrugged, unrepentant. "I don't care about fair. The only thing I care about is keeping you safe, and if Lon has to follow you around the palace to make that happen, then I'm more than happy to help him do it."

"What about me? Don't I get a say in it?"

"Not until the society has been dealt with."

And by then, Tobal wouldn't need a bodyguard anymore.

He rubbed his forehead. This wasn't going to be fun.

CHAPTER NINE

Even days later, Tobal was still thinking about the message and the result of finding it on his bed.

He couldn't take a step out of his rooms without being followed. Usually, it was by Lon, who looked both annoyed and expressionless at the same time. Tobal hadn't known it was possible to look that way, but now he did, and it made him want to poke and prod at Lon until he snapped. He knew better than to do that, but having the other demon follow him around the palace wasn't fun.

He had no privacy. Lon didn't stick around when Tobal was in his bedroom, but he insisted on checking out the place whenever Tobal returned to it. Then he went to sleep in the living area on one of the couches, which meant he could hear everything that had happened in Tobal's bedroom.

The thought made Tobal's cheeks heat.

He didn't have anyone in his life, so it wasn't like there was much action, but he also hadn't dared have any alone time since Lon had started following him around. He had no doubt that Lon would be able to hear it, and if their relationship was awkward right now, he could only imagine how worse it would become if that happened.

All in all, everything about this was incredibly frustrating, and it made Tobal want to scream.

"You should just accept it," Sabin said without even looking up from the list of tasks he was going over.

Tobal stared at him. "What do you mean?"

Sabin looked up. "You know how I met your brother,

right?"

"He saved you from a group of demons."

"Exactly. Well, I wasn't exactly willing to go on that trip. It wasn't my job, and I didn't want to leave the palace. I hate the heat and the sand and everything about the desert."

"Except for my brother."

"Except for him. But anyway, even though I didn't want to go and tried to convince Berith otherwise, I still had to obey his orders."

"Just like I do."

"Exactly. He's the prince, even if he wasn't your brother. I realize it's frustrating, but it'll only be until the society has been taken care of, right?"

"I guess." But how would they do that?

Without using Tobal, they had no way to find out who was part of the society. He still believed his plan of playing bait was the best option they had to move things forward finally, but he knew better than to bring it up to his brother. Berith had refused once, and he wouldn't hesitate to refuse twice or more. He didn't want Tobal exposed to this, and if he had to lock him in his rooms to make sure that didn't happen, he would.

Which meant Tobal would have to be discreet.

He realized it was stupid to think he could do this on his own, but what choice did he have? He couldn't just hang around his rooms, waiting to be rescued. He might not be able to do the rescuing himself, but he also wasn't useless. With Lon dogging his every step, though, how was he supposed to do that?

He'd have to wait. He couldn't contact the society himself because he had no idea who was part of it, but the message had been clear. Either he worked for them, or he died. They'd want an answer, which meant they'd have to contact him again. When they did, he'd insist on having a meeting. It would make sense for anyone in his place to want to talk to the people involved, and he was going to play them. He'd act as if he was tempted to take their offer, if anything because he didn't want to die.

And he didn't. Demons usually had short lifespans, but it didn't mean they didn't want to live longer. Now that Tobal had a family, he wanted years, *decades*, to be happy. He wouldn't get that if he died, but he suspected he also wouldn't get it if he didn't do something about the society.

"I don't know what you're thinking, but I'd stop if I were you," Sabin said. "It doesn't look good."

"I'm just thinking about how annoyed I am that I have to be followed around."

Sabin didn't look convinced, so Tobal was glad when someone immediately knocked on the door. He welcomed the interruption, at least until he realized something had happened. The servant who threw the door open was pale and had eyes so wide it was a wonder they didn't fall out of their sockets.

"What is it?" Sabin asked, getting to his feet.

"The prince's daughter and her mother were attacked," the servant blurted out.

For a moment, the room was silent and still. Tobal's stomach churned as he thought of Cyarea. How was she? Was the society behind this? He wouldn't put it past them to attack a little girl, especially one that was so closely linked to Berith.

This was a sign that the society wouldn't hesitate to get what they wanted. They'd even attack a little girl who had nothing to do with any of this. He needed to do something, and the only thing he could think of doing was infiltrating the society or, at the very least, playing along with what they wanted and see what happened.

"Are they all right?" Sabin asked, already moving toward the door.

"I don't know," the servant whispered.

Tobal was right behind Sabin. Cyarea was his niece, and even if she hadn't been, no little girl deserved to be attacked. *This* was why he needed to do everything he could to deal with the society, no matter what his brothers thought. Cyarea was more important than Tobal ever could be, and not only to Berith.

And Tobal would make sure the society stayed away from her. He had to.

Lon ran into Aloise's living area through the open door. Mikal had reassured him Aloise and Cyarea were both fine, but Lon's heart raced anyway.

He'd failed them. He'd failed *Berith* again, and he hated himself for it.

Mikal stood inside the room, next to the open door, watching Cyarea and Aloise. They were sitting on one of the couches. Reyni was there, quietly talking to them, smiling at Cyarea as if trying to make sure she didn't get worried.

Lon slumped against the wall next to Mikal. "Please tell me they're fine," he begged. He ignored the guards at the open garden door and the one cleaning the blood on the floor.

He already knew Cyarea and Aloise were okay. When he'd been told they'd been attacked, he'd also been informed that both escaped without a scratch. Their bodyguards hadn't been far, and they'd taken care of the demon who'd attacked them, sneaking in from the garden.

"They are," Mikal confirmed as Berith stomped in from the garden.

He looked pissed, which was how Lon felt.

Lon swallowed. He'd always been good at his job, but clearly, that wasn't true anymore. He needed to do something about it, and he knew what that something had to be.

He pushed away from the wall, raised his chin high, and walked over to his best friend. Berith had rushed to his daughter's side, and he hovered by, listening to what Reyni was saying. He looked up when he heard Lon, grimaced, and stepped away from his daughter after patting her shoulder.

"What happened?" he asked.

Lon's mouth was dry. "I'm not sure yet. I was informed Cyarea and Aloise were attacked. Their bodyguards stepped in and neutralized the attacker, but I don't know anything about the attack."

Berith nodded. "We'll find out soon enough, I suppose."

"You will." This was it. Lon sucked in a breath, focused on his next words. "I'd like to offer my resignation."

Berith stared for too long. Lon wasn't quite sure, because he'd never resigned from a job, so he didn't know what the reaction to his words was supposed to be, but there was no other option. Berith had made him head of security, which meant his job was to keep Berith and his family safe.

He'd failed.

"What are you talking about?" Berith eventually asked.

"It's clear I'm unable to do my job. I'm not sure what's happening, but I haven't been able to find anything about the most recent attacks or about the society. I failed, as the day's events have shown. It's time for you to choose someone who will be better at the job."

Berith glared. "I'm sorry, but where do you think I'm supposed to find someone like that? I know you. I know how you work, and my family and I are important to you. No one else would have that kind of incentive to keep us safe, but you do."

"Maybe that's the problem. I might be too close to see things clearly. I worry about you and your family, and I hate that Cyarea had to go through this."

To his surprise, Berith smiled. It wasn't a big smile, but it was there, which told Lon that his friend probably wasn't going to kick him out of the palace for not keeping his family safe. "My daughter is fine," Berith said. "Actually, I think her words were that she had fun."

Lon's eyes widened. "Fun?"

"That's what she said. She managed to get a few kicks in and stabbed the attacker in the thigh."

"She should never have been exposed to this."

"I wouldn't say it was ideal, but even though I've been doing my best to keep her safe and shielded from the reality of our world, I won't be able to do so forever. She's a demon, and she was born in Hell. This is what we have to deal with every day, and it's time she learns."

"I don't think Mel will be happy about that."

Berith's human consort was protective of Cyarea, and he didn't fully understand what being a demon child meant. He never would, but that was all right. He brought a unique point of view to life, and while sometimes Lon didn't know what to do with it, he couldn't deny it made life interesting Mel wouldn't be happy about Berith deciding this was a good life lesson for their daughter, but he'd go along with it—what else could he do?

But that wasn't their main problem. "I still believe I should resign," Lon insisted.

"I'd rather you not waste the paper to write your resignation, to be honest," Berith drawled. "Because I won't accept it."

"Sabin wouldn't let me write it down on a piece of paper," Lon grumbled. "He'd make me use the tablet." That damn device made Lon both afraid and mad just seeing it.

Berith grimaced. "He would, and I'm sure you don't want to have to deal with that."

Lon didn't, but this didn't feel right. "I just can't continue doing nothing."

"You're not doing nothing. I've been watching you. You're working hard to find out who's behind all of this, and the fact that you haven't been able to find more information isn't your fault. Let's be honest—I'm pretty sure things would be much worse if you weren't in charge. Not that I don't have faith in the people who work for you, but I don't trust anyone the way I trust you, not even Mikal."

Lon rubbed his face. "But this isn't working." Neither of them could deny that.

"Which means we'll have to find another way. Maybe we can have a meeting and discuss this with the others. I'm not firing you, though, and I'm not accepting your resignation."

Lon was lucky. Most other princes of Hell wouldn't have hesitated to have him tortured and possibly killed for what had happened. His job was to protect the prince's family, and he wasn't succeeding, no matter why. Berith wouldn't have killed him even if they hadn't been friends, but Lon suspected he *would* have kicked him out.

But they *were* friends. For some reason, Berith still trusted Lon, and Lon wanted to deserve that trust.

The sound of footsteps coming toward them in the hallway made both of them tense. The door was still open, and Lon waited to see who was coming. He hoped it wasn't another guard with more bad news, and he was relieved when Sabin burst into the room, Tobal right behind him. Both of them looked a bit wild, but that expression softened as soon as they saw Cyarea on the couch with her mother.

"She's all right?" Sabin asked, one of his hands fluttering over his heart.

"They're fine, both of them," Berith confirmed.

"Thank fuck," Tobal muttered. "When we were told Cyarea had been attacked, we were terrified."

Cyarea heard her name and looked up. She beamed when she saw Sabin and Tobal, and she got up so quickly that she almost stumbled over her own feet. "Uncle Tobal! I stabbed the bad guy!"

Tobal crouched and opened his arms, and Cyarea threw herself into them.

Lon was a bit jealous. He'd always been Uncle Lon to Cyarea, but at the moment, most of her limited focus was on Tobal. It made sense. She didn't know him like she did Lon and Sabin, and the fact that he was her father's brother was fascinating to her. She always had dozens of questions, and he never hesitated to answer them.

"Did you?" Tobal asked, rising to his feet, still clutching Cyarea against his chest.

"In the leg," she said as she squirmed. She was getting too big to be carried around, and she was vocal about it.

Tobal had to put her down, but he looked more relaxed now. He truly cared about Cyarea—either that, or he was a fantastic actor, but Lon doubted it.

"Sounds great. I'm glad you were able to defend yourself and your mom."

"Next time, I'll stab him in the heart!" she declared.

Tobal was still smiling, but his expression grew more serious as he looked away from Cyarea. She ran back to her mother, who was still talking to Reyni, and Lon stared at Tobal.

Tobal was hiding something.

Lon had been watching Tobal since he'd first arrived at the palace. In the beginning, he'd been suspicious, and sometimes, he still was, although it was easier to dismiss those thoughts now that he knew who Tobal was and what he'd been hiding. Now, he watched Tobal because he enjoyed it, even though he knew better than to try flirting. Tobal was Berith's brother. There hadn't been an official announcement yet, but there would be eventually, and Tobal would have his choice of demons to date. He wouldn't have to make do with

Lon, which meant it was smarter for Lon to stay away.

He wasn't sure his heart understood that reasoning.

But there was something else. Lon could tell, and he'd find out what it was. He didn't think Tobal was involved in the attack, but there were other things he could be involved in, things Berith had forbidden him to get himself into.

After allowing Cyarea and Aloise to be attacked, Lon couldn't let anything happen to Tobal. He'd never forgive himself if he did, and he was pretty sure Berith wouldn't, either.

Tobal was seething. How dare anyone attack his niece? How dare anyone try to hurt a little girl?

He'd been relieved when he'd arrived and had seen that Cyarea was fine, then stunned when she'd told him she'd stabbed the bad guy. He loved that she'd been able to defend herself, but she shouldn't have had to. Her life should be focused on spending time with her parents and going to school, playing with her friends, and doing what she loved. She shouldn't have to wonder if she was about to be attacked every time she turned a corner.

Tobal didn't know how to help with that. He couldn't stay around her the entire day, even though he was tempted to do so just to reassure himself she was fine. He wouldn't stand for his family getting hurt, especially when he knew who was behind the attacks. His brother had forbidden him to get involved with the society, but what Berith didn't know wouldn't hurt him. Besides, once Tobal found out who was part of the society, he was sure Berith would forgive him.

Hopefully.

He chewed on his lower lip and watched Cyarea. He didn't have a plan yet, but he needed to work on it if he was going to do this. There wasn't much he could do at the moment except wait, which he didn't enjoy. He suspected the secret society would reach out to him soon, though. It could be a coincidence, but the attack had to have been to get his attention. In their last message, they'd threatened to kill him and the rest of the family, so this would be the perfect way to show him they were serious. Now that he knew they were ready to kill a little girl to get what they wanted, they'd expect Tobal to go along with their plan.

And he would. Just not the way they expected him to do.

Lon was watching him with narrow eyes, and his expression told Tobal everything he needed to know. Lon suspected Tobal was planning something, which meant Tobal would have to be careful. He couldn't afford to be found out and have his plan referred to Berith. He wouldn't put it past his brother to lock him in his rooms in order to keep him safe, and he didn't want that to happen. He needed to do *something*, and he was the only one who could infiltrate the secret society and find out who they were. He wasn't sure he'd manage to get all the way up to the top, but the more people he could identify, the more people they could arrest, torture, and get answers from.

But maybe Tobal should talk to Lon. Even though he knew how to defend himself, he wasn't a fighter, and he could end up in a lot of trouble if he wasn't careful. On the other hand, Lon knew how to fight. It was his job, which meant he'd know what to do better than Tobal ever could. Tobal wasn't sure it was worth the risk of having Lon go to his brother to tell him about this, though. He couldn't afford for Berith to try to stop him, but he also couldn't afford to make a mess out of it. He needed to get it right on the first try.

He didn't know what to do. He wanted to get Lon involved, both because he needed him and because it would make the situation less scary. The problem was that he didn't know if he could trust Lon not to go to Berith, and he wasn't willing to sacrifice the only opportunity they'd have to do this.

So, no. He couldn't afford to pull Lon in. Lon was loyal to Berith, which meant that if Berith told him to keep an eye on Tobal, he would. Berith had been clear that he didn't want Tobal to reach out to the society, and Lon would follow his orders. He'd try to stop Tobal, and that was the last thing Tobal wanted.

He was on his own.

He chewed on his lower lip as he sat down in one of the armchairs. He looked around the room. Everyone he cared about was here—Berith, Cyarea, Sabin, Zeno, and even Lon. Aloise, Tobal didn't know well yet, but she was Cyarea's mother, which meant she needed to be alive. Tobal had been about Cyarea's age when he'd lost his mother, and he never wanted another child to go through that. It was a dream that would never come true, and he could deal with that, but if he could protect Cyarea from having to go through it, he'd do it.

Even if it meant going against his brother's orders to stay away from the secret society that was threatening all of them.

CHAPTER TEN

The society still hadn't reached out. It had been days since that demon had been sent to hurt Cyarea. Tobal had expected the society to either have a message in his rooms by the time he went back to them or to contact him later that day or the day after that.

They hadn't. Almost a week had passed, and he was still hanging around, waiting for them. He had no way to contact them, or he would have done so himself, but as it was, he was stuck.

How did he reach out to a secret society that was, well, secret?

Tobal hated that there was nothing he could do. Terrified that Berith or someone else in their family would get hurt, he was desperate to do something to stop that from happening. He needed to help, and the fact that there was nothing for him to do, even though he had a plan, made him restless.

The fact that Lon seemed to have caught on that Tobal was planning something didn't help. Every time they were in the same room, Lon stared. It had gotten to the point where Tobal left the room if Lon was in it, but it felt too much like running away and like he had something to hide.

Which, to be fair, he did.

But Tobal didn't want Lon to find out about his plan. He couldn't afford for Lon to run straight to Berith, even though he could use some help. Lon was destroying himself over what had happened, working long hours and barely sleeping. He looked exhausted, with his red skin paler than usual and dark shadows under his eyes.

Tobal wanted to protect him, too.

He'd been surprised to realize that, but as Tobal stared at his bedroom ceiling, he knew he couldn't deny it. Somewhere along the line, he'd started caring for Lon, too. Maybe it was because Lon was Berith's best friend, or maybe there was more to it. There was no way for Tobal to find out as long as he kept his distance from Lon, and he had every intention of continuing to do that. Until this problem with the secret society was solved, it would be better for everyone if Tobal and Lon didn't get involved.

Tobal sighed and rolled to his stomach, grabbing his pillow to hug it.

There was no way to know if Lon was interested in Tobal the same way Tobal was interested in him. Maybe all the attention Lon was giving Tobal was only due to the fact that he knew Tobal was planning something. Maybe as soon as he figured out what that something was, he'd go back to being distant. He might even stop watching Tobal from afar, which Tobal had become used to.

He thought something had changed, though. Before, Lon had been suspicious. It had been obvious in his expression and in the way he watched Tobal, and Tobal hadn't been surprised. But things were different lately, and he wanted to explore how different they could become.

But once again, the secret society got in the middle of things. They were the reason Tobal needed to stay away from Lon, and he didn't like it. If he ever got to meet anyone from the society, he'd give them an earful, dammit.

Tobal pushed himself into a sitting position. He had to do something, and it was time for him to be proactive. He wasn't sure how that would look, since he didn't know how to contact the society, but they had to be watching him. They were observing his reaction, but clearly, they hadn't gotten the message that he wanted to talk to them. Maybe it was because he was still in his rooms at the palace, safe and sound. Maybe there was another reason, or maybe they were just assholes.

There was no doubt they were.

But Tobal hoped that leaving the palace for a bit would help, so he quickly dressed, choosing some of the clothes he'd arrived with rather than the ones he'd been gifted after he'd moved in. He didn't want to look like he was important or for people to think he was rich, because in the end, he wasn't. His brother was, and Tobal was lucky that Berith was more than happy to provide for him. The least he could do was keep Berith and the rest of the family safe.

So he came up with a new plan. He couldn't reach out to the society, but he could try drawing them to him. The way to make that happen was to be on his own away from the palace, and he knew exactly where to go.

Tobal had explored the city, and he knew the perfect spot to spend time in the hopes that the society would reach out to him. His main problem would be to get out of the palace, but it wouldn't be the first time he'd snuck in or out of somewhere. He'd done it many times when he was with his foster parents, and while he'd been younger then, nothing much had changed.

Tobal raised the hood of his jacket, covering his face, and left his rooms. The prince's wing was silent, which was how Tobal had wanted it. It made it easier for him to sneak out using the servants' hallways.

He'd explored those, too. He'd wanted to know everything about the place since it was his new home, and he was glad he had.

He crossed paths with a few servants, but with his hood up, they couldn't see his face. A few looked startled, but he suspected they were used to eccentricity. Tobal had met several demons who never uncovered their faces, and the memory of them had inspired his current attire. Demons were demons, no matter how rich they were or where they lived.

Once he reached the kitchens, he relaxed. The only thing left to do was sneak out through the back door, and he did so, taking advantage of a meat delivery. People were moving back and forth between the kitchen and the area outside of it, so he ducked his head and followed one of the servants past the guards standing by the door. He kept his face down as he quickly walked along the external wall, breathing easier only once he couldn't see the door anymore.

He was out.

He didn't linger around the palace. He couldn't afford to. Instead, he quickly made his way toward the seedier part of town. Every town had these, even when the prince lived there. In this case, it was where most new arrivals stayed and where workers gathered after a long day of work. It wasn't nearly as bad as it had been in the town where Tobal had grown up, but he wasn't looking for trouble, or at least not the usual kind.

He walked past closed businesses and demons pacing the streets until he found the shabbiest tavern. Once there, he walked behind a group of four demons and settled at a table by the door so he could see everyone who walked in and out of the place and have a quick escape if he needed it.

He hoped he wouldn't.

He got a beer but didn't take more than a sip, and not because it was so bitter that he almost spit it out. He couldn't afford to be distracted.

He knew he'd won when a seedy-looking agramon demon stepped up to his table.

Lon wanted to go inside the tavern, but he knew better. He'd attract too much attention, since he was still wearing his uniform, and clearly, that was the last thing Tobal needed. He was in enough trouble as it was.

But as soon as Lon got his hands on Tobal, he'd give him a good shake and demand to know what the fuck he was doing here.

The problem was that Lon would have to admit he'd been keeping an eye on Tobal. He wasn't spying on him using the passages anymore, but he'd heard two servants talking about how they'd noticed Tobal sneaking out of his rooms with a hood on, and he'd known he had to follow. Tobal didn't have a reason to be out of the palace, especially without a guard by his side. Lon was supposed to be that guard, but he'd had to run to his office to solve a problem, and by the time he'd come back, Tobal had vanished. Luckily, Lon had managed to locate him just as he left the palace, and he'd followed.

To this tavern.

Lon had never been here, but he knew the area well. Tobal was up to something. He didn't have a reason to be here, which worried Lon. Had he been wrong? Did Tobal have something to do with the attack, or was he here for another reason? Lon didn't know Tobal that well, so he supposed it could be, but he was trying not to keep his hopes up. Whatever was happening, he didn't like it.

He couldn't go inside, so he'd placed himself in the tight space between the tavern and the building next to it. It was enough that he could see Tobal sitting at a table by the door and the agramon demon standing in front of him. They were talking, and Lon hated that he couldn't hear what they were saying.

He was going to strangle Tobal as soon as they were back at the palace.

He held his breath as he stared at the two. The agramon demon nodded a few times, said something, then turned and left, holding something small that had been on the table.

Tobal stayed there a while longer, sipping on a beer and grimacing every time he did so. Lon had never drunk here, but he could imagine what the beer was like. Tobal would be lucky if his stomach made it out of it in one piece.

Tobal eventually gave up on the beer and got to his feet. He didn't look around the tavern as he headed for the door, and Lon got ready. He couldn't grab Tobal here because he didn't want to make a scene, but as soon as they were close enough to the palace, he'd make sure Tobal knew what he thought of all of this.

Surely Tobal had to know how dangerous it had been for him to come here. Why had he? Lon couldn't think of a good explanation beyond that Tobal had been involved with the society after all, but that didn't feel right, and not just because he had a slight crush on Tobal. If Tobal was truly working with the society, they wouldn't have a reason to meet here. The society hadn't had trouble getting their messages to Tobal in the palace. They'd even snuck a demon into his rooms, for fuck's sake. If they needed to contact Tobal, they could leave another message there, and no one would ever know.

So Tobal was here for another reason.

Lon was still thinking about what that reason might be when Tobal stumbled out of the tavern. Thankfully, he headed toward the palace, and Lon waited a few seconds before falling into step behind him. He didn't want Tobal to notice he was there, and he thought he'd managed until he noticed a group of three demons at the opening of an alley. They were between him and Tobal, and as soon as Tobal walked past them, they stepped out and followed him.

That couldn't be good.

Lon waited, giving those three demons the benefit of the doubt, but he didn't expect anything good to come out of this, and he was right. When Tobal turned a corner, moving into a street that was emptier than the previous one had been, the demons made their move.

One of them called out to Tobal, who had the bad idea of stopping and turning to see what was happening. It gave the three demons enough time to catch up to him, and one of them grabbed his arm when they did.

Lon couldn't let this happen. He didn't know if these demons were planning on robbing Tobal or planning something else, but he wasn't going to waste time to find out. He ran toward Tobal, who was struggling to get himself out of the demon's hold, grabbed one of the other two demons, and pulled back. The demon cried out and stumbled, turning around to face Lon, but Lon was waiting for him. He raised his fist, punching the demon square in the jaw, sending him flying back. The demon hit the wall, his head producing a satisfying crunching sound.

He didn't get up.

Lon turned to the other two. He didn't care if he'd killed the one he'd punched, and he was ready to kill these two if they gave him any trouble.

They did.

Lon wasn't surprised. The two demons rushed him, but it was a piece of cake to defend himself. They hadn't noticed he wore a guard's uniform, but if they had, they'd have understood how bad an idea it was to attack him.

Lon grabbed the wrist of the first demon who reached him and pulled. The demon couldn't keep his balance, and he fell past Lon. It gave Lon a few moments of respite, and that was enough for him to grab the other demon by the throat. He turned and threw the demon he was holding against the other. They crashed together, falling down in a heap. Lon peered at Tobal, who was staring at him with wide eyes.

One of the demons got up, and Lon snarled at him. "You don't want to go against one of the prince's guards," he said.

The demon's eyes widened, and he took a step back. If he

was smart, he'd grab his friends and run.

"What are you doing here?" Tobal asked, distracting him.

Lon almost told him it wasn't the best idea to ask that kind of question while they were still fighting, but he realized the two demons he'd left conscious had taken his advice. They were running down the street, having abandoned the third one, who was passed out on the ground — or dead.

"Saving you, clearly," Lon snarked.

Tobal straightened his back. "I don't need to be saved."

"Are you sure? Because it seemed they managed to startle you, which is never a good start for a fight."

Tobal's hood had fallen back during his altercation with the demons, but the night was dark, so Lon couldn't see his expression. He could imagine it, though. Tobal sounded flustered, and he probably was.

He'd snuck out of the palace, which meant he hadn't expected Lon to be after him. Lon wouldn't have known he wasn't home if he hadn't heard two servants talk about him, and he was glad he had.

That didn't mean he was done chewing Tobal out.

He grasped Tobal's arm, making sure not to put too much force into it, and pulled him toward the palace. "We need to talk," he said through gritted teeth.

"We don't need to do anything. Just let me go."

"Why would I? Berith was clear. He told you to stay at the palace and not try to contact the secret society, yet you did the exact opposite."

Tobal stumbled, but Lon had a good hold on him.

"How do you know I was trying to contact the secret society?" Tobal asked.

"Why else would you be in that dump? What did you think would happen?"

"What did happen. If you were spying on me, you saw that demon coming up to my table."

Lon grunted, not confirming he'd been spying. He didn't have to. Tobal had seen right through him, although he probably didn't entirely understand why Lon had come after him.

Lon didn't, either. He was here to keep Berith's brother safe, of course, but it wasn't only because Berith would be destroyed if something happened to Tobal. He wouldn't be the only one in pain if Tobal got hurt.

Lon would be, too, and that was as confusing as it was terrifying.

Tobal was an idiot. He didn't know how Lon had found out he'd snuck out, but he didn't need to. Lon was the head of security and for now, Tobal's bodyguard. Of course he'd followed him. It was part of his job, and if there was one thing Lon took seriously, it was his job.

Tobal hadn't thought much of it when Lon had said he needed to go to his office for a while. He hadn't even thought of sneaking out right then and there. That idea had come later, and he'd been lucky Lon wasn't already back.

But Lon had somehow found out about this. Tobal wanted to ask how, but he was also afraid of pushing the other demon too hard. Lon was pissed, and while Tobal wasn't afraid he'd hurt him, he also wasn't comfortable with the situation.

Lon gave Tobal's arm a little shake. "Well? You were going to tell me about that demon."

Tobal wasn't surprised Lon knew what demon he was talking about. "He came up to my table and asked me why I was there. It's what I'd been hoping for, so I'd brought a drawing of the society's symbol. I showed it to him, and he knew what I wanted."

"Which was?"

"I told him I needed to talk to whoever was available. He promised to pass on the message, and I think he will."

"Why?"

"They want me to work for them, don't they? That means they'll be happy to find out I'm trying to contact them."

Lon's hold on Tobal's arm tightened. "And why did you do that? Wasn't Berith clear when he told you to stay away?"

Tobal shook his arm, glaring at Lon even though he suspected Lon couldn't see it since it was so dark. "I couldn't just do nothing, especially after what happened with Cyarea. I thought the society would contact me after the attack to boast that they'd managed to get to Berith's daughter and threaten me again, but they haven't. I know they're watching me, though."

"How?"

"I can feel them. Sometimes, even when I'm alone in my rooms, they're still watching."

"That's not possible."

There was something odd in Lon's voice, but Tobal couldn't identify it. "It hasn't been happening lately, but it did before, and I didn't imagine it. Look, I'm just trying to do the best thing for Berith and his family. I don't want anyone to get hurt."

"Just like Berith doesn't want you to get hurt."

Tobal walked in silence for a while. He knew that what Lon had just said was true, which was why it hurt. Berith didn't want to lose Tobal, and he'd be pissed when he found out about this. Tobal didn't want to disappoint his brother. He also didn't want to hurt him, but he did feel like he needed to do more. Berith had opened his home to Tobal, and it wasn't fair that Tobal was the only one gaining something from that.

What also wasn't fair was that his niece might get hurt, and he wouldn't stand for that. Cyarea was young enough that she could manage to stay away from the harsher part of Hell. The fact that she lived at the palace and that Berith was her father could either help with that or make things worse, but

Tobal would do whatever he needed to in order to protect her.

"You could have gotten hurt," Lon almost yelled. "I don't understand how you could be so stupid."

Tobal stopped in the middle of the street. Luckily, they were alone, although he doubted that the demons who lived in the houses lining the street would be happy at hearing them yelling at each other.

Still, he turned to face Lon. "I'm not stupid," he yelled back. He caught himself and swallowed the anger, then softened his voice. "I need to do this for Cyarea, and I haven't changed my mind. If the society contacts me, I'll go along with it and try to identify as many of them as I can."

"You're going to get yourself killed. What will Cyarea do then? You're already her favorite uncle. Do you really think she'll be happy when you die?"

"I'm not going to die."

Lon surged toward Tobal, startling him. Tobal quickly stepped back when Lon reached for his face, but his breath hitched when instead of hitting him, Lon cupped his cheek.

They stood there in the dark, silent street, staring at each other. Tobal couldn't see much, but he could feel. Lon's hand was on his cheek, as gentle as if Tobal were made of glass. He could hear Lon's harsh breath, even feel his chest move, and he found himself leaning closer without thinking about it.

Lon sucked in a breath and stepped back, his hand dropping. Tobal was confused and bewildered, but they'd been having a conversation and needed to finish it.

"Look, if you don't trust me to do this by myself, why don't you do it with me?" he suggested.

Lon was silent for a moment, and Tobal gave him time to think. He started walking again, eager to get back to the palace. His skin itched, and he wanted a bath. It had nothing to do with the tavern he'd been in and everything to do with the society and knowing that they were watching him.

"What was your plan?" Lon eventually asked.

Tobal wasn't about to tell him he didn't have one. "For now, to try to contact the society. I don't know why they haven't reached out yet, but it doesn't matter as long as I manage to get in touch with them."

"And when you do?"

"I'll tell them that I'll work for them as long as they don't hurt Cyarea. They won't believe me if I just change my mind, but I can use her as an excuse. No one would want her to get hurt."

"I'm not so sure about that," Lon muttered.

"I have no doubt they don't care one bit about Cyarea, but they were trying to find a way to convince me to work for them, and I'm sure that's why they attacked Cyarea. Once I'm in, I can get all the names we need, and you and I might be able to take out the entire society and keep Berith and Cyarea safe."

"I have conditions if we do this."

Of course he did. "I'm listening."

"I know you can defend yourself, but you're not trained the way I am. If we're doing this, we're doing it together. That means that when I tell you to do something, you do it, and if I tell you not to do something, you don't."

Tobal resisted the urge to salute and kept his hands by his sides. He wasn't an idiot, and he knew that listening to Lon would be for the best. He might have to stray depending on the situation, but he could promise to do what he could to follow Lon's orders. "All right."

"You also won't put yourself in danger."

"Just going after the society means I'm in danger," Tobal pointed out.

"Then you won't put yourself in any *more* danger. My main goal is to protect Berith and his family, which includes you. I'll find another way to get to the society if I have to, but I'm not allowing you to get hurt."

"I'll do my best to stay out of trouble. You have to see it might not be possible, though."

"I don't care if it's possible or not. If I find you in danger, you're out, and that's that."

Lon didn't wait for Tobal to answer. He stomped ahead, leaving Tobal to stare at his back as he tried to catch up.

Tobal understood why Lon was wary of what they were doing. Berith had been clear—he wanted Lon to protect Tobal, and if anything happened to him, it would strain the relationship between the two friends. That was the last thing Tobal wanted, but he also needed to do what he thought was right, and in this case, that was keeping everyone safe. If he had to sacrifice himself to make that happen, he would.

No matter what he'd promised and who he'd promised it to.

CHAPTER ELEVEN

Tobal stared at the piece of paper on the small table in his living area. He usually kept the table empty, mostly because he didn't own many things. That was starting to change now that he had space and money to buy himself trinkets, but when he'd left his rooms this morning, the table had been empty.

It wasn't anymore.

He wanted to see what was on the piece of paper, but he was also afraid. Its presence meant the society had found an easy way into his rooms, again, which meant he didn't feel safe here. Clearly, they could come in whenever they wanted, whether he was in or not. What if they decided to sneak in during the night while he was sleeping? They probably wouldn't kill him for now, since they wanted to use him, but it was still terrifying to know someone could be there, watching him while he was at his most vulnerable.

But he couldn't continue staring forever. If the piece of paper was what he thought, he needed to tell Lon. They were working together now, which meant they had to do this together.

It was odd. Tobal wasn't used to working with anyone, let alone a guy who knew what he was doing. Lon had been clear that he wanted to be involved, and Tobal was happy about that. It made him feel safer, and it felt good to know he wasn't facing this on his own. He'd been alone most of his life, and it was nice to be able to rely on someone.

Sucking in a breath, he looked around the room one last

time. It was empty except for him. The doors that led to the garden were open, and a slight breeze came through them. From where he was, Tobal could see desert plants and sand, a few paths, and even a bench just outside his room.

The door that led into the hallway was behind him and closed. He hadn't locked it when he'd come in, and he was kind of afraid of doing so. What if there was someone in here with him? He could kill them like he had last time, but they could be stronger than him, so he needed an easy way to escape. He was becoming paranoid, and while he didn't like it, he didn't see a way out of it until the society was dealt with.

It was one more reason for him to want that. He needed to feel safe, and he wouldn't as long as the society was sniffing around him.

Shaking his head, he stepped toward the table. The piece of paper didn't move. It was there, still and silent, waiting for him, and he hated it. He snatched it up and glared at it, not one bit surprised to see the symbol that belonged to the society drawn there. He'd known this was them without having to see it. He'd hoped for it, but now that it had happened, he wanted to throw up.

He unfolded the piece of paper. Someone had written on the inside. The handwriting looked normal enough, with blocky letters, and he tried to focus on what the words said rather than on what they could reveal about the person who'd written them. That would come later.

The tavern. Tonight. Ten.

That was it. Tobal didn't need any more of an explanation, though. The secret society wanted to see him tonight at ten at the tavern, and he'd be there.

That was if Lon agreed to let him go.

One annoying thing about working with other people was that Lon didn't see anything wrong with trying to order Tobal around. Tobal supposed it *was* his right, considering who he was and who he worked for, but Tobal didn't have to like it, especially when it meant he couldn't do what he needed to do. Lon's job was to protect Tobal, but that might not be easy while also hunting the society.

Tobal wasn't sure Lon could see that. He was focused on keeping the family safe, and Tobal suspected that finding out who was in the society took a step back next to that. It wasn't a bad thing, but they needed to know if they wanted to take out the society, and Tobal very much did.

Tobal could keep the message to himself and sneak out like he had last time, but it hadn't been easy, and it wouldn't be tonight, either. He didn't know how Lon managed it, but he always found him, even when he wasn't in the palace. Besides, he had no doubt that Lon had talked to his guards and made sure they understood they needed to stop Tobal if he tried to leave.

So, there was only one thing Tobal could do. He turned around and left his rooms, heading to Lon's office. He couldn't help but wonder if the society was watching him right now. They hadn't said he needed to come alone, but he thought it was implied. What would they do if they found out he'd told Lon about the meeting? He was the prince's head of security, one of his right-hand men.

They probably wouldn't be happy.

But none of that mattered as long as they didn't get their hands on Berith. He rushed through the hallways, hating feeling a prickle on his back. He didn't know if it was real, but it always felt like someone was watching him. That was why he hurried all the way to Lon's office and barely even knocked before throwing the door open.

He should have known better.

Lon blinked up from behind his desk, staring at Tobal. He wasn't alone. Another man wearing a uniform sat on the other side of his desk, and from what Tobal could see, they'd been working.

"What is it?" Lon asked, halfway on his feet already.

"I need to talk to you," Tobal said, stuffing the piece of paper in his pocket.

He didn't know if he could trust the other demon, whom he now recognized as Mikal. Mikal had been nice, and Tobal knew he was close to Lon, but was there anyone they could trust beyond the family?

"I should probably go," Mikal said with a smile. For some reason, he seemed amused.

"I'm sure Tobal can come back later," Lon said with a low growl to punctuate his words.

Tobal tightened his fingers around the piece of paper in his pocket. "I can't. I need to talk to you now."

Lon glared. "What about? As you can see, I'm busy."

Tobal glared right back. Did he or didn't he want to be involved? "You'll want to know this," he said, trying to put everything he was hiding in words.

Lon frowned. At least he didn't look angry anymore.

"I have to go anyway," Mikal said as he gathered a bunch of documents on the desk. "I'll go over what we talked about and let you know."

"Thank you."

Tobal had to resist the urge to tell Mikal to hurry up. Instead of leaving, he kept peeking at Lon and Tobal as if he expected something, and it made Tobal want to scream. Mikal couldn't understand that this was a life-or-death situation, but still.

As soon as the door closed behind Mikal, Tobal pulled his hand out of his pocket and thrust the piece of paper at Lon. "They contacted me."

Lon's eyes widened, and he took the message. There wasn't much to it, but he stared at it for a long time, more than enough to read the short message several times.

"You're not going."

Tobal had known this would happen. "Like hell I'm not."

"It's too dangerous, and while they didn't specify you have to go alone, we both know they won't be happy if I'm with you. Even if they don't recognize me, they won't want you to have the kind of support that might mean they can't manipulate you."

Tobal put his hands on his hips. "You can't tell me what to do."

"I can, and I will." Lon got right into Tobal's face, close enough that Tobal could feel his warm breath on his skin. "My job is to protect you. Allowing you to go would be too dangerous, and it's not something I'm willing to do or compromise about. You're not going, and that's final."

Tobal leaned forward. Their noses brushed together, and all of it was kind of ridiculous, but he couldn't start screaming like he wanted to. They couldn't afford for anyone to hear them fight.

"You're not my father," Tobal hissed. "I don't care what you want or don't want. We agreed we'd do this together, so you should know how lucky you are that I came here to show you the message instead of going on my own."

"It didn't go well the last time you tried doing something on your own," Lon snarked.

Tobal had to resist the urge to hit him. "I'd have been fine."

"Three demons attacked you," Lon said more loudly, pushing forward.

Tobal had to take a step back. Lon was trying to intimidate him, and to be honest, it was working. Lon was an intimidating kind of guy.

But the back of Tobal's legs hit the desk, and he found himself floundering. He reached back, pressing a hand on the desk to keep himself upright, reaching for Lon with the other. It was instinct because Tobal needed to keep himself upright.

Lon's smile was satisfied, and he wasn't done with Tobal.

He leaned close, crowding him.

The door burst open.

Lon jerked away from Tobal and glared at whoever had burst in without knocking. He'd thought it might be Mikal, but instead, it was Berith, and he looked fucking delighted.

"I'm sorry. Am I interrupting something?" Berith asked as he walked in and closed the door.

"You're not," Lon said through gritted teeth.

"Are you sure? Because to me, it looked like I was interrupting something."

Lon didn't often feel the urge to strangle Berith, but when he did, it was overwhelming and usually because Berith was being an idiot.

Today wasn't any different.

Lon sucked in a breath, telling himself to have patience. "Did you need anything?" He knew what the position he and Tobal had been in when Berith had opened the door would have looked like to his friend, and he didn't want to talk about it.

"I just wanted to check in on you, since you were yelling. I didn't expect you to be fighting with my brother." Berith's gaze jumped from Lon to Tobal. "It looked like the two of you were *close*."

"It was nothing," Tobal quickly said.

Berith's expression softened. "You know you don't have to hide it if the two of you are together, right?"

Lon gaped. Where had Berith gotten that idea? He and Tobal weren't together.

Even though part of Lon kind of wished they were.

"What are you talking about?" he croaked.

Berith gestured at both of them. "The two of you have been spending time together, and I like it. There's no reason for you to hide. If you were worried about what I'd think about this, then you don't have to because I'm glad you found each other. I want both of you to be happy, and if that happens when you're together, then it's even better, isn't it? You'll keep each other happy and safe, and in the end, that's all that matters."

Lon blinked, unable to find the words he needed. He couldn't deny he'd thought about whether he and Tobal could be together before, but he hadn't imagined Berith would be happy about it. He should have known better, clearly. Berith wanted everyone to be happy, especially the people closest to him. He seemed delighted that Tobal and Lon were together, even though they weren't.

Lon couldn't lie to him. He opened his mouth to tell him the truth, but one of Tobal's hands shot out, grabbing his forearm. Tobal squeezed to the point of pain, and while Lon glared at him, Tobal's entire focus was on Berith.

"Thank you," he said. "We weren't hiding it, but it's new, and we wanted to be sure it was serious before we told you," Tobal said.

Lon made a strangled sound. The words still wouldn't come, dammit.

Berith's smile was wide. "That's all right. I was hesitant when I first realized I had feelings for Mel, too, but everything went great in the end. I'm sorry I barged in the way I did. I was afraid you were fighting, especially since I forced you to spend time together by asking Lon to protect you, but it was good to see that wasn't the case."

"Berith," Lon started saying. He wouldn't lie to his best friend, dammit. Tobal might not have a problem with it, but Lon sure did.

Tobal turned abruptly toward him and to Lon's astonishment, smacked a kiss on his lips. "He said he's fine with it," Tobal murmured. "We don't have to hide anymore or apologize."

Lon narrowed his eyes at him. "What are you talking about?"

"I'm happy my brother is happy for me," Tobal said. "And that we won't have to hide anymore. We can be together without being afraid someone will see us."

Lon finally got the message. Tobal wanted to use their fake relationship as a way for them to work together without anyone realizing what they were doing. It wasn't a bad idea, but Lon still disliked it. He didn't want to lie to anyone, least of all Berith.

But if Berith found out he and Tobal were investigating the society, he'd be pissed, and Lon didn't want that, either. His job was to keep Berith and his family safe, and right now, he had to decide what it meant.

Lying to Berith, or telling him the truth?

Tobal pushed closer to Lon, wrapping an arm around his waist. He was praying that Lon would go along with his lie, but he couldn't be sure.

He squeezed Lon's waist, silently telling him to confirm they were dating. It would give them a reason to spend a lot of time together, alone. It was what they needed to deal with the secret society without Berith getting involved, but Tobal could see that Lon was uneasy at the thought of lying to the prince.

Tobal kind of was, too. He didn't care much about lying to *the prince,* but he did care about lying to his brother. He and Berith might not have known each other long, but Berith was important to Tobal, and Tobal hated having to do this.

But this was the best way to keep Berith out of it. The secret society wanted to kill him, but Tobal couldn't allow that to happen. If it meant lying to his brother and disappointing him, he'd deal with the consequences when they came.

Berith moved closer to them. He clapped Lon's shoulder, squeezing, and Tobal let go. Lon looked like he was about to explode, and Tobal didn't want to be anywhere near him when that happened.

"I'm not angry you didn't tell me," Berith reassured them. "But you don't have to hide anymore, all right?"

Tobal held his breath as Berith and Lon stared at each other. He wouldn't be surprised if Lon ruined everything, but the demon was smart. Surely, he understood what Tobal was aiming for.

Eventually, Lon grunted. "We won't hide," he confirmed. "I wasn't sure you'd be happy to find out I was dating your brother."

Berith drew Lon into his arms. "How could I not be? You're the best person I could have wanted for my brother. I know you'll never hurt him willingly. You're loyal and strong, and you'll protect him."

Tobal's chest squeezed. He wanted that. He wanted someone to be loyal to him and to protect him, and if Lon was that person, that would be even better.

But he and Lon *weren't* together. Tobal had to keep that in mind, which he could already tell wouldn't be easy. If he and Lon had to act as if they were together, it would be too easy for him to actually fall for the guy.

But when Berith turned to him, Tobal smiled at him. He accepted his brother's hug and shivered when Berith whispered in his ear.

"I'm truly happy for you, brother. It's good to see you settling down at the palace, and Lon is a great man and perfect for you."

Maybe he was. He definitely was a good man, and as to whether or not he was perfect for Tobal, Tobal wasn't sure he'd ever find out.

Berith eventually stepped back. He was still smiling, and

knowing they were lying to him made Tobal feel awful.

"I'll leave the two of you alone," Berith said.

"Why were you here in the first place? Did you need anything?"

Berith's smile turned mischievous. "No, but I crossed paths with Mikal, and he told me the two you were alone in here and that something was clearly happening between you. I thought that maybe, you were fighting, but I'm glad to see that wasn't so."

The fake smile on Tobal's lips hurt, but he kept it in place as Berith left the office. He and Lon stayed silent as Lon locked the door behind Berith, then turned to Tobal.

Tobal let the smile slip.

"What the fuck were you thinking?" Lon demanded to know.

His voice was loud in the office, and Tobal swallowed, wondering if someone outside had heard.

"Tobal?" Lon asked, striding toward Tobal.

The office suddenly felt tiny, and there was nowhere for Tobal to go. He could run out the door that opened into the garden, but he doubted he'd have enough time. Lon looked like a predator right now, and his prey was Tobal.

Tobal licked his lips and raised his hands. "I don't like lying to him any more than you do."

Lon snorted. "Are you sure? Because to me, it looks like you've been lying to him for most of the time you've been here."

That was a low blow, but it was true. "I don't like lying to him. He'd have tried to stop us if he'd found out what we're really up to, and we can't allow that to happen. We need to know what the society is up to."

"And how will lying to your brother about us being in a relationship help with that?"

"It'll give us an excuse to spend time alone together. If

people think we're in a relationship, they won't be surprised if they don't see us around and if we're always attached at the hip. I already know you won't allow me to do this on my own, and I promised I'd follow your orders, so I will. But we *have* to go to this meeting."

Lon's eyes narrowed. "You said you wouldn't put yourself in danger, yet you're about to do just that."

"How else should we do this? They gave us a meeting time and spot. If we don't go, how are we supposed to find out what they want from me?"

"It's dangerous."

"I'm aware of that. I don't like it any more than you do, but I don't see that there's another way to do this. I'm sure it'll be fine."

"I know *I* will be. I'm not sure about you, though," Lon murmured.

At that moment, it felt like he truly cared about Tobal, and Tobal desperately wanted that to be true. He almost moved forward. He wanted Lon's arms around him because even though he'd insisted they had to go to the meeting, he knew how dangerous it was. He wished Lon would reassure him and tell him everything would be okay.

Instead, he stayed where he was by the desk. "If I'm not at the meeting, the society will come after me. I was lucky to survive the first demon they sent. What are the odds I'll survive the second one?"

"I'm supposed to protect you."

"And you are, but you can't be with me every minute of every day." He'd tried, but he had an important job to do, and even though Mikal had been helping, there were things only Lon could take care of.

It seemed like every time he had a meeting or something that took him away from Tobal, the society knew and took advantage of it. That would mean they had someone spying for them in the palace, which wasn't a surprise. Lon suspected that, and Tobal agreed. It was the only explanation for how easily the society got in and out of Tobal's rooms.

It scared Tobal. How was he supposed to know which of the servants he saw every day around the palace worked for the society? Was that demon dangerous? Were they planning to attack Tobal again?

And if they did, would Tobal survive this time, too?

He wanted to believe he would. He *needed* to believe it.

"We'll talk about it later," Lon said with a grunt.

He walked around his desk and sat down, effectively dismissing Tobal.

Tobal watched him for a moment, but Lon didn't look up. That gave Tobal the opportunity to really take him in, and he wondered what it would be like for them to actually be together.

He'd thought Lon would kiss him the night he'd followed him to the tavern. Lon had been terrified Tobal would get hurt, and when he thought about it, Tobal could still feel Lon's hand on his cheek.

But Lon *hadn't* kissed Tobal, and maybe he never would.

CHAPTER TWELVE

The meeting wouldn't happen for several hours, and Tobal was losing his mind.

After leaving Lon's office, he'd gone back to his rooms, but he hadn't been able to stay there. He felt like someone was watching him all the time now, and it gave him the creeps. So he'd headed to Zeno's little house, hoping that being with his brother would distract him. Zeno had been happy to see him, and like always, he'd made Tobal feel welcome.

But Tobal couldn't stop thinking about what would happen later tonight.

He'd insisted they needed to go, and he believed they did, but that didn't mean he wasn't worried about what would happen. There was no way to know how many people the society worked with, and how many of them would be present at the meeting. Tobal doubted the demon he'd talked to the other night would be the one talking to them, even though he'd relayed the message Tobal had sent to the society.

He was terrified, and he wanted to run away screaming, but he couldn't.

His life hadn't been nearly as complicated when he'd been alone in his small town, but he'd never wished to go back to it. Once the mess with the society was over, he could settle into his new life, enjoy his family, and maybe even find someone to share his life with.

As he thought about that, he wondered what Lon was doing. He'd told himself to let go of the idea that the two of them could work as a couple, but it wasn't easy, especially after they'd lied to Berith. It seemed that Tobal's brother hadn't been exactly discreet with the news, and by the time Tobal reached Zeno, he'd already known.

"Thinking about Lon again?" Zeno asked—because of course he did.

Tobal forced himself not to glare. He hated lying to his brother—both of them. He was pretty sure that if he told Zeno the truth, Zeno would find a way to stop him, maybe even talk to Berith. Tobal and Lon could use Zeno's help, but would he keep their secret?

Tobal couldn't risk it, so he forced a smile on his lips. "He's not the only thing I think about."

"I don't see why not. I spend most of my days thinking about Sabin and how I can make him happy. Isn't that what you and Lon have?"

"I don't know that anyone else can have that."

That caused Zeno to frown. "Why not? You shouldn't be with Lon if you don't know for sure that he's who you want. You're not just wasting time waiting for someone better, are you?"

Fuck. Tobal should have known Zeno would get worried. He needed to let some of his real feelings shine through, but that made him feel vulnerable. Still, unless he was honest, at least in part, Zeno would see right through him. Besides, it was almost too easy to pretend he and Lon were actually together.

"I'm not," Tobal promised. "I really like him, but things have been weird, you know? It's not just that I moved here and got my long-lost brother and you back at the same time. There are demons popping up left and right, trying to hurt Berith and the rest of his family, which now includes me. It's kind of scary, even though I'm surrounded by people ready to die to protect me."

Zeno nodded. "I can't imagine what you're going through.

It makes me glad I live here with Sabin and that he's not at the palace more than necessary."

Tobal was glad about that, too. He wanted his brother-in-law to be safe, and Zeno would make sure he was.

Tobal would never have thought to see Zeno in love, but he couldn't ignore it. It made him jealous, and once again, his thoughts drifted to Lon.

Sometimes, he appeared interested in more. It wasn't just what had happened that night near the tavern. Tobal had been so sure Lon would kiss him then, and he'd been disappointed when that hadn't happened. But sometimes Lon looked at him in a way that made Tobal shiver and imagine what would happen if Lon reached for him.

He'd fall right into Lon's arms. That's what would happen.

But they couldn't afford to be distracted, especially not now that the society had reached out again. Lon wasn't going anywhere, so Tobal would be able to find out if there was more between them later. Right now, he had to keep his focus on the important things.

The society.

Besides, even though Lon sometimes seemed interested in Tobal, other times, they clashed. Tobal was pretty sure that Lon thought he was a spoiled brat, but nothing could be further from the truth, and not just because Tobal had never been spoiled a day in his life. Maybe Lon didn't fully understand why Tobal was so insistent that he needed to be involved, but he didn't know what Tobal's life had been like before he'd met Berith.

He'd been alone. He'd even lost Zeno, and he'd thought he'd be alone for the rest of what he expected to be a short life. Now that he was surrounded by people who loved him and who he loved, he'd do whatever he could to keep them safe. He didn't care if that put him in danger or if the society tried to kill him.

He'd survive. He always did.

Berith leaned back in his chair. Lon knew what was coming before the words came out of his friend's mouth, but it was too late for him to run.

"So, you and my brother," Berith drawled.

Lon couldn't tell him it was all a lie. Berith would be pissed and demand an explanation, and Lon couldn't give him one if he wanted him and Tobal to investigate the society. It might be for the best to tell Berith everything, but part of Lon wanted to find out what was happening with the society.

The other part wanted to keep Tobal safe.

But Berith wouldn't hurt his brother. He'd be disappointed and would probably yell at Tobal for a while, but he'd never do anything to hurt him. They hadn't known each other long, but Lon knew Berith had yearned for siblings, and now that he had Tobal, he'd never let him go. He also wouldn't allow Tobal to put himself in danger, which meant that meeting with the society wouldn't happen if he found out about it. Then Tobal, too, would be pissed, and Lon would have to deal with both of them in that condition.

Even he wasn't that brave.

"It's not that serious," he muttered. He and Tobal would need to find a way to break up once all of this was over. Lon could already tell it would hurt Berith, so he wasn't looking forward to it.

"Why not? You don't like my brother?"

"I like him just fine, but me liking him doesn't mean we have to be together forever or anything like that."

"Why not? He's a good person, and you're one, too. You clearly like each other, or you wouldn't have told me about your relationship. Why did you, if it's not that serious?"

Lon would have to lie again, and he didn't like any of it.

"We're just seeing where things can go," he explained. "Things are a bit awkward because I'm also his bodyguard, so it might be too weird for us to be together."

"That's bullshit. You're not planning on dumping him, are you?"

Lon pinched the bridge of his nose. He was running out of patience, and he'd need it for tonight. "I'm not planning on doing anything but getting to know him," he said slowly. He understood why Berith was worried, and he couldn't tell him there was nothing to worry about. "I like Tobal, and being with him is nice, but I don't know if we can do it for the long term. I don't want you to get your hopes up, that's all."

Berith grinned. "Fine. I'll leave you alone as long as you promise you're not leading him on. He really likes you."

Lon arched a brow. "Does he?"

"It's obvious when he looks at you. I don't know him that well yet, but I've been talking to him every chance I get. I remember you didn't trust him initially, and I'm glad you got over that. I just don't want you to keep him at arm's length because you're not sure you can trust him."

"That's not the problem," Lon murmured.

But what *was* the problem? Lon liked Tobal. They weren't together, but it wasn't hard to imagine they could be, and not just for Berith's sake. Tobal was nice, and even though he shouldn't have, Lon had seen him naked. He knew what Tobal hid under his clothes, and if he thought too much about it, he got all flustered at the thought of finding out in the open and maybe even touching.

And that was just Tobal's body. There was so much more about him to like that Lon didn't know where to begin. It wasn't that Tobal was Berith's brother. Lon didn't care about power or social position. Tobal was Tobal, and he liked him just fine.

But Tobal was also stubborn, didn't deal well with orders,

and thought he knew better than Lon. He made Lon want to scream in frustration as much as he made him want to kiss him, which probably wasn't healthy.

Berith was still staring, and he grinned like the asshole he was. "It would be nice to see you two married."

"We're not getting married," Lon said, his voice dry. "Besides, you and Mel would be first if it came to that."

Lon should have known better than to mention that. Berith's expression hardened, then turned a little sad.

The thing was that Berith *wanted* to marry Mel. He wanted to make their relationship official, and not just because he was a prince of Hell. It was important to Mel, but there were so many problems that no one knew how to make it happen. Berith's position and the fact that Mel was human made it complicated.

Mel was acting as Berith's consort, and everyone in the palace respected him—apart from the people wanting to kill him—but there was no way to be sure about the rest of the territory. Sabin had said that not many people knew Berith had taken a human consort, so there might be trouble eventually, even if they never got married. There was also the fact that Lucifer might not see one of his princes marrying a human as a good thing, and Berith didn't want to put his family and Mel in danger by drawing Lucifer's attention.

So they'd decided to wait. It hurt both of them, and Lon wished there was more he could do. He could only keep both Berith and Mel safe and let Sabin and Berith deal with finding a way for Berith to marry his human.

"You'll marry him eventually," he said. He was convinced of that, and he'd make sure they had what they needed to make it happen.

"I know," Berith said. He sounded convinced. "And you'll get married eventually, too. You're too good a man not to have that kind of love in your life. Even if it doesn't happen with my brother, I want you to be happy." He winked. "But I can't deny it tickles me to know that you're now officially family, both you and Sabin."

Lon's mouth went dry. Through his relationship with Tobal, he could officially become Berith's brother, and so could Sabin. since Zeno was Tobal's brother. He could see why Berith was happy about that, and it made him want it to be real. He was surprised at how much it hurt to know it was all a lie, and once again, he wondered if there was any chance for him and Tobal to be together.

Before anything like that could happen, Lon would have to be honest with Tobal. He'd have to tell him about the secret passages and how he'd been spying on him, and he was pretty sure that by the time he was done, Tobal would want nothing to do with him. Lon wasn't happy with what he'd done, but he didn't regret it. He'd been trying to keep Berith safe.

But what if Tobal *could* forgive him? Lon was pretty sure Tobal liked him, or at the very least, that they could be friends. It all depended on whether Tobal's feelings were friendly or more, and it would be easy enough to find out.

Lon told himself he couldn't do that because he didn't want to ruin the mission he and Tobal had taken on, but that wasn't the entire truth.

The truth was that he was afraid of being rejected.

CHAPTER THIRTEEN

Tobal caught himself before he turned to look back. It would have given him and Lon away, and they couldn't afford it. There was no way to know if the society was watching Tobal even outside the palace, but he wasn't about to risk it. Of course, it would have been easier if Lon had agreed to stay back at the palace while Tobal went to the meeting, but Tobal knew that was a lost cause even before suggesting it.

He was right. Lon hadn't even allowed him to say the words. He'd glared and told Tobal that he'd be following him, and that was final. Tobal couldn't say he was sorry. He hoped it wouldn't create problems, but he felt better knowing that Lon had his back.

He had no idea what he was getting himself into.

He could be about to walk in on anything. At the very least, he'd have to deal with a representative of the society, and that freaked him out. These were people who wanted to kill his brother, hadn't hesitated to attack his niece, and had been threatening him every chance they got. They'd kill him if he so much as blinked wrong.

It helped to know that Lon was there, ready to step in.

Tobal just hoped the society wouldn't notice Lon. Lon was head of security, but he wasn't a spy, so he might not be as sneaky as he thought. Still, there had been no changing his mind, which meant that Tobal would have to deal with whatever happened on the spot. It made him uncomfortable, but at least he was doing something to solve the situation and help his family.

Even if it was getting himself killed.

He made his way through the dark, dank streets and headed to the tavern. He was cutting it a bit too close, and he didn't want whoever he was supposed to be meeting to have to wait for him, but he'd had to avoid the guards on his way out of the palace. Lon could have made it easier, but he'd refused, saying they needed to act normal in case they were being watched. They probably were, but it still hadn't been great to have to hide in a dusty closet until the guards had walked past.

The tavern finally appeared, and Tobal breathed a bit easier. He was incredibly nervous, but he was here now, and he needed to get this out of the way. Hopefully, tonight would be the last time he had anything to do with the society.

He'd always been too optimistic.

He sucked in a breath as he reached the door, then pushed it open. The smell of unwashed bodies, rancid beer, and cooked meat hit him in the face. He wrinkled his nose and tugged his hood closer, then looked around.

He didn't have to wonder who he was meeting. Most of the demons in the room were sitting at tables together, but not this one. No, this one was alone, not even touching the beer on the table and staring straight ahead until Tobal came in. When he did, the demon's head snapped up, and their gazes caught.

It was hard to breathe, but Tobal steeled himself, squared his shoulders, and moved closer.

He couldn't tell what kind of demon he was about to face. Most demons were a mix of species, which often made it hard, except when they had characteristics that were specific to a species. This demon had horns but no tail, as far as Tobal could see.

The demon's horns resembled branches from a tree, their texture rough and several small outshoots reaching for the ceiling, so maybe there was some zaron demon in him. The red glowing eyes hinted at that, too, but while Tobal was curious, he had no intention of asking.

He stopped in front of the table. He wasn't sure if he should sit down or introduce himself, so he waited, letting the demon take charge. He and Lon had agreed it would be for the best. Tobal needed to act as if he was interested in what the society was offering but was still a bit reluctant because of what had happened with Cyarea. Tobal wouldn't have to fake that. He *was* more than a little reluctant to be here.

The demon stared at Tobal for a moment. When he spoke, his voice was rough and made Tobal shiver. It was the kind of voice that belonged to someone you wouldn't want to meet in a dark alley — or a stinky tavern.

"You were followed," the demon said.

Tobal froze. He and Lon had known he might be found out, but they'd hoped that wouldn't be the case. There was no way the demon in front of Tobal could see Lon, since Lon was still outside, which meant he had allies out there, staring at them right now.

Tobal swallowed. "Was I?"

"You don't sound surprised."

"That's because I'm not, at least not entirely." Tobal had to come up with an excuse, and fast. "It's the head of security, isn't it?"

The demon arched a brow. His expression was smooth, but Tobal had no doubt he could kill him with barely more than a thought. "You knew he was following you."

Tobal forced himself to grin, then grabbed the chair closest to him and pulled it away from the table. He sat down, and the few seconds of respite helped him find an excuse. "We're sleeping together," he said.

"And I should care, why?"

"I guess you don't, but I thought it would be best to have

an ally close to my brother." It would be useless to act as if Berith wasn't related to Tobal. That relationship was the reason the society had reached out to Tobal to begin with. "I thought it would give me an insight into life in the palace and that it would help me get closer to my brother."

"Why do you need to get closer to him?"

Tobal shrugged. "It always helps. If I show Berith what he wants, he'll give me what I want."

"This meeting was supposed to be secret," the demon pointed out.

"It still is. He won't tell anyone."

"Not even your brother?"

"They're friends, but if I ask him not to, he won't." Tobal leaned closer and lowered his voice. "I have him wrapped around my little finger. He's in love with me and thinks I feel the same." He winked, then leaned back. His stomach churned, and he prayed the demon would believe him. "Anyway, I didn't catch your name," he said when the demon continued staring.

"That's because I didn't give it to you," the demon said.

"Are we keeping our names secret? But you already know mine."

The demon looked exasperated, and Tobal didn't blame him. A lot of people felt that way when they had to deal with him.

"You can call me Dorkel," the demon said with a growl.

"I like it."

"I don't care."

"You're rude."

"And you're here for a reason. You've disobeyed our order to come alone. You don't want to make me angry."

Tobal swallowed. He really didn't, but he had to keep up his act.

He tried to look like he wasn't afraid, even though deep

inside, he was terrified. "Why don't you tell me why I'm here, then? I was told to come here tonight, but no one said what the meeting was about. Can I assume you're finally going to tell me?"

"You can."

"Then I'm listening."

Dorkel stared for a moment. Tobal held his breath, hoping the demon would fall for it. He wasn't sure what he'd do if he didn't. Probably run away screaming while hoping Lon would catch him.

Lon could have kicked himself. He'd really thought he was being more discreet, but clearly he'd been wrong, since someone had noticed him following Tobal.

They even knew who he was.

He wasn't sure how that was possible. Like Tobal, he'd worn a jacket with a hood that hid his face. He'd made sure not to stick too close to Tobal, even though he'd wanted to. He needed to be close in a way that was almost painful and made him panic at the thought that something could happen to Tobal if Lon wasn't there to protect him. Lon couldn't afford to focus on any of this, which was unfortunate. He couldn't stop thinking about what Tobal had just said. It was a ruse to get Dorkel to trust him, even though he knew Lon was there, but maybe it wasn't that far from the truth. The sooner they got rid of the society, the sooner Lon could do whatever he needed to do to solve this *thing* between him and Tobal.

Lon could hear what Tobal and Dorkel were saying. He'd gone to the palace's mage and had asked for a little spell, and the man had been more than happy to give Lon what he wanted. Lon hadn't even told Tobal, which was just as well. He wasn't sure Tobal would have been comfortable with it, and knowing that Lon was listening to what he was saying would probably have made him even more nervous. He already was enough as it was.

Lon leaned against the wall in the alley next to the tavern and held his breath as he listened. He was close enough to intervene if something happened to Tobal, but it would be too easy for anyone, especially Dorkel, to hurt Tobal. Lon couldn't exactly go in, no matter how much he wanted to.

"In your message, you said you were ready to work with us," Dorkel said, his voice soft.

Dangerously so.

"On one condition," Tobal said.

"You can't afford to have conditions."

"Probably not, but this is non-negotiable. I'm sure you can get to my brother through other means, but you haven't yet, which means you haven't given up on using me. If you're going to do that, I want you to leave my niece alone. She's just a child and doesn't deserve to be attacked."

There was a moment of silence, and Lon held his breath. The society didn't have to promise anything to Tobal. Tobal was right when he said they could do this without him. Lon wasn't entirely sure why they weren't, to be honest. He and Tobal would talk about this meeting later, but for now, the only thing Lon could do was listen. The distance he kept between himself and Tobal would hopefully help Dorkel trust Tobal. There was no way for him to know about the spell.

Hopefully.

"What will you do with her once you're on the throne?" Dorkel asked.

"I don't know. I guess she and her mother can leave or something. I just don't want her to die, but it doesn't mean I like her. I haven't known her for long, and she's a kid."

"I can relay your condition."

Lon relaxed, but unfortunately, it didn't last long.

"And of course, we have conditions, too," Dorkel continued.

"What kind of conditions?" Tobal asked.

"You have to prove yourself before we agree to help you."

"I don't need you to help me. I need you to leave me alone and stop attacking my niece and me."

"But you want the throne."

Lon held his breath. He knew Tobal couldn't care less about the throne, but clearly, the society didn't. They thought that was why Tobal was here. It probably made sense to them since they also wanted it. Most assholes didn't understand that other people could want different things.

"Not really," Tobal said. He sounded careless, and it hurt to hear, even though Lon knew it was an act.

"Why are you here, then?" Dorkel asked.

"Because you keep sending people to the palace to attack me, and I don't like it. Look, if you want to get rid of my brother, then that's fine. I don't want the throne, but I do want what comes with it. I'll go along with your plan, but don't expect me to guide this territory or make any kind of decision. I want to live the rest of my life being taken care of and having more money than I know what to do with."

"We can certainly find a way to get you that," Dorkel said.

"Good. What's your condition, then?"

"You have to kill Berith."

Lon sucked in a breath. He wanted to run inside, but he couldn't. Even though Dorkel knew he was there, it wouldn't help Tobal.

Thankfully, Tobal seemed to have things in hand. He chuckled, then outright laughed. "Isn't that your job?"

"It's yours if you want to show us you're serious about helping us."

"I don't think so. You never mentioned me killing my brother. You said you'd do it, and I was counting on that. Find another way for me to prove myself."

"This is our condition," Dorkel insisted.

"I can't kill my brother. There's too much security around him, especially when you've attacked him and his family so many times. He's suspicious of everyone, even me. I might be his brother, but it's not like we grew up together. He doesn't trust me, and as this meeting shows, he's right not to."

"What do you propose, then? We need him dead."

"Then kill him. If you want me to prove myself, I'll kill someone else. He's not the only person you'll have to get rid of if you want the throne."

"We don't need anyone else killed at the moment."

"I'm sure you can find someone."

Lon didn't like how much Tobal was pushing. He was starting to sound desperate, and they couldn't afford for the society to realize how strong their grip on him was. They were important to him because he needed to find out what they were planning, but they didn't care about him. He was just a pawn, and they no doubt had dozens of them.

"All right," Dorkel drawled. "You'll kill Aloise."

Tobal swallowed. He'd known he wouldn't like the answer he'd get since, after all, he'd asked for someone else to kill, but he hadn't expected Aloise. "Why her?"

"Because she's close to Berith. She's the mother of his heir, so she could legitimately take the throne and hold it until their daughter is old enough to take her father's place."

But without Aloise, it would be fairly easy to kill Cyarea. Even though Tobal had asked for her to be left alone, he didn't know if the society would agree. He wouldn't in their place. It would be too easy for Cyarea to rally people around her, especially once she grew up. Besides, even if the society agreed to his condition, he couldn't trust them not to attempt to kill Cyarea anyway.

"If I refuse?" he asked.

"You don't want to refuse."

Dorkel was right. Tobal didn't want to say no because they'd kill him if he did. He also couldn't tell them that even if he said yes, he wasn't about to hurt anyone, let alone his niece's mother. "Fine. I'll do it."

Dorkel smiled, exposing his teeth. "Good. We'll be in touch once her death is announced."

He started getting up, and Tobal panicked. He needed more. "Wait."

Dorkel stopped moving and looked at Tobal. Tobal had no idea what to say.

"What happens when I kill her?" he asked. He didn't want to spend one more second in Dorkel's company, but he hadn't been able to get any more information on the society, which was why he was here.

"We'll contact you." Dorkel's voice was slow, like he was talking to someone he considered an idiot.

"But—"

Dorkel ignored Tobal. He walked away, abandoning him at the table. He didn't head for the front door but rather for the back of the tavern, which wasn't a surprise. Tobal was glad since Lon was probably at the front, waiting for him to come out. He'd bitched about needing more people because he couldn't keep an eye on both exits, but thankfully, everything had gone smoothly. Tobal hadn't needed protection.

But he would if he stayed in the tavern much longer. He could feel the demons around him stare, probably because they'd noticed something was up. It made Tobal want to run, but instead, he stood as tall as he could and walked to the door. His heart raced as he expected someone to grab him, but no one did, and he made it out of the tavern in one piece.

He sucked in a breath, then another, and looked around.

Lon was nowhere to be seen, but Tobal needed him right now. He started walking toward the palace, knowing Lon would be right behind him again. He'd stay away until they got closer to the palace in case Tobal was being followed.

Tobal didn't think he was. The society wanted him to do their bidding, but they didn't care much about him.

Tobal was distracted and didn't see the demon coming toward him. They collided, and Tobal quickly stepped back, an apology already on his lips.

A hand grabbed his arm and pulled him away. Tobal jerked, ready to defend himself, but it was Lon, and he was dragging Tobal toward the palace. Tobal turned, giving one last look at the demon he'd hit, who was standing in the middle of the street.

"Sorry!" he called out.

There was a single-mindedness in Lon's movements that made Tobal realize something wasn't right. Lon had been outside, which meant he hadn't heard what Tobal and Dorkel had been saying.

Right?

"What is it?" Tobal asked as he stumbled, trying to keep up.

"I just got a message from Sabin. Mel has been attacked."

Tobal sucked in a breath. "What? What happened?"

"I don't know yet, but I should have been there."

He should have, and Tobal suspected he'd never forgive himself if Mel was hurt or worse. "You might be head of security, but you can't protect everyone single-handedly. It's why you have Mikal and your other guards. Besides, you're not confined to the palace."

"I shouldn't have left. We knew it was a possibility. They've been attacking more often, and I should have known they'd aim at Mel next."

Tobal suspected the society had taken advantage of the fact that both he and Lon had been away from the palace. Dorkel had known Lon was there, and while he hadn't done anything that made Tobal believe he'd been involved in the attack, he worked with the society. It was enough for Tobal to know he was guilty, if anything, by association.

"Didn't Sabin tell you how Mel is?"

"He said he's all right."

But Lon wouldn't believe it until he got his eyes on Mel. Tobal didn't blame him because he felt the same, and it wasn't his job to protect his brother's consort.

"He'll be fine," he murmured.

"I sure hope so. This needs to end."

Tobal peeked at Lon's face. His jaw was tight, and he was staring ahead, aiming straight for the palace.

Tobal didn't know if what they'd done tonight had been the right thing to do. He'd promised to kill Aloise—which he wasn't about to do—but they'd needed an in with the society, and he'd hoped this would be it. They needed Aloise's death to be announced, though, and the only one who could do that was Berith, which meant they'd have to involve him.

Tobal suddenly felt faint. He stumbled, but Lon was still holding his arm, and he pulled him closer, keeping him on his feet.

"Are you all right?" Lon asked.

"I promised I'd kill Aloise," Tobal whispered.

"I know."

Tobal blinked. "How can you know? You weren't in the tavern." Or had he been? Maybe he'd managed to sneak in while Tobal wasn't looking, but Tobal doubted it.

"I heard your entire conversation with Dorkel, using a spell."

Tobal wanted to demand an explanation, but he was pretty sure Lon would yell at him if he did. Lon was tense, and they were rushing through the streets, both of them needing to check in on Mel.

"So you know he wanted me to kill Berith," Tobal said.

"I do. I'm impressed you had the courage to say no."

"It wasn't courage. It was fear. I know we'll have to involve Berith, but telling him I agreed to kill him isn't something I could deal with."

"So you agreed to kill his daughter's mother?"

"There was no good option. If I had to guess, it was either her, Mel, or Cyarea." And while Berith cared about Aloise, he didn't love her as much as he loved his daughter and Mel. Tobal was surprised Dorkel hadn't told him to kill Mel.

"You did good," Lon murmured. "I heard everything thanks to the spell. I was impressed, and your brother will be, too."

"Impressed enough not to throw me in a cell?"

"I'll make sure he doesn't lock you up." Lon sounded amused, which was a surprise considering the situation.

"Thank you." By now, the palace was in sight, and they moved faster. From the outside, everything looked fine, but Tobal was afraid of what they'd find inside.

He didn't know Mel as well as he knew Berith or even Lon, but he liked the human. From what he'd seen, Mel and Berith were good for each other, and Tobal didn't want his brother to lose the love of his life.

The society was getting too close to obtaining what they wanted, and that made Tobal want to rage. He'd just found his family. Why was the society bent on taking it away from him?

But he wouldn't allow them to do that. He might not be trained, but he didn't need to be. He and Lon were working together, and soon, they'd get to the bottom of this and find out who was behind the society. When they did, they'd kill every single demon involved, and their family would finally be safe.

CHAPTER FOURTEEN

L on was terrified by the time he and Tobal reached the palace. Sabin's message had been frantic, demanding to know
where Lon was and telling him that Mel had gotten hurt. He'd
added that Mel was all right but that Lon was needed, which
was why Lon was running.

The guards by the servants' entrance stepped forward
when they noticed Lon and Tobal, but Lon pushed the hood
away from his face, exposing his face. One of the guards
quickly stepped back while the other stared at Lon with wide
eyes. Lon rushed past them, still pulling on Tobal's hand.

The palace was in chaos.

Lon had no idea where to find Mel, Sabin, or Berith, but he
needed to. He grabbed a servant rushing by, pulling her to a
stop. "Where's the prince?"

She gaped at him but thankfully answered. "In his rooms
with the consort."

Lon wanted to ask her if she knew how Mel was, but he
didn't dare. He nodded curtly, then, still not releasing Tobal,
headed toward the private wing.

Reyni was no doubt already with Mel, and if he knew what
was good for him, Mikal was, too. He'd stay there until Lon
arrived. He'd have to give Lon his report as soon as possible,
but hopefully, they'd managed to catch the attacker this time.

Lon didn't have a lot of hope. He could tell the society had
taken advantage of him having followed Tobal to attack.
There was no way to tell what would have happened if Lon
had been at the palace, but they hadn't taken any chances.

160

They'd known that without Lon there, things would be a mess, and they'd been right.

The main door that opened on the private wing was wide open. Two guards stood framing it, and they nodded at Lon as he walked past. More guards lined the hallways all the way to Berith's rooms.

That door was open, too, but when Lon walked into the living area, he didn't see anyone but Sabin, sitting on the couch with Zeno's arm around his shoulders. He looked up, and Lon's heart broke when he saw there were tears in his friend's eyes.

He finally let go of Tobal. "What happened?"

"I'm not sure. One of the guards came to tell us that Mel had been attacked, but when we got here, Berith only told us he was fine. He's in the bedroom with Mel and Reyni."

That couldn't be good. Lon sucked in a breath, then went to knock on the bedroom door. He normally wouldn't, but he had to know what had happened.

The door swung open, revealing Berith. There was blood on his hands, and his shirt was torn. Lon could see that a set of claws had raked down his chest, but Berith didn't seem to care. He grabbed Lon and pulled him into the room, and Lon went because how could he not?

His knees buckled in relief when he saw Mel sitting on the edge of the mattress. Reyni was in front of him, but Mel was shaking his head. The only wound Lon could see on him was a long scratch on his arm, and he hoped that was all that had happened.

"Tell me," he told Berith.

"I was supposed to be in my office, but I decided I was too tired. I wanted to spend time with Mel, so I came back to the rooms. When I walked in, he was beating a demon with a pillow while also kicking at him."

Lon was impressed. "You killed the demon?"

"Of course I did."

Lon nodded. It would have been better to keep the demon alive so they could interrogate him, but he didn't blame Berith for what he'd done.

Lon had dropped the ball. He was lucky Berith had been there to pick it up, but things couldn't continue this way. He and Tobal were making progress with the society, although having to fake killing Aloise wouldn't be easy. They had to involve Berith now. They couldn't continue doing this in secret, especially when it put Berith and the other members of the family in danger.

"I'm sorry for not being here," he said stiffly.

Birth shook his head. "I don't know where you were, but it doesn't matter. You're my head of security, but even so, I don't expect you to be by my side twenty-four-seven. You deserve to have your own private life, and when I realized that both you and Tobal weren't here, I knew you were together."

They had been, although not in the way Berith clearly believed. Knowing that made Lon feel even more guilty, but he couldn't show it. He needed to do this carefully. Talking to Berith about what he and Tobal were doing could wait. In fact, it needed to wait. because Berith looked like he was about to explode.

"The body?" he asked, knowing they'd have to continue this conversation but also that it wouldn't be now.

"Mikal took care of it. I'm sure he's waiting for you."

"I'll go there now." Even though there was nothing Lon wanted less than to have to deal with this.

"Don't leave my brother alone tonight," Berith quickly said. "I doubt we'll be attacked again, but how can I know?" He rubbed his face. "This is a mess. What's happening?"

Lon's mouth tasted like ash. "I'm working on resolving this, but it isn't easy."

Berith looked up at him. "I didn't mean to imply it was. I

know you're working hard, possibly too hard. I don't blame you for this, and Mel doesn't, either. I apologize if that's what it sounded like."

"I know you don't blame me, but you don't have to. I blame myself enough for both of us."

Berith clasped Lon's shoulders. "Don't. Berating yourself and feeling guilty isn't going to do anything. We need to focus, not lose ourselves in emotions."

He was right, and while Lon wasn't sure he could focus well enough, he'd have to.

He straightened his back, looked at Mel again, and, relieved to see the consort was all right, decided it was time for him to get to work. "I'll send Sabin and Zeno back to their house, then walk Tobal to his rooms."

"Please. Reyni said Mel isn't gravely injured and that the wound on his arm is just a scratch, so I'll put him to bed as soon as this is over."

"Call me if you need anything." Lon would never forgive himself if something happened and he wasn't there. He was never leaving the palace again, dammit.

"I will, but I don't think we'll need anything else. I'll make sure Mel eats and get into bed, but I don't know if I'll manage to fall asleep."

Lon understood because he felt the same way. "Try. The problems will still be there tomorrow morning."

Berith grimaced. "Unfortunately."

Tobal tried to peek into the bedroom, then mentally scolded himself and pulled back. Whatever was happening was private, and Mel didn't need him to be spying.

Still, he needed to know how Mel was.

He paced the length of the living area, looking from the bedroom door to Sabin, who was still on the couch, buried in

Zeno's arms.

"What happened?" Tobal asked. "Did you see Mel?"

"No, but I'm sure he's all right," Sabin said. "Berith promised he was."

Tobal wondered if his brother would lie to Sabin to keep him calm. Probably, but if something were to happen to Mel, it would immediately be obvious from Berith's behavior. If he wasn't yelling and crying, it meant that Mel wasn't dead.

But that didn't tell Tobal whether or not Mel was all right.

The sound of footsteps coming from the bedroom made both him and Sabin jump. Sabin got to his feet and scrambled closer, and they both watched as Lon walked out of the bedroom.

"How is he?" Sabin asked.

Lon smiled at him. It was a weary smile that didn't reach his eyes, but it was there. "Just a scratch. He beat up the demon with his feet and a pillow."

Sabin laughed. "That sounds like him. You're sure he's all right?"

"He is. Reyni is in there with them and didn't even bandage Mel's arm. He just cleaned the wound."

"What about Berith?"

"Well, he fought with the demon and has the claw marks to prove it, but he'll be fine. He's next on Reyni's list."

Sabin slumped, and Zeno was there immediately, wrapping an arm around him and pulling him close. He kissed Sabin's forehead, and while he wasn't as expressive as his partner, Tobal could see he was relieved.

"Everyone is fine," Lon continued. "I need to go see the body, but Berith asked me to tell all of you to go home. He'll take care of Mel tonight and make sure they both eat and get rest, and you should do the same."

"They don't need anything?" Sabin asked.

"If they do, they have plenty of servants to ask. Go home."

Tobal knew it was the best thing they could do. He'd be useless in this situation, anyway. It was best to leave everything in Berith's hands.

"Tobal, I'll walk you to your rooms," Lon murmured as Zeno and Sabin left the room through the garden doors.

Zeno had to guide Sabin outside. He'd keep him safe and make sure he was all right, too. Sabin might not have been attacked, but he was still having a hard time dealing with what had happened.

"You don't need to. They're not far," Tobal told Lon.

"Berith's orders. I think he doesn't want any of us to be alone for too long, especially in the hallways."

Tobal wanted to point out that when he'd been attacked, it hadn't been in a hallway and that the demon had been waiting in his rooms, but it wouldn't change anything. Lon was coming with him, whether he liked it or not.

Tobal felt like what happened to Mel was his fault, and in part, he supposed it was. He'd pulled Lon away from the palace, and the society had taken advantage of that to attack. It made Tobal want to take a step back, but it would be the worst thing to do. He was getting into the society's good graces, and it would be foolish to stop now. They needed as much information as they could get as quickly as possible.

"We'll need to talk to Berith tomorrow," Lon said.

Tobal had been dreading this moment, but he'd known it would come. "I agree. I just hope he won't forbid us to be involved."

"I don't think he can at this point. He won't be happy, and I have no doubt there will be some yelling, but we're *already* involved. Well, you are. The society would probably kill me if I tried getting in contact with them."

That reminded Tobal of what he'd said earlier. "I told Dorkel we were together. He knew you were following me, and he mentioned it. It was the only thing I could think of to justify it."

"It was good thinking. I knew about that already, though."

Right. He'd been using a spell to listen to the conversation.

Tobal wasn't offended, and he didn't feel like Lon had done it because he didn't trust him. He would have felt better knowing the spell was in place, but things had gone all right, except for Mel's attack.

But he couldn't help but wonder what Lon thought of his explanation that the two of them were together. He hated that Lon had heard him lie about him being whipped and ready to do just about anything Tobal wanted. There was nothing further from the truth.

When they reached Tobal's door, Tobal turned to look at Lon. "Since you heard everything, you know what I said about you."

"I do." Lon leaned closer, causing Tobal to suck in a breath. "I don't blame you for what you said, and I won't hold it against you. If anything, it was quick thinking. I'm proud of the way you behaved in the tavern."

Tobal's entire body flushed hot. He shouldn't care what Lon thought, but he did.

Lon hesitated, then pressed a kiss to Tobal's forehead. The touch was there, then gone the next second, but Tobal had felt it. He was stunned, which meant he wasn't quick enough to react when Lon stepped away and opened the door.

"I'll make sure there's no one in there waiting for you," he said before sleeping in.

Tobal stared. Lon had kissed him, but what did the kiss mean to him? It wasn't a romantic kiss or anything like that, just a kiss on the forehead, something he'd only seen Lon do with Cyarea.

But Tobal wasn't sorry. He was afraid to let himself hope, but amongst the evening's chaos, he couldn't help but wonder.

Was Lon falling for him the way he was falling for Lon?

CHAPTER FIFTEEN

Tobal needed to kill Aloise.

How was he supposed to do that? He'd told the society he'd do it, but that had happened days ago, and they'd expect results soon. He still had no idea how to make it happen, but then, he wasn't actually planning on killing her.

But what was he supposed to tell the society? They expected him to kill Aloise, and they wouldn't take no for an answer. If he didn't go along with this plan, he'd never become one of them, which meant he'd never find out who was behind all of this. He'd promised Lon they'd find a way to make it work, but he'd been obsessing over it since the meeting with Dorkel, and he still had no more idea of what to do than before.

But it had been days, which was why he wasn't surprised when he went back to his room after lunch and found a piece of paper on his coffee table. The society didn't have much patience, so he'd expected them to contact him after they saw he wasn't doing anything. He'd hoped to have more time, but clearly, he'd been wrong.

He stared at the piece of paper as if it were a snake about to bite him. It might as well be. The symbol on the paper was the color of blood, a stark reminder of what would happen if Tobal didn't do what he'd promised to do.

But there was no way he'd hurt Aloise, or anyone else for that matter.

He swallowed and stepped closer. The last thing he wanted was to pick up the thing, but he needed to get it to Lon. He'd want to know about this, and hopefully, he'd have a solution. No matter how hard Tobal thought about one, he couldn't come up with anything that didn't sound stupid or wouldn't get him killed.

He looked around the room, but it was empty except for him. He'd left the garden door open, so whoever had placed this message might have come through there, but they also might not have. He hated not knowing how these people kept sneaking in. He didn't feel safe, and while it was a feeling he was used to, it didn't mean he liked it.

He'd thought he'd left all of this behind when he'd moved into the palace, but he felt unsafe again, which was one more reason for him to hate the society.

As if he needed more reasons to feel that way.

Huffing at his hesitation, he grabbed the piece of paper, then stomped toward the door from which he'd just come in. Wasting time wouldn't help. If anything, it would complicate things, so he needed to get over this and get to work.

He didn't open the piece of paper yet. It was for him, but he and Lon were in this together, and to be honest, he was kind of scared. He already knew nothing good would come out of it, but that didn't mean he wanted to be alone when he found out for sure.

By now, he knew his way to Lon's office like the back of his hand. He'd been coming and going, keeping up the pretense that the two of them were dating. Thankfully, none of the people Tobal crossed paths with seemed to care, and neither did the guard following him. Of course, they probably wouldn't dare tease him or Lon even if they did. Lon had a lot of power in the palace, more so than anyone but Berith and his close family. No one would dare disrespect him, and as for Tobal, he was Zeno's brother. That was usually enough for most people to keep their distance. He knew his brother's reputation, and while Zeno was a big softy to him, the same didn't go for everyone else.

Lon's personal assistant was working at her desk, but she looked up when she heard Tobal. She smiled at him, then waved him in, and he wondered if it was because she thought they were dating. Probably. If he were anyone else, she'd have warned Lon he was coming. Instead, she was letting him in as if he belonged there.

Tobal was starting to think he didn't belong anywhere in the palace. He'd come here to be with Zeno and get to know Berith, and he'd gotten both those things, but his life had become much more complicated. What would happen if he left?

His chest tightened at the thought, and he knocked on the office door. He didn't want to leave. He'd settled down, and this was his life now. He didn't care about the money or anything like that, but he didn't want to lose his relationship with his brothers. That was what would happen if he left, and besides, even if he did, it wouldn't keep Berith any safer. The society wanted him to die, and nothing would stop them from obtaining that, Tobal or not.

No, the best thing Tobal could do was to stick around and protect his brother any way he could.

"Come in," Lon called out.

Tobal's heart raced as he pushed open the door. He already knew what Lon's reaction would be, and he wasn't looking forward to it. Lon hadn't been happy about Tobal putting himself in danger, and this wasn't going to help. He'd bitch and tell Tobal he was an idiot, and Tobal wouldn't be able to protest because Lon would be right.

He *was* an idiot. A well-meaning one, but an idiot nonetheless.

He pushed open the door and peeked in. Lon was behind his desk, but he was looking up to see who needed him. Tobal held his breath as he took in his expression, but apart from a flash of recognition, he couldn't read him.

"Tobal," Lon said as he got to his feet. "Is something wrong? I was about to come to join you."

Tobal quickly walked in and closed the door behind himself. He sucked in a breath, then held out his hand. He was still clutching the message, so it only took Lon a few seconds to realize what was happening.

His expression turned to anger. "They contacted you again?" he asked as he walked around his desk.

Tobal's fingers felt frozen, but he managed to let go of the piece of paper and watched Lon open it. His expression revealed nothing, and Tobal was afraid to ask.

"Where did you find this?" Lon asked.

"Same as last time. It was on the table in my living area."

Lon swore. "How did they get in? Didn't the guard check your rooms before letting you in?"

"He did, and they were empty. I have no idea how they got in, but I'd really like to know. Do you know how terrifying it is to know that the society could come in anytime and kill me? I'm having trouble sleeping because I can stop thinking about what might happen."

"Maybe we could move you."

It was tempting, but Tobal shook his head. "It wouldn't solve anything, and it'd look as if I'm trying to run from the society."

"Which is what you're doing. You don't want anything to do with the society."

"I don't want to, but I have to. What does the message say?"

Lon cocked his head as he stared at Tobal. "You haven't read it?"

"I was too afraid." Tobal wouldn't have admitted this to anyone else except maybe Zeno, but Lon wouldn't make fun of him. He'd understand because they were in this together.

Lon nodded. "Well, it's nothing unexpected. It isn't signed, but if I had to guess, Dorkel wrote it. It shows knowledge of your meeting with him the other night."

"Is he asking why I hadn't killed Aloise yet?"

"Not asking as much as threatening you because you haven't. He's losing his patience."

Tobal started pacing. "What am I supposed to do now? I can't kill Aloise. The society expects results, but I can't give them anything. They're going to kill me, then they'll move on to the rest of my family, and I'll be dead, so I won't be able to do anything to stop them." Tobal rubbed his face with both his hands. He was freaking out, and he hated it. He didn't want his heart to race or for his chest to feel tight. He didn't want to worry himself sick over what would happen to Cyarea, Berith, and everyone else.

He felt like he'd brought this trouble with him, even though he hadn't. The society was well-established in the palace, which meant they'd been here for months, if not longer. He was just a means to an end, but they didn't even need him. They could get to Berith in other ways, and they'd do exactly that if they couldn't get Tobal to cooperate.

Tobal's plan had been to infiltrate the society and find out who was part of it, but he hadn't expected them to ask him to kill anyone, which was why it had been a decent idea. Now, it had become a terrible one, and he had no clue how to get himself out of the mess he'd created.

Lon was tempted to burn the message since it was freaking Tobal out so much, but he couldn't do that. They might need it, so instead, he went back to his desk, opened a drawer, and stuffed it inside with the other. Tobal didn't need to read it. He just needed to know that the society wasn't happy with what he was doing — or not doing, as it was.

He'd already known that anyway.

It had been Tobal's idea to meet with the society and go along with what they wanted, but clearly, he hadn't been ready for what they'd asked of him. Lon had been surprised, too. Having Tobal kill Berith would have been easier for the society, but when that had clearly been out of the question, they'd still given Tobal a target that was impossible for him to get to.

Or rather, it was impossible for him to get to Aloise as it was. If he'd truly been working with the society, it would have been easy for him to kill Aloise. He was one of the few people who had easy access to her, which was no doubt why Dorkel had targeted her.

But Dorkel wanted results, and Tobal couldn't give him anything. That meant that the society would strike, and soon.

Lon couldn't allow for that or anything else to happen to Tobal.

Tobal paced in front of Lon, still blathering about what was happening.

"I don't know how they expect me to do this," he said. "I mean, it would be easier than killing Berith, but they have to see that it still isn't that easy. She's my sister-in-law, kind of. Why would I want to kill her?"

"It's not a problem of wanting to kill her," Lon pointed out.

Tobal glared at him. "I guess it's not. They think I don't care about her, that it'll be easy for me to do this."

"I don't think that's the case, either. They're testing you. That's why they asked you to kill your brother. You refused to do anything to him, so they've given you another target. They'll take the next step if you don't show them you can do it."

"What am I supposed to do, then? I can't kill Aloise."

"I don't expect you to."

"Then what? What do I do? Because if nothing changes, I'll be the next one to die. I don't want to die, Lon. I have too much to live for now that I found my brothers."

Lon wasn't sure what came over him. He wanted to protect Tobal, to tell him everything would be all right, even though he couldn't make that kind of promise. Seeing Tobal like this lit a fire in him, and he surged forward, reaching for him.

Tobal squeaked and stumbled back, but Lon was already on him. He cupped one of Tobal's cheeks, but unlike in the alley, he didn't stop there. He leaned forward, giving Tobal time to push him away if that was what he wanted, even though he prayed it wasn't.

Tobal stayed where he was. He stared at Lon with wide eyes, all three of them blinking rapidly. He was holding his breath, clearly waiting for Lon's next move.

Lon kissed him.

Tobal's lips were soft and just a little chapped. When he'd been ranting, he'd kept licking them, which would explain the sensation. Lon loved how Tobal felt against him, though, and with his free arm, he pulled him close. He hooked his arm around Tobal's waist, sighing at the pleasure of finally giving in and having him in his arms. He'd been resisting this for a while now, but that was over. Tobal needed him, and Lon would be there for him.

Tobal let Lon take his weight as if he trusted him, and Lon hoped that was true. He didn't know what would happen with the society, but whatever it was, they'd face it together. Right now, he didn't want to think of the society. He'd wanted Tobal to stop worrying and pacing, and he'd gotten that, but he wasn't sure where to go from here.

He let go of Tobal and took a step back. Tobal continued staring at him as if he'd never seen him before, and maybe that was the case. Lon certainly didn't feel like himself.

"We have to tell Berith everything," Lon said. They should have done it a while ago.

Tobal blinked. "When you say everything, do you also

mean the kiss?"

Lon ignored him and turned back to his desk. He went to grab the messages from the drawer, raising them to show them to Tobal. "I mean the messages and your trips to the tavern."

Tobal grimaced. "He's going to be pissed, especially if I tell him I was almost attacked."

At least now, he admitted he was almost attacked. He'd been protesting that since it happened. "We can skip that bit if you want."

Tobal sighed. "I should probably tell Berith about that, too. If we're going to be honest, we might as well tell him everything."

Lon was relieved that was how Tobal felt. It didn't feel right to lie to his best friend and his prince, but he'd done it because he believed it was the best thing to do, at least under the circumstances. That was over now. Berith needed to know *everything*, and he needed to know it as soon as possible. The society was pushing, and Tobal wouldn't be their only victim if Berith didn't intervene.

"You agree this is the best thing to do?" Lon asked.

He was purposefully ignoring the kiss. They'd have time to talk about it later. For now, they had more urgent things to focus on, like keeping Tobal safe from the society and finding a way around him having to kill Aloise. It would be better if they could stay in the society's good graces. It was what they'd been trying to do from the beginning, and Lon didn't want their work to be for nothing. Tobal had put himself in danger to protect Berith, and it wouldn't be right for him to lose all of that. Lon wasn't sure Berith would see things that way, though.

"Honestly, I don't know. I don't want to do it, but I don't know what else to do. I'm not killing Aloise. I know what it's like to grow up without a mother, and I'm not doing that to anyone. That means we have to find a way around that, and I doubt that'll be possible without getting Berith on board."

Unfortunately, he was right. Lon couldn't say he was looking forward to this, but it was necessary. The prince wouldn't be happy they'd gone behind his back, especially since he'd explicitly forbidden Tobal to do it, but they couldn't change what had happened. They could only move forward, and to do that, they had to be honest.

"Let's go," Lon said, striding toward the door.

It took him a few seconds to realize Tobal wasn't following him. He still stood in the middle of the office, chewing on his lower lip and looking much younger and more fragile than he actually was.

"What is it?" Lon asked. They couldn't afford to waste time. If Tobal wanted to talk about the kiss, they'd have to do so later.

"What if he kicks me out?" Tobal asked.

It wasn't the kiss that worried him. Lon almost laughed at how he'd assumed he was the center of Tobal's world. "He won't," he promised.

"You can't know that for sure."

"I realize Berith is your brother, but I've known him since we were children. I know him better than you, and I can predict how he'll react."

Tobal peered at him. "And how is that?"

"As soon as you tell him, he'll stare at you for a few seconds. He'll be digesting the news. You need to give him time and space, which means you have to keep quiet. Don't try to ask him what he thinks or how he's feeling. Just let him think."

"I can do that," Tobal said eagerly.

"Once he's done thinking and understanding how much danger you put yourself in, he's going to start yelling. He'll ask you how you could do this, why you're such an idiot, and why you went against his orders and put yourself in danger."

"That doesn't sound good."

"It's not, but he's a yeller when he's afraid for his family. The fact that he yells at you is a good thing, even though it doesn't feel like it."

"What should I do while he's yelling?"

"Let him do it. He'll run out of steam after a while and finally cool down enough to focus on what we're supposed to do next. He needs to yell and rant for a bit, get everything out, mostly because he'll be easier to deal with once he's done telling you exactly how he feels about what you've done."

Tobal still didn't look convinced, but he nodded. "I guess we might as well go."

"I'd suggest you stay here, but Berith will want to talk to you anyway. You might as well get this out of the way."

That went for both of them.

Chapter Sixteen

Tobal didn't want to do this. He had to resist the urge to turn around and run back to his rooms. He might have done just that if he hadn't known Lon would come after him and drag him back, kicking and screaming.

That would definitely get Berith's attention.

He sucked in a breath as he and Lon walked past Sabin's desk. Sabin wasn't behind it for once, and Tobal wondered where he was. He didn't have to wonder for long because when Lon knocked on Berith's door, Sabin opened it.

He frowned at them. "It's never a good thing when you visit Berith these days. What's happened now?"

"Nothing good," Lon confirmed. "Is he free?"

"*He* is right here, and yes, I'm free to talk to you," Berith snarked from inside the room. "Sabin, let him in."

Sabin's gaze flickered to Tobal, but he didn't try to stop him from following Lon in. They both knew that if Berith had seen him, he'd have told Sabin to let him in, too.

"I'm staying," Sabin declared, closing the door behind Tobal.

"It would be best if you didn't," Lon said. "You don't want to be here when Berith explodes."

Berith had been behind his desk, but he'd gotten to his feet and had walked around it when Tobal walked in. He looked from Lon to Tobal, his expression already unhappy. "Maybe Sabin should stay in case I'm tempted to strangle both of you. I can tell I'm not going to like whatever you have to say."

Tobal hoped Lon would spend more time trying to

convince Sabin to leave. If Sabin knew, Zeno would, too, and he'd be pissed. Tobal already had to deal with one disappointed brother. He wasn't sure he could deal with a second one.

Sabin crossed his arms over his chest and glared. "Spill it," he ordered.

Lon sighed but obeyed. He handed the pieces of paper he'd been carrying to Berith, launching into his explanation as he did so. "You told Tobal to stay out of the thing with the society, but we've been working together to draw them out. Tobal contacted them and told them he was willing to work with them after Cyarea and Aloise were attacked. We believed he'd be able to get names, at the very least, and we did have a meeting with one of the people who work for the society, but unfortunately, so far, we don't have anything more."

Berith's expression had tightened as Lon explained. He hadn't looked happy before, but now, he looked ready to kill.

Tobal just hoped he wasn't planning on killing *him*.

"You went against my orders," Berith said through gritted teeth.

Tobal tried to remember what Lon told him about the phases of his brother's anger. This was the moment in which Berith should be quiet, right? Why wasn't he?

But Lon was still talking. "We did," he confirmed. "I was with Tobal the entire time. He was never far from me or in danger. I protected him like I would have protected you, so you don't have to worry about him getting hurt."

Berith dropped the pieces of paper on his desk and pinched the bridge of his nose. He sucked in a breath, then another, and Tobal recognized this.

Now, Berith was quiet.

Sabin took advantage of the moment and grabbed the pieces of paper. He examined the symbol on both of them, then opened them to read what was inside. His eyes widened as he did so, and when he was done, he looked as pissed as Berith.

"The two of you went against my explicit orders," Berith said, his voice rising. "I told Tobal to stay away from the society, but he disobeyed." Berith's attention turned to Tobal. "Why did you think I told you to do that? I was trying to keep you safe, but you willingly put yourself in danger instead of obeying. You could have been killed, and they're still threatening you, so you *still* might be killed. What were you thinking? What did you believe you'd obtain by doing something so stupid?"

Tobal opened his mouth to answer, but a quick shake of Lon's head made him pause and snap it shut. Right, they were still at the yelling part of Berith's reaction.

"I *cannot* believe you were so stupid," Berith continued, apparently not caring whether Tobal answered or not. "What would have happened if the society had decided to kill you? How do you think I would have felt, knowing I told you to stay out of this and that you disobeyed? You're my brother, Tobal. I know it might not mean as much to you as it does to me because you also have Zeno, but I care about you. I'd never forgive myself if something happened to you because of me."

Tobal wanted to tell him it wouldn't have been because of him, but he didn't dare. He didn't dare say or do anything but listen to what Berith said and look contrite.

Berith rubbed his face with one hand. "This was incredibly stupid, and I can't believe you went along with it, Lon. What did you think my reaction would be when I found out?"

"I knew you'd react like this," Lon said.

"Of course you did. I should fire you and kick your ass out of the palace."

Tobal sucked in a breath. Berith wasn't going to do that, right? Not only was Lon good at his job, but he was also one of Berith's best friends. Surely, Berith wouldn't kick his best friend out.

"You're not going to do that," Lon said.

He sounded sure of himself, which was impressive, especially since Tobal was quaking in his sandals.

Berith glared at him. "Fine. I'm not going to fire you. I'm extremely tempted, though."

"We were trying to get to the bottom of this. Tobal felt guilty, and he still does. He feels like he's the one who brought trouble to your door."

Berith turned to look at Tobal. Tobal wanted to kick Lon. He'd been fine not having his brother's attention, dammit, and now that he did, there was no getting away from it.

"None of what you did caused the society to come after me," Berith said. "They've been trying to use you, but they'd been coming for me even before you were in the picture. Their goal is to take the throne, and while they're eager to use you as a pawn, it doesn't make you the reason they're doing this."

Tobal nodded. "I know."

"You say that, yet you contacted the society. You knew how dangerous it could be, but you willingly put yourself in that danger. Why?"

"Because I need to do this. I've never had a family, but now, I do. I don't want anything to happen to any of you, and if there's anything I can do to make sure it doesn't, then I'll do it."

"By lying to me and going behind my back?"

Berith sounded hurt, and Tobal hated that he'd made his brother feel that way. What was done was done, though. There was no going back, only going forward.

"I'm sorry," he whispered.

"And what about your relationship with Lon? Was that fake? It allowed you to spend time alone together."

Tobal opened his mouth to tell Berith it *had* been a lie, but he never got to the words out. Lon grabbed Tobal's arm and pulled him closer, so close that their bodies pressed together. "That wasn't a lie," he said.

Tobal blinked. That was news to him, although the kiss they'd shared minutes earlier should probably have been a clue that Lon felt something for him even though they weren't together.

The problem was that Tobal had no idea what that something was.

Lon hated seeing Berith so disappointed and angry. He couldn't change anything about the situation with the society, but he could give Berith at least this.

This was the lie that would have hurt Berith the most. It was personal, especially after he'd told Lon how happy he was that he and Tobal had found their way to each other. It would have hurt him too much to find out it wasn't so.

Besides, that wasn't true anymore. Tobal and Lon hadn't been together in the beginning, so it had been a lie, but they'd grown closer. Lon didn't want to continue lying, but he didn't have to.

Berith stared at him for a moment. "How am I supposed to believe you?"

"I understand why you don't. Tobal and I are still trying to figure things out, but we like each other." At the very least, Lon liked Tobal. He was pretty sure Tobal liked him, too. He wouldn't have allowed Lon to kiss him if he didn't, and Lon had seen how he looked at him when he thought he wasn't looking. It could have only been physical, but Lon hoped that wouldn't be the case. He could get any number of demons in his bed, and he would have if that was what he wanted.

It wasn't.

Maybe it was watching Berith with Mel and Sabin with

Zeno, but Lon wanted something he'd never wanted before and that he'd thought he'd never have. He wanted Tobal in his life, in his bed, and by his side for decades to come.

Hopefully, Tobal wanted the same.

Berith looked from one to the other. "Fine. I'll believe you when it comes to this. You seem to actually like each other, and I hope that's true."

"It is," Tobal confirmed. "And I'm sorry we lied to you. We never meant to."

Berith snorted. "I'm pretty sure you knew what you were doing when you lied to me."

Tobal inched closer to Lon, who wrapped an arm around his shoulders. It was strange to have his loyalty divided between his best friend and Tobal, and before, Lon would have been with Berith a hundred percent. Now, he really hoped he wouldn't have to choose.

"But that's over now," Berith continued. "We have to work with what happened, and since Aloise is involved, we should get her."

"Do we really have to?" Tobal asked in a soft voice. "I don't want her to think I was going to hurt her."

"She'll find this hilarious," Berith said, sounding convinced.

Tobal didn't know Aloise, but Lon did, and Berith was right. She *would* find this hilarious, and once she was done laughing, she'd demand to know how she could help. They had to find a way to fake her death, and having her brains working on it could only be good. Berith tried to shield Mel from everything bad that happened in Hell, and more specifically, in the palace, but Aloise was a demon. Even though Berith loved her, he'd never been in love with her and never tried protecting her beyond making sure she was physically safe. She'd been a warrior, like most demons, and that hadn't changed just because she lived in the palace.

Berith looked at Sabin, who nodded, put down the pieces of paper sent by the society, and headed to the door. He didn't leave, just leaned out to talk to a guard, then stepped back in. He'd been silent through all of this, but Lon had no doubt he'd eventually hear what Sabin thought about all of this.

It would be nothing good.

Instead of yelling at Lon like Lon expected, Sabin stepped toward Berith. "There are a few things you need to go over urgently," he said.

Berith nodded. "I'll follow you to your desk."

They both left the room, Berith glaring one last time at Lon and Tobal. Tobal stayed tense until the office door was pulled behind them. Berith didn't close it, but it was enough to give Tobal and Lon privacy.

Which he wasn't sure he wanted.

When he'd decided to tell Berith that he and Tobal were actually together, it had been an instinctive reaction. It was what he wanted and what he believed Tobal wanted, too, but he couldn't be sure. What if Tobal was about to tell him to fuck off? Lon thought Tobal liked him, but it might be wishful thinking or that Tobal had been trying to convince him of it so he'd help with the society.

Tobal stepped away from Lon, and Lon let him go. There was no other option, even though it was clear Tobal wanted to talk, while Lon wanted nothing more than to run away.

"Why did you do that?" Tobal asked. He kept his voice soft, no doubt so that Sabin and Berith wouldn't hear him from the other room.

"Do what?" Lon was trying to act as if he didn't know what Tobal was talking about, but he did. He was just afraid to answer.

Tobal looked straight at him. "You lied again. You told Berith you and I are together."

Lon would have to be honest. He didn't want Berith to

overhear and believe he'd lied again, especially when he hadn't. He wasn't sure he was ready to tell Tobal the truth, but it looked like he might have to be because it was happening whether he liked it or not.

He reached out and took one of Tobal's hands. "It wasn't a lie."

"You and I aren't together," Tobal protested.

"Aren't we? I kissed you, and I can do it again, if you don't remember."

A flush appeared on Tobal's cheeks. "Maybe not here?"

"I'll kiss you anywhere you want me to kiss you."

"So you want to do it again?"

"More than anything." Except maybe finally getting rid of the society, but he didn't need to say that out loud for Tobal to know. He no doubt felt the same way. "I also want us to be together like Berith and Mel are. I realize I'm not exactly a prize, but if you allow me, I'll cherish you better than anyone else."

Lon might not want to say this, but since he had to, he might as well go all in. Tobal needed to be reassured, and this way, Lon would know what was waiting for him. Whether Tobal wanted him or not, they wouldn't have much time to focus on each other while they also tried to take down the society. This way, Tobal would know how Lon felt, and hopefully, he'd carry that knowledge in his heart until Lon was able to show him.

Tobal stared, and Lon held his breath. Whatever happened next, he'd been honest and hoped Tobal realized that. He didn't want to lie anymore to anyone.

Not even to himself.

Tobal didn't know what to say or even if he *could* say anything. He wanted to reassure Lon that he wanted the same things, but his words wouldn't come. He felt like he and Lon were frozen in this instant, and he was afraid that anything he said would break the enchantment.

How could he not want to be with Lon? In the beginning, he'd found him incredibly sexy, and that had been that. He disliked that Berith had asked Lon to be his bodyguard and follow him around, and he'd been relieved when Lon had found it impossible to do because he still had to work as the palace's head of security. Now, though, he wanted nothing more than to spend hours with Lon following him. He wanted this mess with the society to be over and for them to find out how well they could work together.

Lon was still staring, his gaze heavy, his body poised as if ready to run if Tobal said the wrong word, waiting for an answer.

Tobal wasn't about to do that.

He cleared his throat, trying to make the words come easier. "I want the same," he whispered.

Lon finally relaxed. "Good. That's good. But we have to focus on the society first. I want nothing more than to turn all my attention on you and make you mine, but it's dangerous."

Tobal deflated. Lon was right, but he didn't have to be happy with it. "Fine. We'll focus on the society." But if he had even one chance at being with Lon during this time, he'd take it. He wasn't waiting any longer, dammit. He wouldn't allow the society to ruin this, whatever it was.

He moved forward, ready to kiss Lon again. He was relieved when Lon didn't tell him to go back to his side of the office. He'd said they had to wait, but maybe he meant they had to wait to make this serious, not to be together.

Lon welcomed Tobal into his arms. Tobal wrapped his around Lon's neck, pressing closer as their lips met.

The door opened.

Tobal's first instinct was to jerk away, but instead, he

sighed heavily and pressed his forehead against Lon's shoulder.

"So you really weren't lying about that," Berith said as he walked in.

"Lying about what?" Aloise asked, coming in behind him. "Killing me?"

Tobal pushed away from Lon. "I'd never hurt you, let alone kill you," he declared.

She grinned at him. "You don't have to say it. I already know."

Tobal breathed easier. "Good. I guess they want you dead because you're close to Berith, but I'm not going to do anything to you."

She flopped into one of the chairs in front of Berith's desk and nodded. "I appreciate you not pulling my daughter into this, even though she'd never have been aware of it, anyway." She stretched her legs out, the sides of her red gown sliding to the floor. "So tell me what's going on."

Tobal was happy to let Lon explain everything again. He wasn't proud of the fact that he'd agreed to kill Aloise, even though she didn't seem to mind. Like Berith had said, she actually seemed to find this amusing, which puzzled Tobal. He was terrified of the society, and he'd want nothing more than to hide away if someone had promised to kill him for them. Clearly, Aloise was made of a different cloth than he was.

"So how do you want to do this?" she asked once Lon was done telling her everything.

"We're not going to hurt you," Berith said with a growl.

She waved his words away. "I never expected you to. What is it with all of you thinking I'd believe you can do something like that?"

"What, then?" Lon asked.

"How about we take a day to think about this?" Berith offered. "We all need to focus, which means we have to dispatch the rest of our work to be able to do so. It'll also do us good to spend some time thinking about the situation."

Tobal couldn't say he wasn't happy. He still had no idea what to do, but he was glad he had other people worrying about this and trying to find a solution. He wouldn't have been able to find his way out of this if he'd been alone.

But he wasn't.

It was hard to believe, but Tobal forced himself to do so. He had a family now, people who cared about him, and they'd do what they could to keep him safe, just like he'd do what he could to keep all of them safe. It was odd to have people he cared so much about, but he liked it.

"Lon, why don't you walk Tobal back to his rooms?" Berith offered. "I'll go over what's left of the work I have to do with Sabin, and we can agree to meet here tomorrow. Hopefully by then, someone will have an idea of how to deal with the society."

Tobal wanted to talk to his brother, but he was afraid to. He didn't think he could deal with Berith rejecting him.

"I will. Let me walk Aloise back to her rooms first," Lon said as he moved toward the door.

"You don't have to. My bodyguard is right outside this door," Aloise said, but she allowed Lon to walk her there. Sabin disappeared back into his office, and Tobal was left with Berith.

He swallowed, wondering what he should say.

"I'm really sorry about all of this," he started with. Surely, Berith wanted an apology. "I never meant to lie to you. I mean, I knew what I was doing, but the only reason I did it was to keep you safe. I truly believed I could make a difference in the fight against the society." And now, Tobal realized how stupid he'd been.

But thankfully, Berith didn't seem to blame him. He came closer, his expression serious as he dragged Tobal into his arms. "I don't blame you for doing something stupid. I would have done the same thing when I was younger, and if I remember right, I *did* do things that were probably even more stupid than this. I'm just worried about you. I also don't like that you lied, but I don't blame you for that, either. You couldn't have done this without lying to me."

"I won't do it again. I just found you, and I don't want to risk our relationship."

"You won't. I love you, Tobal, and that's not going to change just because you do something stupid. I hope you know that."

Tobal hadn't been sure, so hearing it from Berith's mouth was good.

Lon cleared his throat, and Berith let go of Tobal. "Go to your rooms and rest. The fight is coming, and we'll all need to be ready to face it," Berith said.

Unfortunately, he was right.

Tobal was relieved to be able to leave this meeting, but it wasn't going anywhere, and neither was the society. They'd have to deal with them soon, no matter how Tobal felt about it.

He followed Lon into Sabin's office, and from there, into the hallway. They stayed silent as they walked toward the private wing. Tobal's thoughts were spinning, and he was already trying to find a way around what he'd promised he'd do.

"How are you feeling?" Lon asked.

"I'm fine," Tobal said. "I was afraid to tell my brother, so it's a relief that he's not going to kick me out. And you were right about how he'd react."

Lon nodded. "Eventually, you'll get to know him as well as I do. There's nothing more important to him than his family, and you should remember that."

Tobal needed to try to do just that, but he suspected it

would take him a long time to believe someone other than Zeno cared about him. He had to make sure he'd *have* time, which meant getting rid of the society.

He was ready for the fight.

Lon walked Tobal to his rooms like he always did lately. Technically, he was still Tobal's bodyguard, but things were shifting so quickly these days that he didn't know where to focus. He was glad to stick with Tobal, but Tobal confused him, or rather, the way Lon felt about him did.

How did Lon feel? He liked Tobal, probably more than he should. Berith had been happy when he'd thought they were together, but what about everyone else? Lon had never cared what most people thought of him, but he didn't want Tobal to have to listen to nasty rumors and whatnot.

What if Lon ignored all of that? What if he only listened to what he and Tobal wanted?

What did he want, then?

He'd have said *nothing* until recently, but he couldn't ignore how he felt anymore. Tobal had barged into his life, pushing his way under his skin and making himself at home there. He was stubborn, fierce, knew what he wanted, and was willing to sacrifice himself for the people he loved. How could Lon not have fallen for him?

"That went better than I expected," Tobal said as they turned the corner.

They were in the hallway where his door was, and their time together was almost over. Lon wasn't used to wanting more time with anyone who wasn't part of his family, although he supposed Tobal was part of his family. Even if they never got together, their lives were intertwined through the people they loved. That meant that their being together might be a disaster. What would happen if they fought? If they decided they didn't want to be together anymore? Their family could implode, and that wasn't something Lon wanted to consider.

Tobal stopped in front of his door and turned to face Lon. Lon had no idea what to do. He was tired of keeping himself in check and away from Tobal, but he was afraid of what would happen if he didn't. This could turn bad.

But it could also turn magnificent.

He opened his mouth to confirm that things had gone well with Berith, even though Tobal didn't need him to, but Tobal took things out of Lon's hands. He reached for Lon, grabbed his shoulders, and pulled him close. Lon didn't resist. He didn't want to. He was fine with Tobal taking control, at least for now.

Tobal kissed Lon like he was precious, which wasn't something Lon was used to. People viewed him as a protector, full of brute force and able to defend himself and everyone else. They relied on him and seemingly never thought he had feelings, too. He wasn't always strong, but he never showed it to anyone because he couldn't. He was the strength, the person who kept their family safe, and he liked things that way. He liked being their shield.

But that wasn't all he was, and Tobal seemed to get that.

The way he touched Lon was gentle, almost as if he expected Lon to break down or maybe reject him. Lon might have before, but not anymore. He wanted to be happy, too. He wanted to have what Berith had with Mel and what Sabin had with Zeno. He didn't know if he could have it with Tobal, but he wanted to find out.

He slid an arm around Tobal's waist and hauled him close. Tobal squeaked, then laughed, and it was the most wonderful sound in the world. It meant that Tobal liked this and that he was happy, and Lon wanted that. He wanted to make Tobal happy, and that realization rocked him to his core.

Luckily, Tobal didn't seem to notice. He kissed the corner of Lon's lips, then twisted enough to reach his door. He opened it, took Lon's hand, and pulled him in, and Lon went. There was nowhere else he'd rather be, no matter what this meant or what would happen tomorrow morning.

The door slammed behind them, spurring Lon to move. He grabbed Tobal's hips and pushed him against the wall, which made Tobal laugh again. Lon cut off the sound with his lips, swallowing it as he thrust his tongue into Tobal's mouth.

Tobal moaned and clung to Lon, his hands stroking up and down Lon's back, then catching his shoulders as if Tobal needed something to hold on to. Lon grinned at the thought. He wanted more of that. He wanted to make him lose his mind.

Dropping to his knees, Lon reached for Tobal's flowy pants and quickly opened them as he pushed Tobal closer to the wall. He looked up, grinning at Tobal's wide eyes—all three of them. They blinked in unison, all of them slightly cloudy. Tobal was still able to think, and that wasn't acceptable.

Lon let out a small growl. Tobal had been driving him nuts since he'd first arrived at the palace, and it was time to do the same to him.

Tobal swallowed heavily, never looking away from Lon. "You're sure?" he asked.

"I wouldn't be doing it if I weren't." Lon understood why Tobal was hesitant, but he wasn't. He'd made his decision. Whatever happened next, he wanted this with Tobal, and as long as Tobal was okay with it, nothing would stop him.

Tobal licked his lips and nodded. Lon hadn't exactly been waiting for him to agree that way, but he was glad he had. He wanted to know that Tobal wanted this as much as he did.

He didn't give Tobal the time to ask himself more questions. He'd already opened Tobal's pants, and he let go. They slid down Tobal's legs easily since they were so large, and Lon wasn't surprised to see Tobal wasn't wearing anything under them. He'd noticed before from the way Tobal's pants moved on his body. He'd wondered, and now he knew for sure, and he loved it.

He swallowed Tobal's cock without hesitating. He was a bit rusty and didn't want to make things awkward by choking, so he didn't take it to the root, even though he wanted to. He needed to get warmed up before he tried, so he spent long minutes worshipping Tobal's body with his mouth and hands.

He pushed his hands under Tobal's tunic, following the red marks he could see with his fingertips, drawing little moans and groans from Tobal. Tobal's cock twitched in Lon's mouth, spurting a tiny bit from the tip, and Lon tasted the salty and slightly bitter essence. It wasn't his favorite thing, but it was Tobal, and that, he loved.

Tobal's scent surrounded Lon. It was stronger here, at the center of Tobal's body. Lon twisted his head so he could take Tobal deeper. His jaw ached, but he wasn't ready to give up. He buried his nose against the place where Tobal's thigh met his groin and inhaled as he swallowed.

Tobal whimpered and grabbed Lon's horns. Lon had no feeling in them, but he could feel the pull in his head, and he loved it. Tobal didn't pull him closer or push him away. He was holding on, which was what Lon wanted.

He was in charge, and Tobal knew it.

He continued sucking and swallowing, letting his hands move lower as he did so. Tobal's ass was naked, and when he pushed his hips forward to give Lon easier access, Lon grabbed his ass with both hands, holding him in place. Tobal's tail wrapped around one of Lon's arms, holding on for dear life. The sounds coming out of Tobal's mouth were becoming louder and more frequent, and while Lon was tempted to get him to completion, he wanted something different, at least this time. He'd see what Tobal looked like when he came in Lon's mouth later.

Lon let the head of Tobal's cock pop out of his mouth and lapped at the head as he looked up. Tobal's yellow eyes were fixated on him, and they were more dazed than before.

Mission accomplished.

The blush on Tobal's cheeks was sexy and adorable at the same time. Lon swooped back down, running his tongue up Tobal's cock before swallowing around the head. Maybe he'd get Tobal to come this way after all. It seemed he wouldn't last long, but Lon could make him come again, and he wanted to drink down everything Tobal was ready to give him.

Lon continued working Tobal's dick with his mouth and one hand—his jaw was sore, dammit—but he reached between Tobal's legs with the other. Tobal widened his stance and thumped the back of his head against the wall. He slid his hands off Lon's horns and tangled his fingers in Lon's short hair, which Lon suddenly wished was longer. Tobal's hold was on the edge of painful as he pulled, silently telling Lon how close he was.

Lon sucked harder and slipped the tip of one finger behind Tobal's balls and into his ass. He didn't dare go too deep because he didn't want to hurt him, but he didn't need to. Tobal sucked him in as he pressed back and moaned. His back arched against the wall as he shuddered under Lon's touch. His cock pulsed, releasing his pleasure into Lon's mouth. He quickly swallowed, but some trickled out. He made sure to look up at Tobal as he licked it from the corner of his lips.

Tobal was slumped against the wall, his chest heaving and his eyes reduced to slits. The blissed expression on his face made Lon want to grab him, tuck him into bed, slide behind him, and hold him all night, but he wasn't done yet. He'd do all of that—later.

Reaching for Tobal, he turned him and guided his hands

flat on the wall. He expected Tobal to protest now that he'd come, but Tobal didn't. He allowed Lon to move him and pressed his forehead against the wall, still breathing heavily.

Lon trusted Tobal to stop him if he did something he wasn't okay with, so he didn't ask if this was okay. He helped untangle Tobal's pants from his feet and threw them away, giving himself easier access. He moved Tobal's legs wider, grabbed his ass cheeks, and pulled them apart.

And realized he didn't have anything to ease his way inside.

Dammit. "Oil?" he asked, barely recognizing his voice. It was low and rough, and it made Tobal shudder.

"Bedroom." Tobal's voice was different, too, little more than a croak.

Lon squeezed Tobal's ass cheeks. "Stay here."

He didn't wait for Tobal to agree or disagree. He pushed back to his feet, his knees protesting pretty much everything he'd done over the past ten minutes, and went straight to the bedroom. Tobal hadn't told him where the oil was in detail, but Lon guessed the small table next to the bed and was relieved to see he was right when he opened the drawer. The jar was small, but it would be enough for tonight.

Lon opened it as he returned to the living area. Tobal was where he'd left him, and Lon took a moment to look at him.

He still wore a loose tunic, and it was long enough to cover the top part of his ass. His pale skin was flushed, which made the red swirls on it pop out. His tail flicked behind him before he wrapped it around his waist, keeping it out of the way so Lon would have easy access to his ass.

Lon didn't drop to his knees this time, even though he wanted to. He was torn between giving himself relief and worshipping Tobal's body, and he told himself that this was just the first time they did this. Many more times would come, and he'd have the opportunity to do everything he wanted to the man offering himself so freely to him.

Lon put the jar on the floor once he'd slicked his fingers with enough solid oil to use on three or four cocks, then focused on the demon spread out in front of him. He pulled one of Tobal's ass cheeks with his dry hand, and while he wanted time to look, his cock was so hard that he felt his balls might explode. It was time for him to get his release.

He slipped one slick finger between Tobal's cheeks and teased his hole, rubbing it, smiling when it tightened and released under his touch.

"Come on," Tobal muttered.

"You already came."

"I want you in me."

That was fine with Lon. He quickly stretched Tobal since that was what Tobal wanted. Tobal wasn't shy about letting Lon know how he felt. He kept pushing back with his hips, tilting his ass up for Lon to take. Lon didn't want to hurt him, so he made sure to be thorough. Once he deemed Tobal ready, he didn't waste any more time.

Lon gripped his aching cock and aimed it at Tobal's ass. Tobal knew what was happening, and he looked over his shoulder. They stared at each other as Lon pushed inside of him, but it didn't last long. Tobal moaned and pushed back, neither of them stopping until Lon was fully lodged in his body.

It was both heaven and hell. Lon had yearned for this, and now that he had it, he felt almost lost. He cared so much about Tobal that the thought of losing him was enough to petrify him.

But he wouldn't lose him. He'd make sure of that.

He gripped Tobal's hips and pulled back, then slammed into him. Tobal moved with him, and Lon wasn't surprised to find he was hard again when he slid a hand around his waist to touch his cock. He jacked him off, trying to keep the same rhythm with his hand and his hips, but it wasn't easy when he was chasing his pleasure. He wanted Tobal to come again, though, and it needed to happen fast because he was ready to go.

Tobal bucked under him, pushing back and taking his dick even deeper as his body rippled around Lon's cock. The movement made his tunic slide to the side, exposing his neck and part of his shoulder. Lon pressed his face there and kissed Tobal's skin, then lightly bit down.

Tobal cried out and jerked in Lon's hand. His cock twitched, erupting in Lon's hold, while his ass tightened around Lon's cock. Lon bit down harder, making Tobal whine and push back against him as he came, feeling like he was making Tobal his.

Hopefully, he was. He never wanted to lose this, not now that he had it.

He never wanted to lose Tobal.

CHAPTER SEVENTEEN

When Tobal woke up the next morning, he expected to be alone in his bed. Lon had followed him there after what had happened in the living area. They'd woken up during the night for a second round, and Tobal had fallen asleep sated and sticky, hoping Lon wouldn't run but knowing he probably would.

It would make sense. Even though Lon had said he wanted to be with Tobal, he wasn't used to being in a relationship. Tobal wasn't, either, and it was kind of overwhelming to think about. More importantly, Lon needed to be easily found. If something happened during the night, his guards wouldn't have been able to find him if he hadn't been in his rooms. Tobal and Lon hadn't talked about it, and Tobal wasn't angry.

Just disappointed.

He stared at the ceiling for a moment. He felt like he could stay in bed for a week and still not want to get up. The problem was that he had to face reality, both with Lon and with the mess he'd made with the society. Berith would expect a solution to the problem Tobal had created, and unfortunately, Tobal didn't have one. He hadn't had the opportunity to think, and now, it was too late.

"You're thinking awfully hard for someone who just woke up," a voice said from beside Tobal.

Tobal's eyes widened, and he rolled sideways. Lon was there, stretched out against Tobal's pillows, looking like he belonged. Tobal's heart raced as he threw himself forward, knowing Lon would catch him.

He did. He grabbed Tobal's shoulders and dragged him closer, wrapping him in his arms as Tobal snuggled against him.

"You stayed," Tobal murmured.

He felt a kiss pressed against his hair. "Where else would I go?"

"You didn't want to do the walk of shame through the hallways?"

"It wouldn't have been of shame. I'm not ashamed of what happened between us."

Tobal couldn't stop smiling. "That's not what I meant. I didn't expect you to be here still."

"There's nowhere else I'd rather be."

"I guess it's a good thing nothing happened during the night."

Lon sighed. His chest moved under Tobal's head, and Tobal took a moment to enjoy what was happening. He was in his bed with a wonderful demon he was falling for. He still had to deal with the society, but he couldn't think of anything better than waking up in Lon's arms.

Although actually waking up in his arms would have helped Tobal freak out a little less first thing in the morning.

"Nothing happened," Lon confirmed. "But I can't wait for the moment the society is dealt with. I don't like going to bed wondering if I'm going to be woken up because someone has died."

Tobal hadn't thought about that. He had trouble sleeping lately because he couldn't stop himself from imagining someone sneaking into his rooms while he was out, but last night, he'd slept like a baby. Lon's presence had made him feel safe, and he understood better why Berith had made Lon his head of security. It almost didn't feel fair to take Lon away, even if only for the night, but Tobal wouldn't change anything that had happened last night.

"Unfortunately, we can't afford to stay in bed forever," Lon said, as if he'd read Tobal's mind. "It's time for breakfast, and I'm sure Berith is waiting for us. We need to talk about the society and decide what we'll do about them."

"We need to talk about how we're going to kill Aloise," Tobal muttered.

He expected Lon to tell him that this was his fault, but instead, Lon hummed as he stroked a hand up and down Tobal's naked back. "You know, that's not a bad idea."

Tobal jerked up into a sitting position. "What's not a bad idea?"

"Killing Aloise. Not for real, of course, but her death would be easier to fake than Berith's, and since it's what the society wants, knowing she's dead would allow you to dig deeper."

Tobal couldn't even begin to think about how that would work. "How?"

Lon shook his head and pushed away the sheets. "I'm not sure yet. We need to talk to Berith, though."

Tobal watched him as he got out of bed. He was tempted to flop back against his pillow but couldn't afford to. Even though it felt like the moment between him and Lon had been broken by both their lives pushing back in, there was no way to avoid it. If he was lucky, Lon would be right back in his bed tonight.

Tobal yelped when Lon grabbed one of his ankles and pulled him to the side of the bed. He tried to stay where he was, but the only thing he could grab was a pillow, which he dragged right along with him. Lon grinned down at him, and he glared, but there was no heat in it. How could there be?

Lon towered over Tobal, looking down at him. "You're absolutely gorgeous naked in bed, and I can't wait to come back to this, but it's better if we wash up and head out."

Tobal sighed and let go of the pillow. "I know."

"I promise this won't be our only night together," Lon said, his voice soft. "I want to ignore the world for a bit longer, but I'd never forgive myself if something happened while I did so."

He was right, and since he didn't have a choice, Tobal pushed up and finally got out of bed. Lon grabbed him by the waist and pulled him close, kissing him even though Tobal protested he had morning breath. Lon did, too, but Tobal found he didn't care much. Just being in his arms, kissing him as their bodies were pressed together, made him feel like he'd found a slice of heaven in Hell.

At least until Lon slapped his ass.

Tobal jumped away, glaring again. "What was that for?"

"Just because I could. Come on. Let's take a bath, then go grab breakfast. It won't do us any good if Berith has to drag us out of your rooms."

Tobal didn't want to do anything that would displease his brother after what he'd already done, so he went along with Lon's plan. The bathroom was big enough for an entire sports team to clean up together. So far, the spell was still on him and Lon, but reality would soon break through, and Tobal was afraid of what would happen then. The only thing he could do was have faith in himself and Lon, so he allowed Lon to guide him out of his rooms once they were clean and dressed.

They quickly stopped in Lon's rooms so he could change, then headed to the dining room. From the sounds coming from inside, Tobal could tell most of the family was already gathered, so he wasn't surprised when he walked in and saw that everyone was there except for Cyarea. They could have this meeting in Berith's office, but what would be the point when everyone was present now?

Aloise grinned at him when she saw him. "You're going to kill me," she declared.

Tobal's steps faltered. He would have stopped entirely if Lon hadn't pressed a hand against his back and pushed him forward.

"What do you mean?" he asked.

"Exactly what she said," Berith said with a smile. He was sitting next to Mel, feeding him bits of pancakes as Mel read a book. It wasn't the first time Tobal saw them do this, and it was kind of adorable. How could Mel focus on anything that wasn't what Aloise had said, though?

"You're going to have to explain," Lon said.

Berith nodded. "I know. We were talking and thought the best thing would be to fake Aloise's death. The society expects her to die, so we're going to give them just that."

For some reason, that didn't reassure Tobal as much as it should. Clearly, they were going to fake Aloise's death, but would the society fall for it?

Tobal couldn't think of any other way out of this, no matter how hard he focused on it. That meant he'd have to go along with the fake death thing, and while he wasn't sure it was the best idea, he was willing to listen to what his brother had come up with.

Who was he kidding? He'd do whatever Berith asked of him, and not only because they were in this mess because of him. His brother was a prince of Hell, used to this kind of action. He knew what to do.

And Tobal would only have to follow his orders.

Faking Aloise's death didn't sound like the worst idea. Lon hadn't come up with anything else since he'd been busy and was willing to listen to what Berith had to say. Tobal seemed in shock, though, so Lon gently guided him toward a chair at the table.

Tobal flopped down into it, still frowning. Lon had been

observing him since he'd arrived, so he knew what Tobal enjoyed eating in the morning. It didn't take more than a few minutes for him to grab a plate and fill it with every food Tobal liked, then place it in front of him.

Tobal blinked at the plate, then up at Lon. "Thank you. You didn't have to do that."

"I didn't have to, but I wanted to," Lon said. He hesitated, then leaned forward and kissed the top of Tobal's head.

Tobal seemed frozen, so Lon turned to grab himself a plate. He quickly filled it, and when he sat next to Tobal, he looked up and noticed Berith was staring at them. He arched a brow in question, and his friend grinned and winked.

Clearly, Berith was glad to see that Lon and Tobal were actually together. It was the one thing they hadn't lied to him about, or rather, they *had* lied, but that lie didn't matter anymore. It wasn't a lie now that they were together, and Lon wasn't planning on hiding their relationship. If anything, Tobal should be the one to hide the fact that he was dating Lon. He was Berith's brother, meaning he could have almost anyone he wanted.

And for some reason, he'd chosen Lon.

"You two are adorable together," Aloise said.

Lon couldn't imagine himself being adorable doing anything, but he agreed when it came to Tobal. "Thank you. Now, what's the plan?"

She grinned. "And here I thought you couldn't wait to gush about your boyfriend."

"I don't need to gush about him. Everyone can see how amazing he is for themselves."

Tobal made a strangled sound, so Lon turned his attention to him. He rubbed Tobal's back as Tobal struggled to get his breath back, and while he was worried, he gave Tobal time to gather himself.

"Everything okay?"

Tobal nodded. "I'm fine. I just didn't expect you to be like this."

"Like what?"

"I thought you might want to hide the fact that we're together." Tobal's voice was little more than a whisper.

"I don't. I'm not ashamed of being with you, and there's no reason for us to hide the fact that we're together from our family."

"You're right."

Unfortunately, it was time for all of them to work. The sooner they got rid of the society, the sooner they could return to a peaceful life, and Lon and Tobal could learn to be a couple in their everyday lives.

Lon couldn't wait.

"If we fake Aloise's death, Tobal can go back to the guy he talked to and tell him it's done. Hopefully, the society will see this as proof he was serious about becoming part of it. Once they do, they'll hopefully allow him deeper, and he can find out more about the people who are part of this group," Berith explained. "He can give you the names, and you can do your job and take care of them."

"The only thing I'm worried about is that the two of you aren't hiding the fact that you're together," Aloise said. "Won't the society have a problem with that?"

Tobal had been chewing a piece of bread, but he quickly swallowed. "I don't think so. When I met with the society's representative, Dorkel, he knew Lon was following me even though I didn't. He asked me about him, and I had to come up with an explanation on the spot. I told him that I seduced Lon and that he'd do whatever I asked him to do."

Aloise didn't seem convinced. "If he believes that, he doesn't know Lon well."

"I don't think the society knows any of us well. They have their idea of what they want to happen, and they don't care about the people. Their only goal is to kill Berith, so they're focused on him. They know who Lon is and what he does, but I don't think they ever really looked into him. They'd know he's not the kind of guy to let himself be guided by lust otherwise."

Berith nodded. "So your relationship won't be a problem. How do we do this?"

Everyone started throwing out ideas, and Lon thought as he finished his pancakes. He was still hungry, which wasn't a surprise after the night he'd had, so he got back to his feet and went to get more food.

He wasn't surprised to see Zeno following him. He'd expected the demon to want to talk about Tobal, but he had no idea which way things would go. He waited, not wanting to make an enemy out of Zeno.

"So, you and my brother," Zeno said, never looking up at Lon.

"Me and your brother," Lon confirmed.

Zeno chuckled. "You don't have to look so scared. I'm not going to tell you to stay away from Tobal, and I'm not going to threaten to kill you if you hurt him."

Lon breathed easier. Normally, he wouldn't have been worried about any of this, but Tobal was important to him. He didn't want to be at odds with Tobal's family.

"You know, I feel that the more time passes, the more similar we become to humans," Zeno said.

Lon couldn't deny that. "Mel's presence hasn't helped."

"Or maybe it has, in the best of ways. I don't care what other demons think Hell should be like. I like my life, and I don't want it to change. I'm fine being more human than demon." He peered at Lon again. "And I'm fine with you and my brother being together. It's none of my business, anyway."

"I agree it's not, but I don't want you and Tobal to fight over this."

"We won't. Tobal is an adult, and I'm sure he knows what he's doing. As long as you can make him happy, I don't have a problem with the two of you being together."

Lon licked his lips. "I can't make promises, but I'll do my best." He had no idea how to make Tobal happy, but he was nothing but stubborn when he wanted something, and he wanted Tobal. If he didn't want Tobal to leave, he'd have to keep him happy, and he was ready to do just that.

"I know you will."

That was all Zeno said. Lon was a bit surprised but relieved. It seemed that everyone was on board with him and Tobal being together, which lifted a weight off his shoulders. If he didn't have to worry about how their family would react to the news, it meant he could focus on the next step in their plan against the society.

Lon looked around the table as he sat back down. Everyone here wanted the same thing — to get rid of the society. They were willing to work as a group to make it happen, and it was a good reminder that Lon wasn't alone in this.

Together, they'd make it happen.

CHAPTER EIGHTEEN

Tobal wasn't sure this would work. "Can we go over it again?"

Thankfully, Aloise didn't seem bothered. She smiled at him, then launched herself into yet another explanation of the plan. "Berith will make an announcement that I'm sick," she said. "He'll say he suspects someone poisoned me, and of course, that someone would be you. He'll explain he's not sure I'll make it and demand privacy, and no one will want to bother him after that."

"But people will know you're not actually dying," Tobal pointed out.

"Not if I stay here in my rooms. Berith can use the excuse that I was poisoned to limit the number of people who can come in to those we trust, like Mel. He agreed to go along with this and to bring me food."

"But people will still notice he's bringing food to a woman who's supposed to be dying."

She winked. "That's where the secret passages come in."

They'd already told Tobal about the passages, but he hadn't seen them yet. It was hard to believe that an entire network of them ran behind the walls, yet at the same time, it was also easy. Of course the palace had secret passages.

Aloise got to her feet. "I'll show you," she said.

"Show him what?" Lon demanded to know as he looked up from his tablet.

He was on board with the plan but didn't like it. Tobal didn't, either, but he didn't see another way out of the situation. They had to kill Aloise, and since he wasn't about to do it in real life, faking her death was the best they could come up with. Hopefully, the society would believe it, and they'd finally open up to Tobal.

"The secret passages," Aloise explained as she moved toward the bookshelves on the wall.

Lon made a strangled sound that caught Tobal's attention. He looked at his lover, frowning when he saw that Lon looked uncomfortable when Aloise opened up the secret passage in the wall.

It was a simple arch that opened on a narrow hallway. The only thing Tobal could see when he peeked in was stone.

"What's going on?" he asked, leaning back. Maybe Lon hadn't known about the passages. That didn't sound right, though. He was head of security, which meant he had to know there was a hidden way to travel the palace.

"See?" Aloise said. "We can use them to get me food and so I can see Cyarea. Maybe I can even use the passages to spy around the palace."

The back of Tobal's neck prickled. "Is that something people could do?"

"Spy from the passages? I don't see why not. There are holes in the walls that were created for that purpose."

Tobal turned to look at Lon again. "Is it possible that someone has been using these to spy on me? Because I *know* I felt like someone was watching me in the past, but I couldn't see them, and I was alone in my rooms."

Lon sighed and rubbed the back of his neck. "It was me," he said.

Aloise made a squeaking sound, but Tobal was stuck on Lon's words. "I'm sorry?"

"It was before I got to know you, when I believed you were working with the society. I spied on you using the passages because I wanted to catch you while you were doing it."

"You spied on me?" It was what Lon had said, but Tobal had a hard time wrapping his mind around it.

"I did, and I'm sorry. I shouldn't have, but I was trying to protect Berith and the family. I thought you were behind some of what had happened, so it made sense for me to keep an eye on you."

Aloise made a strangled sound, but Tobal continued ignoring her. He wasn't sure how he felt about Lon's admission. He understood why Lon had done it and where he'd come from, but it didn't mean he was comfortable with it. What had Lon seen? Tobal had nothing to hide, and he hadn't done anything he shouldn't have that Lon didn't already know about, but still. It made him slightly uncomfortable to know that Lon had been watching him, and he hadn't known.

Lon sighed and stepped forward. "I'm sorry," he whispered. "It was a breach of trust, and I shouldn't have done it. Will you be able to forgive me?"

Tobal might not be sure how he felt, but he was sure there was nothing he needed to forgive. "I understand why you did it, and while it makes me uncomfortable, I'm not going to hold it against you. You were doing your job."

Lon nodded. "I was."

They stared at each other until Aloise cleared her throat. That got both of them back in motion.

"We should go," Lon said. "Aloise, I'll lock you in your rooms on our way out. You know what to do."

"Get in bed and act as if I'm dying. I needed a vacation, so this is going to be great rest." She almost sounded happy.

Tobal suspected she was doing the most with what the situation was giving her, and he didn't blame her. He wouldn't want to be in her place, having to act as if she was dying, but she was making a sacrifice for all of them, and the least he could do was help her deal with it. He had his own job to do, and he'd do it.

After making sure she had everything she needed, Tobal and Lon left her rooms. The sound of the lock snapping into place was final, but Tobal told himself that wasn't really true. Aloise was perfectly fine, and nothing was going to happen to her.

But the society had to believe Tobal had done his job.

"Berith should be making the announcement about now," Lon murmured as they walked down the hallway.

"Should we be there?"

"It would be for the best if we tried acting normally. What would you do if this was actually happening?"

"Try to be there for my brother. Let's go." Tobal might not like any of this, but the plan was in motion, and they needed to play the game.

Sure enough, they found Berith on his throne, Mel sitting next to him. Berith had already started talking to the people gathered in the room, but they'd decided together what the announcement would be about, so Lon knew what he and Tobal had missed.

"We still have hope she'll recover," Berith was saying. "She's my daughter's mother, and I don't want Cyarea to lose either of her parents. I'm only making this announcement so that people know what's happening and don't worry about not seeing her around."

No one dared ask questions, but Tobal could see people whispering to each other. It wasn't a surprise. Berith had just announced his heir's mother had been poisoned. Gossip in the palace would be wild.

Lon moved away from Tobal as they'd planned. Tobal wanted him to stay, but until the society contacted him, he needed to be alone as much as possible to give them the opportunity to reach out. He stared at his brother, wishing they could have avoided all of this. He didn't like the mess the society had created, and he couldn't wait for all of it to be over.

Lon focused on what he'd do if the situation was real, ordering guards around and making sure the rest of the family was safe. He wouldn't put it past the society to attempt to kill someone else now that Aloise was supposedly out of the picture, but he hoped that wouldn't happen.

He knew the plan had worked when he noticed a servant approach Tobal. Tobal was focused on Berith, and he was startled when the servant touched his elbow. They had a quick conversation, and Lon waited, holding his breath. He expected Tobal to look up at him in confirmation that he was doing the right thing, but he never did. He kept his focus on the servant, then on the piece of paper the servant gave him. He was a good actor, but Lon was able to tell who had sent the message from Tobal's reaction when he opened it.

The society had already gotten in touch, which meant their plan was working. It was time for the next step.

Burning the society to the ground.

He wanted to rush to Tobal's side, but instead, he gave Tobal space. The servant still hovered close, looking around as if he expected someone to catch them in the act of betraying their prince. Lon made sure not to stare, even though it was hard.

Thankfully, he had enough work to do. He'd kept in contact with Mikal the entire day, and having Mikal know about the plan helped. It meant one more person could help shoulder all of these responsibilities, which freed some time and space for Lon to focus on the family. Aloise might not actually be dead, but the family was supposed to behave as if she were dying, which wouldn't be easy for anyone. Mel had promised he'd stick with Cyarea, who was the one person they all worried about.

They couldn't tell the little girl her mother wasn't dead in case she blurted out something she shouldn't in front of someone who wasn't part of their family, but they also couldn't allow her to believe her mother was dead. It would destroy her, and they were doing this to save the family, not to hurt it. Right now, Cyarea was probably with her nanny, but Mel would take over soon. They'd thought about leaving Cyarea with Aloise, and maybe they'd end up doing just that, but for now, they needed to behave as if this mess was true.

Even though Lon didn't dare move closer, he kept an eye on Tobal and the servant. Tobal was done reading the message, and they were quietly talking again. He nodded a few times, and when the servant offered him something to write, he took it, and, using the same note he'd just been given, he wrote a message back to the society. Lon didn't know what he was writing, but he trusted Tobal.

As soon as the servant left, Lon rushed to Tobal's side. Tobal didn't look at him, but Lon knew he was aware of his presence. Thankfully, Berith distracted everyone in the room when he got to his feet. He offered Mel his hand, and together, they left the room. This gave Lon and Tobal the opportunity they needed to vanish, too.

Lon stuck to Tobal's side as they left the throne room. They headed straight for Berith's office, and Lon dragged Tobal into his arms as soon as they were in.

"I'm fine," Tobal said.

"Has something happened?" Berith asked.

"The society's already contacted me," Tobal explained. "A servant approached me and handed me a note from Dorkel."

Berith looked exhausted, which Lon didn't like. They were all tired, and hopefully, they could sleep for a week and relax once the society had been dispatched.

"What did the note say?"

"Not much. It confirmed they knew I was behind Aloise's poisoning and that they'd contact me."

"How did they know you did it?" Lon asked.

"No idea, but the servant who approached me clearly works for the society, and there's no way to know how many more do. I sent him back with a message to confirm I'd be waiting for the next note."

So they had to wait again. Lon hated waiting, dammit.

A quick knock on the door made all of them jump. The tension was high, and they were all worried about what would happen next.

Sabin opened the door and peeked in. His expression was grim, so something had to have happened. He knew Aloise was faking, which meant it couldn't be that.

Lon almost groaned. What now?

"What is it?" Berith asked.

"The ministers are demanding to talk to you."

Berith grimaced. "Is it about Aloise?"

"Yes. They demand to be informed and given more details than what you explained earlier."

Berith and Lon exchanged a glance. Lon was glad he wasn't in Berith's place, but he'd have to be present at the meeting anyway.

Berith groaned. "Fine. Can you organize a meeting in fifteen minutes?"

"Of course. Are you sure you want to do this?"

"I'm sure I *don't* want to, but what choice do I have? They'll hound me until I give them what they want, which clearly is information about Aloise. Organize a meeting, please. I'll deal with the ministers."

Sabin nodded and disappeared back into his office. Tobal moved toward the door, too, and while Lon wanted to ask him to stay, he wouldn't be allowed at the meeting anyway.

"Let me know if there's anything I can do," Tobal murmured. "And if Mel needs help with Cyarea."

They were all worried about the little girl and trying to

shield her from what was happening as much as possible, but unfortunately, they couldn't isolate her. She had to learn to live with all of this, which Lon didn't like one bit. She didn't deserve any of this, but unfortunately, this was life in Hell.

"Mel should have things in hand, although I'll make sure he knows to contact you if he needs anything. He told me he was planning on taking Cyarea to her mother eventually," Berith explained.

Tobal nodded. "I'll be in my rooms, then."

Lon didn't want Tobal to be out of his sight, but they all had to deal with being uncomfortable right now. Just to be sure, he sent Roque along. Yakim was with Mel and Cyarea, while Zeno had agreed to keep an eye on Aloise, which meant everyone was protected.

It made it easier to let Tobal go.

Since almost ten minutes had already passed, he and Berith decided they might as well go to the conference room.

Sabin had worked his magic, and the room was set up for the meeting. Most of the ministers were already there, and Lon wasn't one bit surprised when Nowla was the first to jump down Berith's throat.

"I demand to know what happened."

Berith dropped into his chair. "I'm pretty sure I saw you in the throne room when I made the announcement. You know what happened."

"The mother of your heir was poisoned?"

"She was. We're still looking into it, so I'm not sure how it happened yet, but I wouldn't worry if I were you. I doubt whoever was behind this will come after you."

"Considering who she was, she was supposed to be kept safe. If you can't even protect the mother of your child, how do you think you can protect the rest of your territory?"

Lon almost rolled his eyes. Thankfully, he wasn't the one who had to answer these stupid questions. He'd have growled at her to fuck off and left.

"What happened to Aloise was a fluke. I don't see why it means I can't do my job, but please, explain it to me. I'm all ears, even though I'd rather be with Aloise and my daughter."

Several of the ministers wiggled in their seats, clearly uncomfortable with where things were going, but Nowla didn't seem to care. She was one of the harshest, so Lon wasn't surprised. He also wasn't surprised that she was trying to use this against Berith. Anyone decent would have given him time to be with Aloise and Cyarea and to grieve, but not Nowla. She was striking the iron while it was still hot, and Lon despised her for that.

Once again, he wondered why Berith didn't fire her. Nowla had a lot of power and wasn't afraid to wield it. It was safer for Berith to stay on her good side, but Lon couldn't help but wonder if she *had* a good side. He'd never seen anything coming from her that could be called that.

But Berith had a lot of power, too, and if she tried to use hers against Berith, he wouldn't hesitate to strike back.

Tobal was still nervous when he reached his rooms, maybe even more than before. He couldn't help but wonder if someone was walking through the passages, spying on him. He wouldn't put it past the society to know about them and to be using them, which would explain how they managed to get into his rooms in the past so easily.

"I'll check your rooms," Roque declared, gently pushing Tobal to the side and stepping in ahead of him.

Tobal was used to this by now. He let Roque do his job as he leaned against the wall in the hallway, his mind spinning, thinking about how many things could go wrong.

"It's empty, but there's a piece of paper on the table in the living area," Roque said as he came back. His voice was harsh, and between that and his words, Tobal's heart started racing.

"From the society?" he whispered.

"Their symbol is on it."

Tobal was glad Lon was able to trust several of his guards with the secrets. Apparently, Roque, Mikal, and Yakim had been guarding the family for years, and everyone trusted them with their lives. Tobal did, too, which meant he wasn't alone as he walked into his rooms and headed straight for the small table in the living area.

The note was there, and Tobal stared at it for a moment. Wasting time wouldn't help, so he snatched it up and quickly unfolded it.

"They agreed to a meeting," he said out loud.

Roque nodded. "It's what we were expecting."

"And hoping for, yes." But Tobal was still terrified.

Clearly, it was obvious because Roque patted his shoulder. "Don't worry too much. It won't help you. And besides, you have to remember you're not dealing with all of this alone. I doubt Lon will allow you to go anywhere alone, especially when it comes to meeting these people."

Tobal chuckled. "I *know* he won't. It doesn't mean I'm not terrified of what will happen. This note says I won't just be meeting Dorkel."

Roque frowned. "Who else will you meet?"

"His boss." Tobal swallowed. He couldn't have wished for anything better. They were in this to get to the head of the society and eradicate the entire operation from the palace and the entirety of Berith's territory, after all. Still, he'd thought he'd have to meet many more people and prove himself several times before actually meeting whoever was in charge.

He supposed it wasn't a bad thing that it would happen so quickly. This way, he wouldn't have to fake it for much longer, and Aloise could return to her life sooner than any of them expected. But he was surprised at the eagerness. Until now, the society had threatened Tobal and kept him at arm's length. Could it really be so easy for him to infiltrate?

"What if it's a trap?" he asked, even though he didn't expect Roque to know the answer.

Roque grimaced. "Then, we'll deal with it. You won't go in there alone," he repeated.

That was what Tobal had to keep in mind. No matter how scared he was, he was doing it for his family, and his family would be behind him as he did it. He wasn't used to being in this world, to the danger that came with being Berith's brother, but it didn't matter.

He was in, and the only way was forward.

CHAPTER NINETEEN

The plan was in motion. It didn't matter how much Lon didn't like it, Tobal would meet with Dorkel and Dorkel's boss, and that was that. It was why they'd done all of this and why Aloise was hiding in her rooms, faking her imminent death. Tobal wouldn't back down even if Lon asked him to. He wouldn't want to have done all of this for nothing, and Lon understood. If he was in Tobal's place, he wouldn't want to take a step back, either.

But he *wasn't* in Tobal's place. That meant he'd have to watch the man he'd fallen in love with put himself in danger, and it wasn't something he knew how to deal with.

It was one thing for Berith, Lon's best friend and a prince of Hell, to put himself in danger. He knew how to defend himself, and he could be savage. It was another thing entirely for Lon's partner and lover to put himself in danger because some assholes wanted to kill Berith. If Lon could, he'd go instead of Tobal.

But he couldn't.

That didn't mean he wouldn't be present. Using the excuse that Lon was his lover might have worked, but no one was willing to try. It would be too easy to mess things up, and Lon had no intention of doing that. Tobal was doing this once, and that was that. That meant they had to get it right the first time around, which in turn meant they had to be extremely careful not to mess things up.

And that was why the plan was for Lon to follow Tobal through the palace using the secret passages, then, once he was out, to keep his distance.

He wouldn't be the only one going with Tobal. Roque had volunteered, and while Lon didn't want to take away one of his best men from protecting Berith and the family, he wasn't willing to put Tobal in danger. He and Roque wouldn't be following Tobal together. That way, even if one of them was found, the other would still be able to have Tobal's back. Lon had reinforced security around the family as much as he could, but he'd be taking Mikal, Roque, and a good number of guards with him, so the sooner this was over, the better.

Lon leaned against the wall in the passage, listening to Tobal move around his rooms. It was a bit awkward now that Tobal knew Lon was there, but he'd forgiven Lon for what he'd done. Lon still felt guilty about spying on Tobal, but he shouldn't. He'd been doing what needed to be done, and he'd do it again if he had to.

It wouldn't be with Tobal the next time, though. Lon trusted him a hundred percent, just like Berith did. He'd been slow on the uptake, but not anymore. Tobal had never wanted anything but a family and an easier life, and as soon as the secret society was dealt with, that was what he'd have.

And Lon would be part of that easy life.

He'd always known he'd had it easy next to some of the demons who lived in Hell, but he'd never fully realized how much until he met Zeno and Tobal. Some of the things they'd told him about their childhood had made him want to throw up, and he was glad Tobal had a chance to change things. He was working with Sabin, or rather, he had been, until he had to take a step back because of the society. That would be over soon, and Tobal would be able to settle into his new life. Lon had no doubt it would take them a while to find a way to make things work, but they'd have all the time they needed.

"I'm going," Tobal whispered, his voice close even though he wasn't in the passage with Lon.

Lon didn't answer, just in case, but he quickly knocked on the wall with his knuckle. That way, Tobal knew he was listening and that he was ready to go, too.

It wasn't exactly easy to follow Tobal using the passages. Lon couldn't cross through hallways or anything like that, but being hidden also meant he didn't have to deal with the people around the palace. Many of them were trying to get in Tobal's good graces now that they'd seen he was close to Berith. Berith was planning on announcing Tobal was his brother as soon as this mess was over. Tobal was hesitant, which was understandable, but Lon thought it was the right thing to do. Tobal's life would change again, something Tobal might not be ready for, but he deserved for everyone to know who he was. Berith wouldn't keep him a secret like their father had, and Lon had seen how pleased Tobal was about that.

By the time Lon was out of the palace, Tobal was way ahead of him, barely visible in the distance. It made Lon grit his teeth because of how uncomfortable it made him feel, but he quickly followed, careful not to expose his face. He had no doubt Tobal was being watched, so he kept an eye open for that, too.

Dorkel had decided the meeting would be at the tavern, which made things easier. Lon had sent Mikal ahead, and they were using a spell to communicate. Mikal was inside the tavern, which meant he'd be able to keep an eye on Tobal in a way Lon wouldn't. He could step in if anything happened, and Lon had no doubt something would.

He also had a gaggle of guards standing by, ready to act when he called on them to arrest Dorkel and the person he was working for.

They were prepared for pretty much anything, but Lon still felt like he was missing something. He'd never forgive himself if something happened to Tobal, and he prayed nothing would. He and Tobal had just found each other. Lon was unwilling to lose him so soon.

It became harder to breathe once the tavern was in sight. Lon couldn't go in, so instead, he slid into the tight space between the tavern and the building beside it. Tobal knew he was listening this time, but also that Lon was too far to be able to intervene quickly.

That was where Mikal would come in. If he didn't keep Tobal safe, Lon would have words for him.

Tobal had agreed to sit at the same table he'd sat at the first time he'd met Dorkel. That meant that from where he was, Lon was able to see him. It was a relief, although it would make things more complicated for Lon because he could see what happened but wouldn't be unable to move quickly.

Tobal ordered a beer, and once he had the mug, he wrapped his fingers around it. He didn't drink, but Lon hadn't expected him to.

Once Tobal was at the table, the only thing they could do was wait. Lon shuffled his feet, hating this part of the job. He wasn't used to sitting around. He might be head of security, but he was always in motion, walking around the palace and checking in on his guards and the people they were protecting. He hated having nothing to do, and the tension of the moment made everything worse.

Who would Dorkel arrive with? Who was betraying Berith and the family? Not knowing put Lon on edge, but there was nothing he could do but wait.

Dammit.

He was shuffling his feet again when movement inside got his attention. He sucked in a breath and watched as Dorkel walked toward the table Tobal was sitting at, a hooded figure next to him.

The figure was completely hidden by a hood and the long clothes they were wearing. It was quite dramatic, but it made Lon want to grab and shake them. Couldn't they make things easier on him for once?

Dorkel and the person with him stopped in front of Tobal's table. Dorkel held one of the chairs out as Tobal scrambled to his feet, and Lon knew what expression Tobal had on his face. His eyes would be wide as he looked from the figure to Dorkel, and his heart would be racing. He'd be afraid, but he'd still be ready to do whatever he had to in order to finish this mission.

"Just wait," Mikal suddenly whispered through the spell.

Lon couldn't see him, but he wasn't surprised Mikal had known to tell him to wait. Lon wanted to step in right away and arrest these two assholes, but it would be better to get them to betray themselves first.

Not that Berith would care about what they had to say. He'd send both of them to the dungeon by the time this was over, and Lon would be more than happy to get them there. They had many ways to get information, even from people unwilling to give it up.

But torture was messy, and it wasn't a guarantee. It would be best if Dorkel and his boss told Tobal who else was involved of their own volition, which was the only reason Lon pressed harder against the wall and stayed right where he was.

Tobal swallowed and stared at the person in front of him. He still had no idea who they were, since they wore a hood, and he wondered if they'd take it off.

"You did quick work," Dorkel said as he tapped his fingertips onto the table.

Tobal forced himself to relax. It would be normal for him to be nervous but not to freak out. He had to behave as if he was reluctant to kill more people but willing to do it if it meant the society wouldn't hurt him.

"You were convincing with your threats," he said.

Dorkel nodded curtly. "We had to be. You were wasting time."

"Was I? Well, it seems to me *you've* been wasting time, too. Isn't your goal to kill my brother? Because I haven't seen a lot of that happening."

Dorkel growled and started getting to his feet, but the person beside him raised a hand. They wore gloves, so Tobal couldn't see anything about them. He couldn't help but wonder if they'd stay covered the entire time. What would happen if he didn't have a name to give Lon and the others? All of this would be for nothing, and that wasn't something he was willing to let happen.

They needed results, and they needed them now.

Tobal held his breath when Dorkel's boss reached for their hood. He didn't know who to expect, and he didn't have much of a reaction when the demon's face appeared. He'd seen her around the palace, but it took him a moment to recognize her.

It was the eyes, mostly. They were completely black with no white in sight, and they gave him the creeps. He'd noticed them at the palace, too, and he'd made sure to stay far away from Berith's minister.

But now, he couldn't because she was sitting in front of him.

"You recognize me," she said.

"I don't know your name, but yes. I've seen you with my brother."

"I'm one of his ministers."

Of course the betrayal had come from close to Berith. From what Tobal had heard about some of the ministers, Berith should have suspected them. Maybe he had, but he hadn't had any proof any of them were involved.

He did now.

Tobal tilted his head in agreement. "I see."

"Do you? Why don't you tell me what happened to Aloise?"

"I already told Dorkel in the note I sent him."

"I want more details."

Her voice was smooth, and she didn't sound scared. She probably wasn't. She believed she was doing the right thing, or at the very least, she didn't care whether or not she was. She wanted something and was ready to do pretty much anything to obtain it, which Tobal could understand up to a certain point.

He cleared his throat. "I poisoned her. I thought it would be the best way to kill her so I wouldn't be suspected, and it was fairly easy since we eat together. I made sure to sit next to her at breakfast yesterday, and I slipped something in her drink."

"What poison did you use?"

Tobal was relieved Lon had insisted they choose one. He wouldn't have known how to answer this question otherwise. "Spider flower."

"I see. An odd choice, but not surprising. You care about her."

"How could I not? She's a nice person." He swallowed. "Or I should say was."

Nowla — Tobal remembered her name now — stared at him. "*Was*? Has she died?"

"Yes. My brother's keeping it quiet for now, but you got what you wanted. I killed Aloise." He leaned forward, but not so close to make Nowla angry. "What's next for me? You said you wanted to kill my brother and put me on the throne, and I'm fine with that. I don't want anything to do with his death, though. It was hard for me to kill Aloise, but it would be impossible to kill Berith."

Nowla stared at him as if he were an interesting specimen. He was convinced she'd ask him to kill Berith or possibly

Cyarea, so he was relieved when she didn't.

"You won't have to kill anyone else," she said. "I want the satisfaction of doing that myself. Once your brother is dead, I'll need you to take his place on the throne. You won't make any decisions. You'll be my puppet, and if you're not okay with that, you need to make your peace with it. I won't hesitate to kill you if you ruin this for me."

Tobal leaned back. "The only thing I wanted when I decided to come here was a life of luxury. I've had enough hardship in my life. I want food and money, but not power. It gives me a headache."

"So this would be perfect for you."

"It sure sounds like it. As long as you don't expect me to make any kind of decisions, I'm on board with the plan." Saying the words made Tobal's stomach churn, but he and the important people in his life knew he was faking it, and that was good enough for him to be able to say them.

Nowla smiled, but it didn't look nice. If anything, it was terrifying and made Tobal want to run away screaming.

"We have a deal, then," Nowla said.

She didn't offer Tobal her hand, but Tobal wasn't sure he'd have taken it, anyway.

That was when the tavern door burst open.

Lon stood in the doorway, looking like an avenging hero. If his eyes could have shot fire, Tobal had no doubt they would have. Lon was as angry as Tobal, but unlike Tobal, he could do something about it.

"Dorkel, Nowla, the two of you are under arrest for treason," Lon declared, striding into the tavern.

A movement to the side captured Tobal's attention. He'd known Mikal was here somewhere, but he hadn't looked around to find him. He was relieved to see both him and Roque, and he allowed himself to relax.

That was a mistake.

Dorkel jumped to his feet. A knife appeared in his hand out of nowhere, and before Tobal could try to stop him, he lunged at Lon.

Tobal saw the knife move in slow motion. Lon could defend himself, but he'd been as surprised as Tobal about the attack, and Tobal was terrified it would be enough for Dorkel to hurt him. It wasn't his job to protect Lon, but it didn't mean he couldn't do it.

So he did something stupid. He threw himself in front of Dorkel, cutting off his path to Lon. Lon yelled behind Tobal, but Tobal was too focused on the pain as the knife Dorkel had been wielding sank into his shoulder.

He didn't think he'd ever felt anything like that. He'd been wounded before, but never with a knife, and he hadn't known what to expect.

He now knew he should do everything he could to avoid being wounded by a knife again.

The blade sank into his body as if he were made of butter. Dorkel growled in displeasure and tried to pull the knife out, but Tobal wouldn't allow him to keep his weapon. He threw himself backward, his shoulder pulsing in protest, the world around him turning slightly wobbly and black at the edges.

He wasn't afraid of what would happen next. Lon was there, and he'd make sure Tobal was fine. Tobal didn't think the blade had hit anything vital, anyway.

He supposed he'd find out soon enough.

Lon watched Tobal fall. His entire world was reduced to watching the man he loved, and he couldn't have looked away even if he'd tried.

That blade had been for him. He'd have been able to take it easily, but maybe Tobal hadn't known that. Maybe he had, and he'd decided to protect Lon anyway.

It was stupid, but Lon couldn't blame Tobal because he'd have done the same thing. Tobal wouldn't die from that wound, but he'd be in a world of pain, which was almost as bad. Dorkel had hurt Tobal, and Lon wouldn't stand for it.

He roared and threw himself at Dorkel.

The demon had been stunned by Tobal's move, and he hadn't been able to get the knife back. It meant he was weaponless and that they'd do this with their bare hands.

Lon was fine with that.

Tobal's back hit the wall, but Lon knew he couldn't afford to look back at him. He had to trust Mikal and Roque to help Tobal. If he allowed Dorkel even one inch of space forward, it would be the end for him, and he wasn't ready for that to happen. He had too much to live for, too much to experience.

But that didn't mean he wasn't ready to kill Dorkel.

Lon folded himself forward as he collided with Dorkel. He pressed his shoulder into Dorkel's stomach and grabbed his thighs, hauling him up. Dorkel scrambled to get hold of Lon's horns, but Lon moved quickly, slamming the other demon to the floor. The impact jarred even Lon, but the fight wasn't over yet.

Good.

Dorkel wouldn't let Lon win easily. He'd managed to take hold of one of his horns and used that to pull Lon down with him. Lon rolled forward, avoiding Dorkel's body and dislodging the demon's hand from his horn. He got to his feet in the same movement and turned, ready to go again.

This time, it was Dorkel who threw himself at Lon.

Lon had expected him to, so he twisted out of the way and grabbed the back of Dorkel's head. Dorkel's momentum was pulling him forward, but Lon stopped it with his knee.

He raised his leg, slamming his knee against Dorkel's nose. It exploded, blood dripping everywhere. Dorkel didn't even make a sound, though. Instead, he twisted his upper body and wrapped his arms around Lon's waist. He had enough force to push Lon away, then to the floor. He straddled Lon's waist and cocked a fist, ready to hit.

Lon raised his legs and folded them around Dorkel's upper body. He rolled until Dorkel was under him, and just like Dorkel had before, he raised his fist. The impact on Dorkel's face broke more bones, and blood spurted from Dorkel's wounds. It wasn't enough to stop Lon, and he continued hitting Dorkel even after Dorkel stopped trying to push him away. The only thing that stopped him was a hand suddenly landing on his shoulder.

He twirled, ready to attack, but stopped in time. Tobal stood there, his eyes wide, his hands raised as he made sure Lon knew he wasn't dangerous. The knife was still lodged in his shoulder, and the sight was enough to finally jolt Lon out of it.

He scrambled to his feet, reaching for the knife but not daring to touch it. "We need to get you to the palace," he declared.

Tobal smiled. "I'll have to agree with that. It would be great if someone could take the knife out. It kind of hurts."

Lon was careful as he pulled Tobal into his arms. "Why did you do that?"

"I'm not sure. I mean, I know you can defend yourself. You just showed it to everyone in the room. I was terrified he'd manage to hurt you, though. I reacted before I could truly think."

"And you got hurt."

"I'd do it again if it meant keeping you safe."

Lon had no doubt that was the case, but he'd make sure Tobal didn't have to do it again.

"Let's get you back to the palace," he said as he leaned down. Tobal squeaked and flailed as Lon hauled him up into his arms. He'd made sure that Tobal could lean his good shoulder against him and had one of his arms secured around

Tobal's back and one under his knees.

"You don't have to carry me," Tobal protested. "I was stabbed in the shoulder, not in the leg."

"I'll carry you anyway. You're losing blood, and I don't want you to faint while you're walking back. Besides, I need to feel that you're all right."

Tobal's expression softened, and he kissed Lon's cheek. "All right. Take me home, then."

Dorkel was still on the floor, either unconscious or dead. Lon hoped it would be the first one because he had questions to ask. Nowla was framed by Roque and another guard, with Mikal tying her hands together behind her back. She held her head high, glaring around while the people who'd been peacefully drinking in the tavern watched with wide eyes. This would be all over the city in just a few hours, but Lon would deal with that when it happened. He had other priorities.

"You'll get both of them to the palace?" he asked Mikal.

Mikal's expression was grim. "I have everything in hand. Take your man back to the palace and make sure he's all right. I don't like his new accessory."

Tobal laughed, then winced.

Lon was pretty sure he didn't like his new accessory, either.

He left everyone but a few guards behind. They followed him to the palace as he carried Tobal, and he was glad for that because it meant people stayed away. The crowd was gathering around the tavern already — everyone was curious to find out what was happening. He had no doubt more people would gather at the palace's door, but he and Tobal would be safe inside when that happened.

The guards opened the doors for him, and Lon barged into the servants' courtyard. There were guards here, too, and as soon as they saw Tobal was hurt, they snapped into motion. One of them ran inside, and Lon knew without asking that he was fetching Reyni. Lon hesitated between taking Tobal to the infirmary or his rooms, but Tobal made the decision.

"I want to sleep in my bed tonight."

Lon headed in the direction of the private wing. He was glad Tobal had picked this option because Mikal wouldn't have trouble finding Lon, and even though Tobal was hurt, the wound wasn't that bad. He'd be more comfortable in his rooms, especially since Lon had every intention of spending the night there. It would take a while for him to be ready to go to bed since he had to make sure Dorkel and Nowla were secured, but it would feel good to know Tobal was here, snuggled under the sheet, waiting for him.

They reached Tobal's rooms as Reyni turned the corner. He arched a brow when he saw the knife in Tobal shoulder, but thankfully, he didn't have anything snarky to say about it. Instead, he opened the door and gestured at Lon to take Tobal inside.

"I think you can go now," Tobal said as he patted Lon's shoulder. "Reyni is here, and you have work to do."

"I'm not going anywhere until I know for sure you're fine."

"I was stabbed in the shoulder. I'm not going to die."

"It doesn't have anything to do with dying. I need to be sure you're fine before I focus on anything else. If I'm not, I'll worry about what's going on and how you are, and I won't be able to do my work. Berith needs to know what happened, and I'll go to him as soon as Reyni is done with you, but for now, you're stuck with me."

Tobal's smile made it worth it. He wasn't used to people choosing him, but Lon was planning on doing just that for the rest of their lives.

Tobal had tried to convince Lon to go back to work, but he was secretly glad Lon wasn't going anywhere. His shoulder hurt like a bitch, and he didn't dare look at it. He didn't have a problem with the sight of blood, but the wound felt pretty gnarly.

"Put him down on the couch," Reyni ordered.

"Not on his bed?"

"I need to examine his shoulder, not his leg or his torso. The closer I can get, the easier it'll be for me."

Lon obeyed without asking any more questions. He was gentle as he helped Tobal settle into a comfortable position, growling a bit when Tobal winced. Tobal suspected he'd be doing a lot of wincing in his near future, but at least now, he was home, and both Dorkel and his boss had been arrested. Tobal felt like he could finally breathe, until Reyni tugged on his tunic.

Tobal gritted his teeth and glared at the healer. "You really have to do that?"

Reyni gave Tobal a blank look. "Would you rather I leave bits of your tunic in the wound when I close it? Because I can if you want, although I won't listen to you whine about infection if that's the way you decide to go."

Tobal stared at the healer. He wouldn't do that, right? Still, Tobal couldn't be a hundred percent sure, so he nodded at Reyni to continue.

It was easier to focus on Lon, who'd sat on the arm of the couch and hovered over Tobal. Tobal leaned against him, relieved he didn't have to deal with this on his own. Lon would have to go back to work soon, so Tobal needed to get his comfort now while he could.

"Are you surprised about who Dorkel's boss was?" he asked to distract himself while Reyni slid out the blade from his shoulder. He made sure to keep his gaze on Lon.

"Not really. I always suspect most people of wanting to hurt Berith. His ministers already have a lot of power, but it's not enough for some. I try to keep an eye on them. I'm not sure how she managed to do all of this under my nose, but I'll find out."

Tobal had no doubt Lon would. He was like a dog with a bone. Now that he had it, he'd get to the end of it.

Reyni poked and prodded at the wound before declaring it just a scratch. It didn't feel like it, but Tobal had no intention of making him angry again, so he nodded. Reyni moved on to cleaning it while Lon leaned closer and kissed Tobal's forehead. "He'll survive?" he asked Reyni.

"Without a problem. He lost some blood but nothing that would create problems. I'll ask the servants to bring him food and water. The wound will take a bit to heal, but as long as it doesn't get infected, Tobal will fully recover."

Lon's shoulders slumped as soon as Reyni was done explaining himself. He hadn't shown it, but he'd been terrified, and now that he was letting go, Tobal could see it. He wasn't surprised that was how Lon felt. He'd been scared, too, when Dorkel had launched himself at Lon holding a knife.

"I really need to go to Berith," Lon murmured. "I also have to check on Mikal and see how things are going with the prisoners. I don't want to leave you, though."

"You heard Reyni. I'll be fine and will be waiting for you in my bed once you're done. I just hope you don't get angry if you find me asleep." Getting stabbed was fucking exhausting.

Lon chuckled. "I won't hold it against you."

He got to his feet just as someone quickly knocked on the door. Lon tensed, and Tobal held his breath as he waited for Lon to answer. Hopefully, it wasn't anything bad.

Tobal was pretty sure it was when Lon opened the door to find Roque standing there.

"What?" Lon barked out.

Roque didn't seem offended or scared by his tone. "Dorkel escaped."

"How is that possible?"

"We thought he was unconscious, but he was biding his time." Roque looked behind Lon. "How's Tobal?"

Tobal straightened, then hissed when Reyni slapped his thigh and leaned back. "I'm fine," he called out.

Roque nodded. "Good." He turned his attention back to Lon. "We're going through the buildings around the tavern, trying to find him. In the state he was in, he won't go far. It's a miracle he managed to run."

"Find him," Lon ordered. "What about Nowla?"

"She's already in a cell."

The sound of someone running in the hallway made Tobal sigh. What was it now? Had Nowla torn down one of the walls and escaped, too?

He didn't dare move after Reyni had already hit him for it once, but it was a near thing when Berith barreled into the room. He pushed past Lon as if he knew Tobal had been hurt, and Tobal was sure that was the case when his brother rushed to his side.

"What happened?" Berith asked.

"Your brother got himself stabbed," Reyni explained, still focused on the wound. "But he'll be fine. You can yell at him later."

Berith squeezed Tobal's good shoulder. "No yelling. I'm just glad you're all right."

"So am I."

Berith straightened. "Lon? Can you give me your report?"

Lon sent Roque away and started to explain while Berith turned his gaze back to Tobal as he listened. His gaze flickered behind Tobal, and Tobal twisted slightly to see what had caught his attention. He ignored Reyni's glare because he couldn't focus on anything but the demon standing there.

Where had he come from? Who was he? Was Tobal about to be attacked again?"

But Berith was relaxed. He gestured at the demon to come closer and sat on the couch next to Tobal. "Dimri. What do you have for me?"

The first impression Tobal had of Dimri was darkness. He'd seen demons like this a few times, so he was pretty sure Dimri was at least part mahli. He couldn't be full-blooded because he wasn't tall enough, but his arms and fingers were long enough for Tobal to do a double take. Dimri was fully covered in tight, black clothing except for his face. His skin was a dark gray, and his eyes glowed white. It reminded Tobal of Lon's eyes, but Dimri's glowed in a way that made him uncomfortable. Dimri's black curls partly hid two short horns, and he was thin enough that Tobal wondered when was the last time he'd eaten.

"You should have come directly to me when you realized you were in trouble," Dimri said.

His voice made Tobal shiver. It was as dark as the rest of him.

"I would have if I'd known how to find you. You always disappear without taking your tablet with you."

"That's because it would be too easy for someone to find me through it. What do you want me to do?"

"Interrogate Nowla. You'll get every answer we need from her."

Dimri was silent for a moment before nodding. "I'll go right now."

"Thank you. And if you could keep an ear open, we're still looking for the demon who was with her at the tavern."

"I'll make sure he's found."

Tobal watched Dimri walk away and vanish into the darkness of the garden. "Who was that?"

"My spymaster."

It made sense, although Tobal thought Dimri was a little bit too memorable to be a spymaster. All his darkness couldn't hide the fact that he was impossible to ignore.

Berith patted Tobal's shoulder and got to his feet. "Lon and I have to go to work. I'll tell Aloise she can stop faking her own death, but I don't think any of you should leave your rooms for tonight."

"I'm not going anywhere," Tobal promised.

And he really wasn't. He'd told Lon he'd be here when he was done working, and he had every intention of keeping that promise. The palace was home, but more importantly, Lon and Berith were home. The entire family was where Tobal belonged, and even though he'd been hesitant in the beginning, he wouldn't have it any other way now.

He'd found his place. He was very fortunate that it was such a good place and that everyone had welcomed him with open arms, making him feel like he was one of them. As long as he had a say in it, he was never leaving.

And if he was forced to, he had no doubt his family would come after him.

CHAPTER TWENTY

Lon jumped when Dimri suddenly appeared next to him. He pressed a hand to his chest and glared at the spymaster, who looked unbothered by his reaction.

Lon suspected he did it on purpose. He liked being sneaky and making people jump, and to be honest, Lon would do the same if he could. It *was* kind of funny — when he wasn't the one jumping.

"I'm going to put a bell around your neck," Lon threatened.

"I'd just take it off. I need people not to hear me."

Lon shook his head. Dimri did need people not to notice him. He wouldn't be a good spymaster if everyone knew who he was and what he did. "Any news?"

Dimri raised a hand and examined his claws. Lon could be mistaken, but he thought he saw a hint of blood under them. It made him shudder, even though he wasn't a stranger to interrogations and torture. It wasn't his job, though, which meant he usually avoided the most brutal part. It wasn't exactly part of Dimri's job, either, but for something this important, he'd wanted to be there.

"I have a list of names," Dimri said.

"Good. We'll finally be able to get rid of everyone."

"I wouldn't be too sure about that. Some of the names were surprising. Berith will have to be careful if he wants to get rid of them."

"He wants to." Lon didn't have to ask his friend to know. After everything the society had put them through, Berith would burn it to the ground.

"It'll be fairly easy to take down the people who worked for the society in the palace, but it goes deeper than that, almost up to Lucifer."

Lon's stomach turned heavy. "Lucifer himself is involved?" If that was the case, they were in trouble.

"No. But people close to him are, and we can't be sure he'll believe us when we tell him about it. We also can't deal with it ourselves since these people are so close to him. Berith will need to involve him, and I don't know how he'll take it."

Lon was getting a headache. He hadn't expected the society to run so deep. He'd thought it was a group of people in the palace, unhappy with how Berith did things. Knowing it went so high up was a complication no one needed.

"What do you suggest?" he asked, hoping Dimri had an answer.

"To have Berith contact Lucifer directly. They're friends, aren't they?"

"Friendly, at the very least." Lon wasn't sure anyone could be Lucifer's friend considering who he was.

"Hopefully, it'll be enough. Berith has to tell him what I found."

Dimri held out a piece of paper. It was folded, and there was a drop of blood at the corner. Lon took it, making sure not to touch the blood, but he didn't open it. He wasn't sure he wanted to know right away.

The society wasn't going anywhere, clearly. It was a problem that had grown and grown, and it was too big for Lon to be able to take care of it. He didn't like it because he was head of security, and he should be able to deal with this kind of thing. He could still have all the people who lived at the palace and were involved arrested, and he would, but what about the others? How was he supposed to protect his family from them?

He couldn't. He didn't have any reach when it came to Lucifer's people or his palace, and he found Lucifer kind of terrifying. He wasn't looking forward to having to deal with him, although hopefully, they wouldn't need to. Surely Lucifer had people who took care of this stuff for him.

"Thank you," Lon said as he pushed away from the wall. He'd been waiting for Dimri outside the dungeons, and he regretted it. He should have stayed with Tobal longer.

"Good luck."

Lon turned a glare to Dimri, but by the time he looked up, the spymaster had already vanished. Lon rolled his eyes. Dimri was as dramatic as he was annoying.

Lon was glad to leave the dungeons. He spent his fair share of time there, but it made him uncomfortable. Mel hadn't gotten to it yet, and he probably wouldn't because he realized there were some things he didn't have a say in, but it wouldn't be awful to stop torturing people. Of course, Lon wouldn't get all the answers he needed if they did. It wasn't like if they'd asked nicely, Nowla would have told them the names of the people she worked with.

Lon's headache was back.

He made his way to his office, avoiding most of the people he crossed paths with. A few servants tried to stop him, but he told them to make an appointment. He didn't have the energy to deal with whatever they had to complain about, and he was on a mission, anyway. He had to tell Berith about all of this as soon as possible because they needed to make a decision.

Sabin was at his desk when Lon went in. He looked up, squinted, and cocked his head, then sighed. "I can see you don't have good news."

"Do I ever have good news?"

Sabin snorted. "Right. You can go in. Should I come along?"

"Not unless you want nightmares."

Sabin grimaced. "Better I stay here, then. I'll be ready when you're done. I can feel he's going to need me."

Since Sabin would be the one to contact Lucifer's people, he was right. He'd probably wish he hadn't been by the time this was over.

Lon quickly knocked on the door of Berith's office, then opened it when Berith told him to. His friend was behind the desk, but he got up when he saw Lon and walked around it. He went to flop onto one of the couches in the corner by the window, and Lon followed him there.

"Please tell me you don't have more bad news," Berith lamented. "I don't think I can take it if that's the case."

"Dimri got some results."

Berith groaned and closed his eyes for a moment. Lon didn't push, giving him the time to gather his thoughts and probably his energy. Berith had been working hard since Nowla had been arrested, and more than ever, Lon was glad he wasn't in his friend's place.

"Tell me," Berith ordered.

Lon held out the piece of paper Dimri had given him. "This is a list of names."

"Dimri got them from Nowla?" Berith took the note and opened it.

"Yes. I can take care of some of these people since they live at the palace and are under your jurisdiction, but other names are going to be a problem."

Berith stared at the list. "I recognize some of these."

Lon nodded. "You should. They work for Lucifer."

Berith rubbed his face. "You're telling me the society goes all the way up to him?"

"Yes."

"But why? It doesn't make sense for anyone in Lucifer's court to be interested in me and what I do."

But that wasn't exactly right. Berith was only one of many princes of Hell, but he was an oddity. He treated his people nicely—for being in Hell, anyway—tried to be a fair leader, and he'd recently taken a human consort who wanted to teach children and keep them safe. Some people had been convinced Lucifer would put an end to that union, but as far as Lon knew, he'd been amused more than anything.

What did the society expect him to do? Punish Berith when he hadn't done anything wrong? Although of course, that was a vague description. Some people thought Berith was doing a good job, while others believed he was doing the opposite. Lucifer was the guy in charge, but it didn't mean other people, especially those close to him, didn't have influence, power, or opinions.

"This is a mess." Berith shook his head. "I'll have to contact Lucifer," Berith said.

"Better you than me."

Berith chuckled. "I can't say I disagree, but he's not a bad person."

"I'll have to take your word for it. Be careful, all right?"

"Don't worry about me. It's not the first time I've had to contact him."

"Maybe not, but it's the first time you have to tell him that people close to him tried to kill you." And there was no way to know how he'd take it.

Lon was happy to be able to leave the office. Sabin didn't ask him what was happening, but they both knew Berith would tell him soon. In the meantime, Lon was fine stepping away from the entire situation, so he made his way to Tobal's rooms.

They'd been sharing since Tobal was stabbed a few days earlier, but they hadn't talked about it. Lon wanted to ask Tobal to move into his rooms, but even though he was more comfortable there, he'd be happy to do the opposite and move in with Tobal. As long as they were together, everything was right in the world as far as Lon was concerned.

This was what he wanted to think about. Even if it was only for a few minutes, he needed to leave Lucifer and the society behind and focus on the demon he loved.

Tobal glared at the ceiling. "There's no reason for me to stay in bed," he said. "I was stabbed in the shoulder, but my legs are perfectly fine."

Roque chuckled from the chair he was sitting in by the bed. "I have my orders."

Of course he did. Tobal was pretty sure Lon had threatened to fire Roque if he allowed Tobal out of bed. He briefly wondered what Roque would do if he tried sneaking away. Would he restrain him? Would he tie him down?

Tobal wasn't willing to find out, but he was still annoyed.

He turned his glare to the demon. "I'm bored. I have work to do."

Roque had been reading a book, but he looked up. "There's nothing for you to do right now. Sabin isn't working on your project. He has too much work to do with the society."

"Exactly. I could work on it alone, and we'll be further ahead by the time I'm healed."

"I'm not letting you out of bed."

Tobal sighed. "I didn't think you would."

The sound of the living area door opening made both him and Roque sit up. Roque slid out of his chair and vanished so quickly that Tobal would have missed him if he hadn't been staring at his bedroom door. His heart raced as he waited, even though he knew it wouldn't be anyone from the society.

All of that was over. They hadn't found Dorkel yet, but it was a question of time, and in the meantime, they had Nowla, and she was talking. She'd confessed that the society had found out about Tobal being Berith's brother through Tobal's foster parents. They'd known about the diaries, and Tobal was lucky they'd been too stupid to destroy them. They'd probably wanted proof that Tobal was Berith's brother, but keeping the diaries had meant Tobal had found out about it.

Tobal shuddered at the thought of how Lon had gotten this answer from Nowla, but he couldn't find it in himself to feel sorry for her. She'd threatened his family. She'd wanted to kill his brother. She deserved everything she was getting, and once it was over, she wouldn't hurt anyone ever again.

Lon appeared at the door, and Tobal relaxed. "Didn't you go to work?" That was what Lon had said when he left earlier.

Lon smiled, but he looked tired and a bit out of sorts. Tobal wanted to ask what was going on, but he was never sure he should. He wanted to know what was going on in Lon's life, but if it was related to work, it was none of his business.

Lon came closer. He tucked up the blankets, checked Tobal's glass of water, and fussed over him. It made Tobal feel warm and gooey inside, and he wanted more. He wasn't used to having people take care of him, even when he was in pain. When he'd been a kid, his mother had done it, but it had been so long ago. It made him feel loved, and even though Lon hadn't told him how he felt using those words, Tobal had no doubt he was telling him through his gestures.

"Sit down," Tobal gently said. "You look tired."

Lon sat on the other side of the bed, propping his back against the pillows. "I am. Hopefully now that the society is being eradicated in the palace, I'll be able to get more rest."

Tobal didn't miss the words Lon used. "Only in the palace?"

Lon grimaced. He opened his arm, silently asking Tobal to move closer. Tobal was happy to do so, and he snuggled against Lon's side, careful of his shoulder. It didn't hurt as much as it had right after he was stabbed, but he needed more time to heal, and it wouldn't do him any good to reopen it by moving too quickly or not thinking about what he was doing.

"Dimri got the names we needed from Nowla," Lon explained. "I went back to the office before coming here, and I've given orders to have those people arrested, but the problem is that it goes much higher than we expected."

Tobal didn't like the sound of that. "How high?" Berith was the highest it could go in his territory, which meant the society's reach was much longer than any of them had expected.

"A few people who work with Lucifer are involved," Lon said.

Tobal hissed. "What? What about Lucifer himself? Is *he* involved?"

"I don't think so, but who knows?"

"You know what it means if Lucifer was behind all of this, right?" Tobal couldn't even begin to wrap his mind around that possibility.

"I don't think he is. Lucifer likes Berith. He appointed him to this role, and as far as I know, he never complained about the way Berith does things."

"But Berith has been unconventional lately. He's opening safe houses for children and took a human as his consort. What does Lucifer have to say about that?"

"I know Berith contacted him to tell him about Mel, and he wouldn't have taken Mel as a semi-official consort if Lucifer hadn't been on board. I don't think we have to worry about him."

"But even if he isn't involved, someone almost as powerful as him is, and that's a problem."

"Exactly." Lon sighed. "There's nothing we can do about it. Berith will tell Lucifer, and we'll have to see what he decides to do. In the meantime, we'll take care of the pieces of the society at the palace."

Tobal tried to relax. Lon was right. If things went that high up, they wouldn't be the ones taking care of it. They also couldn't live their lives afraid of what would happen next. They had while the society had been threatening them, but that was over, and Tobal wanted to finally relax.

He had everything he could ever have wanted. Zeno was with him, and he'd found another brother. He'd made his home in a palace, and he never had to worry about food or being in danger.

Well, no more than usual.

With the society gone, Tobal wanted to savor having all of this. Reality would be there once he was healed, and he'd have to deal with it then.

But now wasn't then. Now, he could close his eyes and allow himself to drift off to sleep against Lon's shoulder. Lon would protect him from whatever or whoever tried to get to him. He'd love him, and that was all that mattered in the end.

EPILOGUE

The palace was a mess of people running around, and Tobal wasn't sure he liked it.

He looked down at himself, straightened his tunic, and wondered if it was good enough to welcome Lucifer. He hadn't seen the demon yet, but he would soon, and while there was no reason for Lucifer to notice him, he still needed to make a good impression. He was Berith's brother, and he wanted to make him proud.

"You're fine," Sabin muttered from his chair next to Tobal's.

Tobal swallowed. He'd gotten used to his new position at the palace, especially after he moved into Lon's rooms with him. The rooms were on the small side because Lon liked things that way, but Tobal didn't mind. He didn't need a lot of space, especially when he had the entire palace to run around.

But tonight was different. Tobal felt incredibly out of place and wanted nothing more than to run back to his rooms.

"Are you as nervous as I am?" he asked.

Sabin shrugged one shoulder. He looked beautiful tonight, with his purple hair neatly arranged and his makeup glittering under the light. "Maybe not as much as you. It's not the first time I've had to deal with Lucifer."

"Deal with him? I won't have to talk to him, right?"

The corner of Sabin's lips curled. "Probably not tonight. You *are* Berith's brother, though. I wouldn't be surprised if Lucifer took an interest in you."

Tobal suddenly wasn't hungry anymore. He stared down at his plate, which was still empty because they hadn't started dinner yet. People were still arriving to the party, and no one had seen Lucifer yet. Berith and Mel weren't here, but Tobal had been too nervous to stay in his rooms and be fashionably late.

He couldn't even take advantage of Lon's presence to calm himself. Lon was one of the people running around the palace, keeping an eye on every single guard and the people who'd arrived with Lucifer.

Everyone had been stunned when Lucifer decided he wanted to visit. His official reason was that he wanted to meet Berith's consort, and that might as well be part of the truth, but in reality, Berith and Lucifer wanted to talk about the society in a place they knew was safe. Now that all the society's members in the palace were dead, there would be no one to impart what was being said to the rest of the society. Lucifer had made sure to leave the people involved behind, even though it had caused a few problems.

Tobal was glad he didn't have to be involved anymore.

"Here they are," Sabin said, suddenly getting to his feet.

The door behind the throne opened, and Berith and Mel came through, arm in arm. Both of them were beautiful, Mel especially so. He looked so fragile next to Berith, but anyone who knew him knew he was anything but. His body might not be the body of a demon, but that didn't make him weak.

Right next to them was Lucifer. Tobal had never seen the demon, and he hadn't been sure what to expect, but he wasn't surprised.

The king of Hell wore all black. Unlike most demons, he didn't wear flowy clothing that would help with the desert heat. No, he wore a black suit and shirt that had to have come from the human realm.

He looked human, too. Just like Mel, it didn't mean he was

weak, although not in the same way. Mel was strong mentally and in spirit. Lucifer had powers no one could rival, and from what Tobal had heard, he could kill with barely a thought. There was a reason every demon in Hell feared him, and probably hated him.

Lucifer's long black hair was gathered at the back of his neck like a slick waterfall, and his black eyes glittered as he looked around. Tobal and Sabin were seated at the same table as Berith and Mel, but Tobal hadn't realized it meant he'd have to sit with Lucifer, too.

Fuck.

When the king looked his way, he quickly tilted his head forward in respect. Lon had told him how to behave, but Tobal hadn't been listening as much as he should have. He'd been distracted, like always when he was with Lon. Now, he regretted it, but it was too late. He couldn't allow panic to take over, so he stared down at the table, hoping Lucifer wouldn't notice how flustered he was.

"Sabin," Lucifer said, his voice smooth.

Sabin quickly bowed. "My king. It's a pleasure to see you again."

"You're as beautiful as always. Berith told me you've taken a life partner?"

Even though Zeno had tried getting out of the party, he hadn't been able to. He was sitting on Sabin's other side, and while his expression was thunderous, probably because of how Lucifer had talked to Sabin, he bowed, too.

"My king," he murmured.

"I have to say that you have good taste, Sabin," Lucifer drawled. "And this has to be Berith's long-lost brother," he continued.

Tobal swallowed. Lucifer's attention was on him now.

He hoped he wouldn't mess things up.

He looked up, his gaze crossing with Lucifer's. "I am," he confirmed. "It's an honor to meet you."

Luckily, Lucifer settled down next to Berith, on the other side of the table. There was an empty chair next to Tobal, which was reserved for Lon, and Tobal really hoped it wouldn't be long before Lon arrived. He didn't think he'd ever been as uncomfortable as he was now, with the king of Hell staring at him.

"I'm glad Berith found you," Lucifer said, his voice making Tobal shiver. "He's always wanted brothers."

It was a surprise to realize that Lucifer and Berith had to be somewhat close. "I was glad to find him, too. I was alone before, but having a family is much better."

Lucifer's expression turned pensive. "I suppose it is. Now, where is your other half? I've been told you and Lon have moved in together recently."

Tobal quickly glared at his brother, who seemed amused, before nodding. "We have. He should be here any minute."

Luckily, Lucifer's attention moved away from Tobal after that. Tobal breathed easier. He felt like he had no idea what had happened, but also like he'd narrowly escaped a painful death. He was even more relieved when Lon finally sat next to him, and he leaned closer, smiling when Lon did the same and pressed a kiss to the corner of his lips.

"Sorry I'm late," Lon announced to the table. "How did it go?" he asked Tobal in a whisper.

"He's terrifying," Tobal whispered back.

Lon chuckled. "He is, but he's not a cruel person. You don't have to be afraid of him. If you don't attack or work against him, he won't hurt you."

Tobal wanted to believe that, but it wasn't easy. He was sitting at the same table as the most powerful demon in Hell, and no matter how many times people told him to treat Lucifer like he was a friend, he didn't think he'd ever be able to do that.

But dinner was fine. Tobal kept his attention on Lon and

the people around him, happy to leave Lucifer to his brother and Mel. Mel seemed a bit intimidated, but he relaxed during the meal, and so did Tobal. He'd known Lucifer wouldn't attack them or anything like that, but sitting next to him and eating dinner with him made him look almost normal.

After dinner, the dancing started. Tobal had been looking forward to it and shot to his feet almost immediately. Lon groaned, but when Tobal extended his hand, he took it and allowed Tobal to pull him to his feet.

"I'm not a dancer," he warned for what had to be the hundredth time.

"I don't need you to be. Just follow my lead."

"Can I have the next dance?" Lucifer suddenly asked.

Tobal didn't know what to say. "Of course. With Lon or me?"

Lucifer's smile exposed his fangs. "Both of you. It's been a while since I've danced with such beautiful people." He left his chair and offered Mel his hand. "But first, I'd like to dance with the most beautiful of all."

Mel's cheeks flushed, but he took Lucifer's hand. Tobal was impressed by how smooth the king of Hell was, but he probably shouldn't be. Lucifer was kind of nice, though, and it helped Tobal relax, even though he was going to be dancing with the king soon.

But first, he'd focus on Lon.

They twirled on the dance floor, wrapped around each other. Tobal couldn't see anyone but Lon, and on impulse, he leaned forward and kissed Lon's jaw. Lon smiled down at him, his gaze soft.

"Are you in pain?" Lon asked.

"I promise to tell you if I am, but I'm fine."

"As long as you're sure. I don't want you to be uncomfortable."

"Oh, I've been plenty uncomfortable tonight, but it's

getting better. Lucifer isn't as intimidating as I thought."

Lon laughed. "Only because you haven't seen him when he gets angry. He *is* a nice person, though."

"But my favorite is still you."

"I better be, because you're *my* favorite."

There it was. Lon was telling Tobal he loved him without using those words, but Tobal heard them all the same. He leaned his cheek against Lon's chest, his heart racing. "I love you," he whispered.

Lon's arms tightened around him. It was enough of an answer, and as they danced the night away, Tobal almost couldn't believe how fortunate he'd been.

ABOUT THE AUTHOR

Catherine is the creator of several series, most of them paranormal, including the Whitedell Pride Series and the Gillham Pack Series. While she graduated in translation, she decided to go the writer's way because it was more fun to create her own stories and characters.

She's been living in Italy for more than twenty years, but she's a daughter of the North — Belgium to be precise — and she misses it so much that she's already planning to move back.

She loves pizza — probably too much — her son, her pets, and of course, books. She sneaks some reading time into her schedule every time she has five minutes free from writing, demands from her various pets and son, and lastly, housework.

Connect with her:

lievens.catherine@gmail.com
BookBub: https://www.bookbub.com/authors/catherine-lievens
Website: https://authorcatherinelievens.com/
Facebook: https://www.facebook.com/catherine.lievens.9
Facebook Group: https://www.facebook.com/groups/411788002341528/
Twitter: https://twitter.com/authorCLievens
Newsletter: http://eepurl.com/c-uvKn